SILENT WITNESS

A Cass Leary Legal Thriller

ROBIN JAMES

D1265303

Robin James Books

Chapter 1

AN EERIE STILLNESS settled over Finn Lake. Sugary snow fell, brushing against my cheeks as I stepped to the water's edge. Pure white filled the sky and covered the lake. It was hard to know where one began and the other ended. I took that first, halting step out, waiting to hear the ice break. It didn't. It wouldn't. Winter magic. The lake would stay frozen like this for weeks now.

This pureness wouldn't last though. By morning, ice fishermen would dot the landscape with their tents. Behind me, I heard my brother Matty rummaging through the shed to set up his own. I smiled. He'd been staying with me since Christmas. His wife Tina had thrown him out claiming it was for good. I expected her divorce complaint in my inbox any day now.

Even with all Matty's family turmoil, things had been peaceful with my family over the last two months. We all spent the holidays together. The last time that happened was before my mother died. Only my father was missing, but that's what accounted for the peace.

The snow crunched beneath my feet as I trudged up the

hill toward the house. Left to his own devices, Matty might tear the shed apart to find what he needed. A small beach chair flew by my head as I approached. I ducked neatly, barely avoiding having it crash against me.

"Do you mind?" I asked. "Joe said he put all the winter stuff in the hall closet upstairs. He didn't want it to get wet."

Matty made a noise and let out a stream of obscenities as he crashed into a few more things on his way out of the shed. Before I could get the words out to warn him, he banged his head on the doorframe as he came out. Blood trickled down his forehead as he looked at me with wild eyes.

"Nice work," I said. "Don't hurt my door!" But I was still smiling as I walked up to him. I pressed my mitten against the wound as I led him up to the house.

"Joe was supposed to fix the roof on that piece of shit," Matty said as he took a paper towel from me and planted himself on the living room couch. "We wouldn't have to worry about anything getting wet out there if ..."

"Save it," I said, pulling the first aid kit out from under the kitchen sink. I tossed a bottle of antibiotic cream at my brother. He caught it one-handed and grumbled some more as I ripped off a wad of paper towels. Regardless of his temper, I was proud of him. Matty had stayed on the wagon all through the holidays, his break-up with Tina, and his current employment status. He'd been working odd jobs around the lake, waiting for a callback at the machine shop in town. Though no one would admit it, I felt fairly certain his layoff had more to do with my choice in clients than anything else.

Late last year, I'd defended the girl accused of murdering the town's basketball coach and former hero. It had ripped the town apart and things hadn't completely returned to normal. Maybe they never would. There would always be those who blamed me for busting up a piece of the good ol'

2

boy network of Delphi, Michigan, population 8953. No matter how far I went, how high I flew, I was still a Leary to the people of this town. Still east-side-of-the-lake trash.

"I'll take a look at it after my damn head stops bleeding," he said.

"Good idea. I've got to go into the office for a little while. I've got a hearing to prep for. And don't be a baby. It's barely a scratch."

His scowl melted me. Matty had been giving me the exact same look since he was a baby. From the time he was six years old on, I'd done most of the mothering in his life. He was twenty-six now, but some things never changed.

"What are you smiling about?" he asked. "I know that look. You're about to get all weepy on me or something."

I went up to him and smoothed the wild hairs away from his forehead. He had our mother's eyes, clear, blue, and mirroring everything he thought. Right now, he was about to flip me off.

"It's nothing," I said. "It's just, for the first time since I came back here, things are starting to feel almost normal." I'd spent over a decade working for the Thorne Law Group, a high-powered law firm in Chicago. I might be there still if it hadn't gotten too dangerous. Some of my client's dealings had landed me in the crosshairs of the FBI. I'd danced with the devil and barely lived to tell the tale. But now I was home.

He raised a brow. "You know what Granny Leary would say. Quick, two Hail Marys and an Our Father or you'll jinx us."

I grabbed my coat off the hook by the door and slid the strap of my leather messenger bag over my shoulder. "Shows how much you know. It was five Glory Bes."

Matty sat back and put his feet up on the coffee table. Two brown chunks of ice slid off the tread of his boots. He at least had the decency to wipe it with the paper towel before steam came out of my ears.

My phone buzzed as a text came through from Miranda, my secretary. I'd left my phone on the coffee table about two inches from Matty's boot sludge.

"Told ya," Matty said. "That's probably hell breaking loose right now."

"Shh," I said. "You're the jinx." I was only able to read three words of Miranda's text from the home screen before the message disappeared. "Better call Detective …"

I picked up the phone to unlock it and read the rest of it. Call Detective who? Other than a few speeding tickets, I mercifully didn't have any criminal cases for the time being. I'd asked to be taken off the court-appointed list after the Coach Drazdowski trial in November. My civil docket was keeping me more than busy these days.

"I'm tellin' ya," Matty said, smiling. "You're teasing the devil." He managed a fairly accurate impression of our grandmother's thick Irish brogue as he recited her favorite saying. Bridget Leary was also convinced each and every one of us was headed straight for hell. Some days, I thought she might be right.

I pulled up my contacts, ready to just call Miranda back. Better to have a heads-up about what detective needed my attention than to just dive right in. I never got the chance. Instead, my phone rang from a number I didn't recognize. It was a 734 area code though.

"Cass Leary," I said, bracing for the answer. It was probably just Matty's superstition getting under my skin. Still, a shadow fell across my heart in the time it took for the caller to take a breath.

She was crying. No. More like screaming. Her voice was so loud, Matty heard it all even though I didn't have the phone on speaker.

"Help me! Please. They're here. They're saying ... God!"

"Whoa," I said. "Just hold on. Slow down. I don't know what ..." I meant to ask who it was. Something was happening in my brain. It was as if I were on a time delay. The woman on the other end of the phone kept screaming. She was frantic. Frenzied. Panting. But time caught up with me and I recognized the voice with cold clarity.

Vangie. It was my little sister Vangie. And she was scared to death.

"Help me," she screamed. "Oh God. Help me!"

Chapter 2

"Vangie?" I asked, trying to keep my own voice calm. "Vangie, are you hurt? What's the matter? Where are you calling from?"

It didn't make sense. After the Drazdowski trial, Vangie had gone back to Indianapolis. She'd been a key witness for me, laying her personal life wide open to save my client. Without her, an innocent girl would be serving life in prison for a murder she didn't commit.

But now Vangie was screaming. She was terrified. I tried to calm my brain. No. Vangie was safe. She'd gone back home. She had a good job there, tending bar at an upscale restaurant. We'd seen her for two days at Christmas just a few weeks ago. She shouldn't be calling from a 734 area code.

There was shouting on the other end of the phone. Two deep male voices.

Matty was off the couch. He'd heard enough to know something was very wrong. I put a hand up to quiet him.

"Cass," she screamed. "You have to ... I didn't ..."

I took a breath and realized I was trying to will my sister into doing the same thing from the other end of the phone.

"Vangie, I need you to calm down and tell me what's going on. Are you okay?"

She sobbed into the phone. I heard more shouting and then some pounding, like running footsteps. Matty pulled on my arm.

"I can't … just sit down," I ordered my brother. My heart flipped. Then, from the other line I heard one of those deep voices again.

"Ma'am, put the phone down. Put your hands up." A cold chill went through me. He sounded like a cop.

"Vangie, goddammit! What's going on?"

She cried again and I heard more running. A door slammed. "Cass," she sobbed. "I don't know what's happening. They just showed up here. They're going through everything. Hey, that's my purse!"

"Who is it?"

"Ma'am, I'm going to count to three." I heard the man's voice again. "And I'm not going to ask you again."

"Jesus, Vangie, is that a cop?"

"This is my sister!" Vangie screamed. "She's a lawyer. She's my lawyer. You can't do any of this. Tell me what's going on! I didn't do anything."

"Vangie," I said, trying to make my voice steady. "I need you to listen to me very carefully. I don't know what the hell is going on over there, but you need to shut up right now. I mean it. Are you under arrest? Have they read you your rights?"

"Cass!" Matty shouted. He tried to take the phone from me but I gave him my shoulder and turned my back to him.

"Vangie!" I shouted.

"I know, I know," she said. "But I need you. Right now!"

"Where are you? Give me an address."

There was a muffled sound. My blood went cold. It sounded like a struggle. I heard Vangie cry out and a loud crash like the phone hit the floor.

"Goddammit, Cass. What's going on?" Matt blurted.

"I don't know. It sounds like ... I think it's cops."

I squeezed my eyes shut and strained to hear what was going on from the other end of that phone. In the distance, that deep, muffled voice came through.

"You have the right to remain silent. You may refuse to answer questions. Anything you say can and will be used against you in a court of law. You have the right to an attorney ..."

I let out a hard sigh and looked up at the ceiling. "She's being arrested, I think," I said. Then, I yelled at the top of my lungs. "Somebody pick up this phone!"

There were a few more shouts and some muffled yells. I pulled the phone away from my ear and looked again at the caller ID. Matty followed my line of thinking and grabbed the pen and pad of paper off the fridge. I turned the phone toward him and he wrote down the number, for all the good it would do now.

"Let me talk to my sister," Vangie's voice cut through. "I told you. She's my lawyer. You have to let me talk to her."

I couldn't make out what the officer said back. God, I hoped she was cooperating. I loved her more than anything, but my little sister could be a scrapper, especially if she had a beer or two in her. She got that from our father. But it wasn't even noon and I'd never known Vangie to be a drunk. That said, I'd learned a lot of things about her in the last few months that I'd never known before.

The line went dead.

"Shit," I muttered.

"Call it back," Matty said. I could have kicked myself for not thinking of it first.

I pressed the redial button and waited. The phone rang, going unanswered. It felt like an eternity. I was just about to click off and try again when finally, someone picked up.

"Hello!" I shouted, not even waiting for a response. "My name is Cassiopeia Leary. I'm an attorney. My sister is Evangeline Leary. She just called from this number."

I heard some throat clearing on the other end. Whoever picked up must have muffled his end. He was talking to someone but I couldn't make it out.

"Ms. Leary?" he said. "This is Detective Brett Carey, Ann Arbor Police Department."

"Great. Detective Carey. Do you have my sister there? I'd like to talk to her."

"You'll need to come here to do that," he said. "She's been arrested."

I knew it. Still, when he said the words, my heart twisted. "I'm sorry. On what charge?"

"She'll be processed at the Ann Arbor Police Station on East Huron. Are you familiar with it?"

Ann Arbor? What the hell was Vangie doing in Ann Arbor?

"I know it," I said. "So we're clear, my sister has requested counsel. I need your word you understand that. *I* am her counsel. She may not be questioned outside of my presence. I'm holding you personally responsible if ..."

"Ms. Leary, you can save it. We're doing this by the book. You can meet your sister down at the station."

"Detective," I said, swallowing hard. I had that time-delay feeling again. "Detective Carey, what is my sister being charged with?"

Carey took a breath. I felt suspended in mid-air. In some detached corner of my brain, I felt like this was my fault.

Matty was right. I should have said my five Glory Bes. But as I waited for Carey's answer, I could *feel* the bottom dropping out all over again.

"Ms. Leary, your sister's been charged with double murder."

Chapter 3

Forty minutes. That's how long it should have taken me to drive from Delphi to Ann Arbor, Michigan. With Matty driving like a bat out of hell, we were about to make it in half that time. I gripped the dashboard and pressed my feet against the floor as if I could will the car to go even faster. Just as we were about to veer into our exit lane, my phone rang and everything flipped all over again.

"She's at U of M hospital!" my older brother Joe shouted at me. In the time it took me to grab my purse, Matty had called him and told him what we knew.

"She's what? How do you know that?"

"I'm still listed as her emergency contact. I just got the call from a nurse there. They took her to the ER. I don't know anything else. I'm maybe five minutes behind you."

Once again, Matty could hear everything. He swerved and stayed on the highway until the next exit. A semi behind us laid on his horn. Matty rewarded him with a middle finger and cut him off to get to the off-ramp first. If he didn't watch it, two more Learys would end up in the ER for Joe to deal with. But we were lucky. Matty parked in a hospital loading zone and we ran for the doors together.

I don't know how I got my legs to work as we made our way in. The U of M Medical Center is a massive complex with labyrinth-like halls. For a moment, I wondered if we'd taken a wrong turn. Then, I lost my heart as I saw a half-dozen uniformed officers standing guard in front of one of the rooms. I knew. No one had to tell me. My sister was inside.

I pulled out a business card and put a steadying hand on Matty. We'd worked it out in the car. He was to let me do the talking and keep his temper in check.

"My name is Cass Leary. I'm here for my sister, Evangeline. I'm also her attorney."

A nurse in pink scrubs stood off to the side. The officers looked to her. She held a tablet in her hands and pulled something up.

"I'm not her patient advocate," I said. "My brother Joe is. He's on his way. But I very much need somebody to tell me what's going on."

Another man walked out of the hospital room, shutting the door behind him. He wore an ill-fitting gray suit and his tie was crooked. My blood boiled as he introduced himself.

"Detective Carey," he said, extending his hand to shake mine.

"Did I not make myself clear on the phone?" I asked. "Miss Leary has counsel … you can't …"

"Now, just hold on. I take it you're the sister."

"I'm a hell of a lot more than that …"

"Cass," Matty shouted. It was his turn to put a hand on me. He drew me away from Detective Carey. "I don't really give two shits about this legal stuff right now. Somebody needs to tell me what the hell's wrong with Vangie."

Just then, the elevator doors opened and Joe stepped out.

My heart lifted. I hadn't realized how much I needed his strong presence. It was this place. The sounds. The smells. One night, almost twenty years ago to the day, we'd stood in a hallway just like this waiting for word on our parents. Back then, only our father survived. My mother lived just long enough to talk to the police, then she died on the operating table while I fed my younger siblings dinner from a vending machine.

"Follow me," the nurse said once Joe identified himself. She led us into a small conference room. A young red-headed doctor came right behind her and introduced herself as Dr. Louise Hopperton.

"I'm the ER attending," she said. "I was here when they brought your sister in. First of all, you need to know that she's physically fine. There's some bruising on her arm and a laceration across her cheek. I don't even think it will need stitches. You can speak to the officers, but she's under arrest. When you go in there, you'll see she's in restraints. That's as much for her protection as anything else. Evangeline was altered when they brought her in."

"Altered?" I said. "As in under the influence?"

"We've run a BAC and toxicology labs. There's no alcohol in her system."

"I need to stop you right there. Joe, tell this doctor you do not give permission for those results to be turned over to the police without a warrant and neither does Vangie."

"What she said," Joe answered, drawing a hand over his face.

"I understand," Dr. Hopperton said. "And I know the law too. To be honest, my sense is, Evangeline's mental state has more to do with trauma as opposed to any illicit substance."

"What trauma?" Matty asked.

The doctor let out a sigh. "She's calmer now. A few

minutes ago, she started asking for you, Ms. Leary. I think it's better if you just talked to her yourself. Her vitals are stable."

"I don't get it," Joe said. "What the hell happened?"

Dr. Hopperton looked at her feet. She was a small woman, maybe five feet tall. She wore little makeup and had fine features, her hair pulled back in a high bun with wisps of her red hair framing her face. I couldn't place her age. She could have been thirty or fifty for all I knew.

"Mr. Leary, I've given your sister a Valium, to help calm her down. I was afraid she might try to hurt herself. And that's still my biggest concern. You can get the story from the police. But they brought her in as a precaution. She was resisting arrest and they say she took a swing at one of the officers before they could get her cuffed. That's how she scraped her cheek. They wrestled her down to the ground."

"Son of a bitch!" Matty punched the side of his fist against the wall.

"Enough of this," Joe said. "We need to see our sister."

Dr. Hopperton nodded. "I think that's best."

The nurse still stood in the doorway. She peered over her shoulder. The cops were out there and wouldn't leave. But they weren't going to keep us from Vangie's side.

As we filed past them and into Vangie's small hospital room, my heart went stone cold. My sister looked so small, so scared. She was in soft restraints around her ankles and legs; her right wrist was handcuffed to the metal bars of the bed. She stared out the window, her eyes wide and vacant. The cut on her cheek was really more of a scrape, but it stuck out in stark contrast to her pale skin. I called her name and for a moment, it was as if she was someplace else. Then she finally turned her head and met my eyes.

"What the fuck happened?" Joe got to her first. He leaned over the bed and smoothed Vangie's blonde hair away from her forehead. She bit her lip to keep from crying. I could clearly see the effects of the Valium or whatever Hopperton had given her. She looked drowsy, docile. The fire I normally saw was out of her eyes.

"They won't listen," she said. "Oh God. They won't tell me."

"Tell you what?" Matty asked.

I looked behind me and pulled the door shut. "Listen," I said. "We have a lot to talk about. Most of it, we can't do here. Do you understand? I need to go out there and talk to that detective and about your ... legal situation. Right now, I just want to know if you're okay."

Vangie blinked hard. "Yeah."

"Did you really punch one of those cops?" Matty asked. I wasn't sure I liked his tone. My little brother had his run-ins with the law over the years. But every single time, he'd brought it on himself.

"They're dead," Vangie said, hiccupping.

"Who?" I asked. I took the chair on the other side of Vangie's bed, opposite Joe. Matty stood at the foot.

"S-Sarah and Ben. It can't be real. They have to be lying."

My mind raced. Sarah and Ben. Who the hell were Sarah and Ben? Vangie started straight at me. She could see the confusion running through me. She tried to sit up, her arms straining against the bindings. The clang of the hand-cuffs against the side rail made a hollow sound that seared straight through me. This was happening. This was real. My sister was in trouble.

"Sarah and Ben Dale. Jessa's adoptive parents." The cold truth slammed through me. Sarah and Ben. Jessa. Last year, my sister had revealed a secret that had nearly ripped my family apart. She ran away at eighteen after being raped by Coach Drazdowski, the murder victim in my big trial. Vangie hid the resulting pregnancy from all of us and gave the baby up for adoption. That baby was Jessa. Her daughter. I'd never met her, but she was now six years old.

"Wait a minute," Joe said. "You're saying Jessa's parents are dead? How? When? What's that got to do with you?"

I rose slowly from my seat. Double murder. They'd arrested my sister for double murder. Did they think she'd killed her daughter Jessa's adoptive parents?

Vangie slowly nodded. Tears spilled from her eyes. "Somebody killed them. They think it was me. I swear to God, I didn't do it. I would never …"

"Okay," I said, switching back into lawyer mode. "I told you we have a lot to talk about. I don't want to do it here if we can avoid it. You did the right thing calling me, honey. Let me take care of what I can. For your part, you talk to *no one* but me about these charges. I'm sorry, not even Joe or Matty right now."

I leveled a hard stare at Joe. He gave me just the slightest nod to tell me he understood. I would leave my sister in their care and trusted they'd keep her calm. I needed to find out what kind of mess she was in.

I stepped out into the hall. Detective Carey was a big guy, bald, barrel-chested. He looked like every hardened cop you see in the movies with the cheap suit to match. I headed straight for him. He was in a huddle with Dr. Hopperton and another woman who towered over the pair of them. Dr. Hopperton looked relieved as I showed up. She put her hands up in a gesture of surrender and backed out of the circle. The other woman turned to me.

I recognized her as Rayna DeWitt. Like me, Rayna was in her mid-thirties. We'd graduated from the same law school class though I barely knew her then. She was pretty, with kinky brown hair that she wore piled on top of her head. A few ringlets escaped near her temples and she gave me a pleasant smile.

"You're the lawyer?" she said, her voice hard, accusatory.

"We need to question your sister," Carey said. "They're discharging her."

"So you're fine with violating her HIPPA rights along with everything else?"

Rayna put a hand on Carey's arm. "Let's all just take a breath. Nobody's violating anything."

"Great," I said. "You have a copy of my sister's charging document? I'd love to take a look at the warrants you served on her."

"Of course," Rayna said. "You'll have everything you're entitled to as soon as humanly possible ..."

"Enough of this bullshit!" Carey turned on me. He was a huge, looming presence and he advanced on me, backing me against the nurse's station. "I don't give a good goddamn about your sister right now. I've got two murder victims still lying in a pool of blood on their kitchen floor. And I can't even care about that right now. But every second I gotta stand here talking to you and not your sister, there's a little kid out there that needs my help."

I couldn't breathe. Rayna DeWitt's smile faded and I saw her anger rise to match Detective Carey's.

"What the hell are you saying? You don't have Jessa Dale? Jesus. Where is she?"

Carey slapped his hand to his thigh. "That's what I need your sister to tell me. You can have my badge after this for all I care. It'll be worth it."

I side-stepped. My heart pounded in my ears. Jessa. Vangie's daughter. They didn't have her. Her parents were lying in a pool of blood. Dear God in heaven.

"You don't have her," I said, my throat dry.

"No," Carey said through gritted teeth. "I've got a team of officers out there canvassing. She's vanished. She didn't show up for school yesterday and the neighbor found the parents dead this morning. It's been over twenty-four hours already."

I met his eyes. Twenty-four hours. We both knew what that meant. For a missing child, that was an eternity. The case was already growing stone cold. My sister's behavior began to make sense. No wonder she'd resisted arrest. She was desperate. Frantic.

My six-year-old niece was missing and her parents were dead. From the hard look in Detective Carey's eyes, I knew he believed she was already dead.

Chapter 4

IT FELL to me to break the news to my sister that her six-year-old daughter was missing. For the first time, I was glad she was in restraints. She pulled against them, throwing her head hard against the pillow. Vangie let out a choked sound, like a wild animal in pain. My heart broke in a million pieces.

"What are they doing about it?" Joe said quietly. He hadn't moved from the chair beside Vangie. His fists tightened in his lap. Vangie wailed, but I sensed an equal, quieter reaction in my brother. He had a daughter of his own. Of course he was thinking about how he would feel if anything happened to Emma.

"There's been an Amber Alert issued," I said. "They're questioning the neighbors, her school friends ... but ... I don't know. Vangie, the police want to question you about Jessa. When was the last time you saw her?"

She went still, sinking against the pillow; she turned her head to the side. "Cass, you have to find her. She's just a baby. God. She must be so scared. If they hurt her ..." She turned to me, tears falling from her eyes. "They won't hurt her, will they?"

I had far more questions than answers. I still had no idea what evidence they even had against her. All I knew was Ben and Sarah Dale had been murdered in their home and their little girl had been missing for over twenty-four hours. The cold, clinical part of me knew the statistics. I couldn't let my mind go there.

"Two days ago," Vangie said. "I went to see her after she got home from school. She's in kindergarten, Cass. She's so smart. She read me a book."

"Vangie," I said, lowering my voice. "Why do the police think you killed her parents?"

Vangie's eyes darted back and forth. I was afraid of losing her to rage or despair all over again. She'd made her situation even worse by resisting the police, but I understood it. Though they hadn't given her hard answers, of course my sister worried about little Jessa when she found out what had happened to the Dales. But I needed to know what evidence they had against her, and fast.

"I don't know," she said. "They won't tell me anything. They wouldn't even tell me about my baby. They have to find her. Oh God. Cass, they have to find her!" Her voice rose and she started to thrash again. Her blood pressure monitor went off and a nurse came in.

"She's okay," I said. "My sister is just upset." The nurse adjusted the leads on Vangie's monitor and left us alone with a stern look. I wanted to get her out of here. But she was better off strapped to that hospital bed than she would be in jail. I was hoping to run out the clock and get her out on bail before that happened.

"Vangie," I said. Joe moved over and I took his seat. "Do you have any idea who might have hurt the Dales? You said you saw them two days ago, you were in the house?"

She nodded and my heart sank. So there would be physical evidence. My sister had been at the crime scene a mere hours before the murders. But that alone wasn't enough. She was Jessa's mother and she'd told me the Dales allowed her to see Jessa on a semi-regular basis. What else could they possibly have? The way my sister's eyes flickered, I got the sinking suspicion she had more to tell me that I wouldn't like one bit.

I didn't get the chance to ask her more before Detective Carey and Rayna DeWitt came back in. Rayna motioned for me to follow them.

"I'll be back," I said. I followed Carey and DeWitt into the same room where I'd met with Dr. Hopperton. Rayna had a thin case file under her arm.

"Listen," she said, turning to face me. "We've got more than one plate spinning at a time on this. Right now, our priority is finding out whatever we can to get that little girl back home. To the extent your sister can help with that, she needs to."

"She doesn't know anything," I said.

"Of course she doesn't," Carey said under his breath.

"Look," I said. "You're doing your job. I get that. I want nothing more than for you to find my niece too. I won't stop you from questioning my sister on that, as long as I'm right there with her."

"Your sister is scheduled to be arraigned in two hours," Rayna said. "I've got the charging document right here."

She slid a packet of paper out of her file and handed it to me. I scanned it quickly. They had Vangie on two counts of first-degree murder. Each would carry a life sentence with no possibility of parole if she were convicted. It was sparse on details except for the most chilling. Sarah Dale was shot three times, twice in the back and once in the head. Ben Dale died of blunt force trauma to the head.

"Where are your warrants?" I asked. Rayna pulled those out of the file and handed them to me.

I didn't like working like this. DeWitt and Carey stood there as I tried to absorb what little information I had, quickly. Though it was in me to stall for time, the sooner I got in front of a judge on this, the better. With any luck, I'd get Vangie released to me from the hospital instead of the county jail.

She'd been arrested at an address on Ellsworth Rd. just inside Ypsilanti. What the hell had she been doing there? They searched the place on a warrant, but it looked like they probably didn't even need it. It wasn't Vangie's house. It belonged to someone named Travis White. I had far more questions for my sister than answers but no good could come from tipping my hand.

"I'll meet you in court in two hours," I said, glancing over the documents as I left the room.

"Every second you stall me is one more second your sister's kid stays in danger," Carey shouted.

Blood roared in my ears. "My sister has no idea what's happened to that little girl. But we're on the same page as far as her safety. You can talk to her now."

DeWitt and Carey passed a look. Carey didn't need to be told twice. He barreled past her and followed me back into Vangie's hospital room. Matty and Joe bristled, but they dropped their shoulders and left the room at my command.

"Vangie," I said. "Among other things, Detective Carey is trying to help find Jessa. I said it would be all right for him to finish asking you a few questions about that."

Vangie sat up and gave him a frantic nod. "Anything," she said. "Anything you want. Just ... you have to find Jessa."

"When was the last time you saw her?"

"The day before yesterday," Vangie said. "I already said that. After school, about four o'clock."

"What was she wearing that day?"

Vangie's eyes darted to mine. I gave her a small nod. "Um ... she had on a pair of jeans. Pink light-up tennis shoes. She's learning to ride her bike without training wheels. She wanted to show me but it's too cold. God, it's so cold. If she's out there ... She has a pink parka. You know, one of those that has a hood with fuzzy white fluff on the inside. It's got white snowflakes all over it. Did you find that? Do you think she's got it? She'll need it."

Carey wrote it all down. His expression betrayed nothing. I watched my sister grow even smaller in that bed as she struggled to remember anything that might help find Jessa. But when the questioning veered to what happened at the house, I had to step in and shut it down.

Carey wasn't happy, but he knew he'd reached the end of that part of Vangie's story. His look was stone cold as he finished taking notes and left the room.

"It's freezing out there," Vangie said. "Cass, he wouldn't say if they found Jessa's coat."

"I know," I said. "You did great, though. Now, here's what's going to happen. You're being discharged and the sheriffs are going to bring you down the street to the district courthouse. You're scheduled for arraignment and a bail hearing this afternoon. You're going to plead not guilty. Then I'm going to argue like hell to have you released into my custody instead of holding you over in jail."

Vangie nodded. No sooner had I said it before two Washtenaw County deputies filed in, ready to transport my sister. Dr. Hopperton had worked some magic to get her discharge papers through. More than anything, I just wanted to bring my sister to the courthouse myself, but there was no way I could. I gave Vangie a grim-faced nod. She'd been so brave over the last year. Now I needed her to tap into that well of strength yet again.

I waited in the hall with my brothers. A few minutes later, Matty nearly lost it as the two female deputies led my sister out. She was shackled and had changed from a hospital gown to an orange jumpsuit. If luck was on our side, that would only be temporary.

Chapter 5

Two hours later, I walked into the District Courthouse in downtown Ann Arbor. My brothers stayed glued to my side. They wouldn't listen to me that they were better off waiting for me at home.

"I need you two to promise to behave yourselves," I said. "No outbursts. Actually, I'd rather you just go home and wait for me to call you."

"Bullshit," Matty said. "I'm not going anywhere. That's our baby sister they're trying to railroad."

"We don't know that yet," I said. "I don't even know what they've got on her." What I *hadn't* said was that the police felt it was enough for probable cause to arrest her. It had to be a hell of a lot more than just her visit to the Dales' house two days ago. What in the actual hell was going on with her?

I had no time to get into it. The judge called Vangie's case first. I dusted off my skirt, gave a stern look to my brothers, and headed up to the podium.

Vangie was led in with another group of criminal defendants. They were all chained together and my sister looked so scared.

Judge Ruiz took the bench. I didn't know her. She was newly elected and I didn't spend much time in District Court, let alone one county over. She wore a white lace collar over her robe that reminded me of Judge Judy. I wasn't sure if that was good or bad.

They brought Vangie to my side. The deputies loomed over her. Judge Ruiz read the charges against her and Vangie pled not guilty in a loud, clear voice.

"Your Honor," Rayna DeWitt said. "The state recommends no bail in this case. With the severity of the charges and the defendant's flight risk, I think no amount of bail is warranted."

Ruiz looked at me. "I disagree," I said. "As the court has likely surmised, Ms. Leary is my sister. I, along with our two brothers sitting in the gallery behind us, am her only family. I'm asking that you release her into my custody. There is also the matter of her child, the victims' adopted daughter. Jessa Dale, as the state is aware, is currently missing and endangered. My sister wants desperately for her to be found and is cooperating with law enforcement to the extent she can. She's not going anywhere. And, as an officer of the court, I'll vouch for her and can guarantee she doesn't leave town."

"Where do you live, Ms. Leary? Ms. Cassiopeia Leary?" the judge asked.

"In Delphi," I answered. "Out of county but it's only twenty miles from here."

"You're willing to post bond for her if I set it?" Ruiz asked.

"I am," I said, hoping like hell she didn't pick a figure I couldn't afford. Screw it. I'd mortgage the lake house if I had to and have Joe do the same to his place.

"Here's what I'm going to do," she said. "The state has a

point. These were heinous crimes. The status of that missing little girl makes me inclined to keep your sister behind bars until the police can make some headway on that investigation. I'll split the difference, so to speak. I'm setting bond at $500,000. If you can make it, I will release her on house arrest. She's not to leave your home, Ms. Leary."

Judge Ruiz banged her gavel before I could so much as close my mouth or breathe. A half a million bond meant I needed to come up with $50,000 for the surety company. It would hurt. I'd have to drain my meager savings, and take a hefty cash advance on my two credit cards. But Vangie would be under my roof by nightfall. It was worth every penny.

I turned to her. "You need to bear with me a little longer," I said. "There's some processing that still has to happen. The sheriffs will set you up with an ankle tether. They aren't the most comfortable things in the world, but …"

Vangie was crying. Sobbing actually. "Cass, I don't care. Thank you. I just want to hug you. Are you going to make this okay?"

In that brief moment in time, my sister was five years old again. She'd asked me the exact same question the day after our mother's funeral. Would I make this okay? Would I take care of her? I swallowed hard and gripped her shoulder.

"Yes," I said, hoping like hell I could make good on that promise.

Chapter 6

"WE'LL STAY WITH HER," Joe said, handing me the keys to his truck. "You go find out what you can. We'll meet you back at the house tonight."

My shoulders sagged with relief. Joe knew exactly what to say. I'd have to scramble to get the financial pieces in place for Vangie's bond. But in the meantime, I'd already called Miranda, my secretary. She sent a runner over to the prosecutor's office to get a copy of the lengthier police report on Ben and Sarah Dale's murder. By the tone in her voice, I knew she'd already taken a look at it.

"I'll be there in half an hour," I said. "Can you call Jeanie and see if she can pop over? I think the sooner I get good brains on this, the better."

"Will do," Miranda said. Jeanie Mills was my mentor and sometimes law partner. I pulled her out of retirement last year when I caught the Drazdowski murder case. I had no idea it would be less than three months before I was right back here with another one. My sister had helped me win that case. Now her own life was on the line.

Certain that Joe and Matty could keep their heads long

enough to get Vangie home safe, I rushed out of the court-house. After a quick stop at the bank to line up the bail money, I headed back to the office.

Miranda had put a closed sign on the front door. I didn't get much walk-in traffic, but it was a good call, nonetheless. I heard booming voices from upstairs. She was waiting for me in the conference room, the Dale file spread out on the table.

At first sight, Jeanie Mills didn't look like the bulldog she was in court. She was short and wide, yes, but had an almost grandmotherly face with soft eyes and a ready smile. At seventy, she didn't have any actual grandchildren of her own. She had my siblings and me. Two decades ago, after my mother died, she'd gone to bat with us against Child Protective Services and the probate court to keep us all under the same roof. My dad was barely fit to care for us back then, or ever, really.

"What do we have?" I asked, unbuttoning my coat.

"How is she?" Jeanie asked. It was six o'clock in the evening now, but she was sipping from a large mug of coffee, ready to pull an all-nighter if I asked her to.

"She's scared," I said. "They still haven't found Jessa."

"God." Jeanie took a step back, almost as if I'd delivered a gut blow. I guess I had. She learned about my sister's baby right along with me in the middle of the Drazdowski trial last year. We were both still working through our guilt on that score. Vangie hadn't wanted to tell either of us about what happened to her when she was only eighteen years old.

Jeanie went to the table and started laying out the crime scene photos. She printed them from a digital file, four to a sheet of paper. My heart twisted. They were devastating.

I'd never met Sarah or Ben Dale. They were young, both attractive. Vangie had shown me a picture of them just a few months ago. Ben had sandy-blond hair and bright blue eyes. He could have been a print model. Sarah was tall and pretty with a charming dimple in her cheeks, sleek dark hair and a wide jawline.

In the photos, Sarah lay on her back, spread eagle. She had on a pink tank top stained red with blood and checkered pajama pants to match. I noticed little details in the photo, my brain trying to shield itself from the grisly horror at the top of the frame. Sarah was barefoot, her toes perfectly pedicured with blue polish. Her dark hair fanned out beneath her. Part of the left side of her head above the forehead was gone. My stomach rolled and I pressed my hand flat against it.

The police report said she had also taken two shots to the back. Those wounds weren't visible in these photos, but the blood trail they left was. It led in an arc all around the kitchen island she lay beside.

Then there was Ben Dale. He lay at his wife's feet, face down, perpendicular to her body. His hair was stained completely through with dark, blackish blood. In the background, their stainless steel refrigerator could be seen. It was papered over with crayon drawings and what looked like a spelling list. Jessa's things.

I sank slowly into a chair at the conference table and sifted through the rest of the documents. I found the arrest warrant and read through it. Jeanie took the seat beside me and waited.

"Well," she finally said. "What are we dealing with?"

I looked again at the laundry list of evidence they'd based their warrant on. I could read the words, but my brain wouldn't process them. Jeanie put a hand on my wrist, pulling me back to the present.

"Come on, Cass," she said. "Let's go through it one by one."

"Right." I slid the photos of the bodies aside and fished for another one mentioned in the warrant. Jeanie had picked up the warrant itself. She let out a low whistle as she brought herself up to speed.

"Okay," I said. I went to the whiteboard I kept on an easel in the corner of the room.

"They've got a witness here, a neighbor," Jeanie noted as I started writing the bullet points. "Mrs. Kimberly. She saw Vangie at the Dales' house the evening before the bodies were discovered."

My hand trembled as I wrote in my shorthand. Vangie hadn't yet told me any details about her visit with the Dales. Would the Kimberly woman testify to anything damaging besides Vangie being there? Could she possibly have over-heard anything? "And we don't know yet how long the Dales were dead before the other neighbor found the bodies."

"Right," Jeanie said. "They were found at 10 a.m. the next morning by a Lisa Speedman. She's a friend of Sarah Dale's and their daughters are in the same grade. Speedman says she thought it strange Jessa didn't come to the bus stop that morning and when she walked by the house she noticed a service door to the garage wide open. She went in."

"There's no sign of a robbery," I continued. "Nothing was removed from the house as far as the investigators think. They found Vangie's fingerprints on Sarah Dale's cell phone."

Jeanie had picked up one of the photos. I looked side-ways. It was taken from the house where they arrested Vangie. She still hadn't explained that part to me either. With each bullet point I put on the board, my questions and fears deepened.

"This," Jeanie said, waving the photo. "They found a woman's shirt wadded up on the bedroom floor where Vangie was staying. It had bloodstains all over it. We're waiting for a complete analysis but what if it ends up being from one of the victims?"

I jotted down more notes. More questions for Vangie.

"And they found just one thing taken from the scene," I said. In another of the crime scene photos, a smashed picture frame rested face down on the stairs. There was a glaring space missing from a large gallery wall the Dales had in the foyer. The photo inside of it was missing.

"Whoever Ann Arbor's got in their computer crimes department knows what to look for," Jeanie said. "She found a picture of the wall in one of Sarah Dale's Facebook albums. The one in that frame was a family photo of the three of them taken just last year."

"And they found it on my sister." I had to sit down. None of this made any damn sense.

"Is she ready to talk?" Jeanie asked.

"She doesn't have a choice," I answered, my voice rising.

The office phone buzzed on the conference table. "Jeanie?" Miranda called up from the intercom. "That phone call you've been waiting on from the clerk's office is ready on line one."

I gave Jeanie a questioning look. She held up a finger and took the call. I couldn't tell much from the things she said. Just a yes, a no, and an "I see." But Jeanie's scowl deepened and when she met my eyes, I knew I wouldn't like whatever information she was getting from the other end of that phone. When she hung up, I couldn't sit a second longer.

"Jeanie, what?" I said.

Jeanie sat back hard in her chair. "That was my friend down at the Washtenaw County court clerk's office. I was just trying to figure out what Vangie and the Dales would have to argue about. I wanted to see if anything had made its way to the family court."

I shook my head. "Vangie doesn't have any rights to that child. The adoption has been final for years."

"Well, last week, the Dales petitioned for a personal

protection order against your sister. The judge signed it three days ago but it hadn't been served on her yet."

My heart dropped. Oh Jesus. This was getting worse and worse.

Before I could unleash the rant I wanted, my cell phone buzzed in my jacket pocket. It was Joe. Vangie had been processed. He was on his way back to my house with her. I texted him back that I would meet them there.

Jeanie rose and rested her hands on the table. I did the same on the other end. The evidence against my sister was already damning and it was only getting worse. And yet, my sister couldn't have done this. There had to be a mistake. Or she'd been framed. That was my heart talking and I trusted it. But before last year, I hadn't seen or spoken to my sister in over six years. She'd hidden her pregnancy from me. She'd kept the secret of Coach Larry Drazdowski and her rape from me.

Though my heart told me one thing, my head grew suspicious of something else.

Chapter 7

THE NEXT MORNING, we turned my living room into a war strategy session. Joe had helped me move the big whiteboard from my office and drilled holes in the wall so he could hang it there. For the duration, Vangie couldn't leave my house except to go to the courthouse and her follow-up appointment with a medical doctor. She was still frantic, pale, and she hadn't slept in going on three days.

"I can't stay here," she said. My sister was literally tearing at her hair. "She's out there. Somewhere. I have to be out there looking too."

There was still no word on Jessa's whereabouts. She'd been missing for over forty-eight hours. Even Vangie knew what that meant. The odds of her daughter being found alive dwindled by the minute. My heart broke for her. But there was nothing I could do about it. She was in trouble. Big trouble, and I needed her to understand it and come clean with me.

Joe and Matty were gone. The Ann Arbor police had set up a hotline for tips on Jessa's disappearance. The search party was focusing on a wooded area not far from the Dales' house. My brothers went to join it. This left me time to question Vangie outside their presence. It was better for all of us. Jeanie showed up with fresh donuts and a determined look on her face. I'd babied my sister up until now. That had to end and Jeanie was ready, willing, and able to back me up.

Jeanie set the coffee and donuts up on my living room table. I kept the worst of the crime scene photos away from my sister, but we had plenty to confront her with.

"Vangie," I said. "You have to tell me everything. I mean ... everything. Good, bad, ugly. You're facing two murder charges. If they stick, you'll never see the outside of a prison cell for pretty much the rest of your life."

"I didn't do it," Vangie said. She sat in the big recliner chair in the corner of the room, her knees tucked up under her chin. She looked every bit the little girl I used to dress and send off to school. But now, I needed her to grow the hell up.

"Why didn't you tell me about this?" I waved the personal protection order at her. Jeanie had picked up copies from the courthouse early this morning. "What was going on between you and Ben and Sarah?"

Vangie wiped a hand across her face. "It was all getting blown out of proportion. They weren't going to go through with that."

"They *did* go through with it!" I started to yell. Jeanie gave me a stern look. She knew my sister almost as well as I did. If I wasn't careful, she might shut down on me before I even got started. "Vangie, this is a signed ex parte order. That means Ben filed a petition. He presented evidence to the court. The judge found it to have enough merit to enter an order against you without a hearing. That's as serious as it gets. This was entered four days ago. You told me you went to their house three days ago. You violated a court order."

"They didn't tell me about it!" Vangie said. "It was bullshit. Sarah was freaking out. She was really pissed at me for going public with Jessa's paternity. I did that for *you!*"

I clenched my fists at my side. My heart tore with equal parts guilt and pure frustration. Vangie's testimony in the Drazdowski trial had been gut-wrenching and compelling. Her child was conceived by rape just before she turned eighteen.

"But why the P.P.O.?" Jeanie asked. "A personal protection order seems like a drastic step."

Vangie stared out the bay window at the placid lake. An inch of snow covered it making a picture-postcard scene. Tall, snow-dusted pines broke up the white landscape on the opposite shore. "I didn't think they'd do it," Vangie said, her voice small and quiet. "Sarah wanted to take what she called a cooling-off period. With all the publicity surrounding the trial, she thought it wasn't good for me to be around them."

"What did you say?" I asked.

Vangie had tears in her eyes as she looked at me. "What do you think I said? I love that little girl. She's my heart, Cass. She's a miracle. She's beautiful and smart and she's got this wild streak that drives her parents nuts. Jessa is amazing." Vangie's voice cracked. I went to her.

"Tell me the rest," I said. "Vangie, I need to know it all."

"I got angry," she said. "A few weeks ago, Sarah said she wasn't going to let me see Jessa anymore. She said it just got too complicated. She and Ben were even thinking of moving. He's had offers to work for another firm near his aunt and uncle in Florida. Boca Raton or somewhere. They always say no. Part of that is because Sarah liked that Jessa had this connection with me. But now …"

I sat on the footrest near her. I hated to admit it, but it made a certain amount of sense. The Drazdowski trial had ripped Delphi apart and made national news. I could understand her mother's desire to protect Jessa from any of that.

My sister was brave to tell her story, but it also meant Jessa's paternity was public knowledge. She had been conceived during a rape.

"Did you ever threaten them?" I asked.

Vangie dropped her eyes. "No. But ... I just couldn't *not* see Jessa. I went to her school a couple of times. They know me there. I brought her lunch."

"Christ. Without the Dales' permission?"

Vangie's eyes said it all. I wanted to shake her. I wanted to scream at her and ask her why she hadn't come to me with all of this. Why was she *still* hiding the biggest parts of her life from me?

"Okay," I said. "So they got the restraining order. Why did you go there the other night?"

"I just wanted to talk. I swear I didn't know about the order. I don't know why they never mentioned it. I don't know. Maybe they changed their minds about it? They never told me not to come. They never told me they got that paper. I didn't hear from their lawyer about it. Nothing. But Ben was really cold to me that night. He'd never been like that before. Things got a little heated. I'll admit, I said some things I regret now. I'm not proud of that. But I did *not* kill them over it. Jesus. I don't even know how to shoot a gun. The cops said someone shot S-Sarah in the head."

"All right," Jeanie said, practically reading my thoughts. "Let's focus on some of the rest of this. What the heck have you been doing in Ypsilanti? You're supposed to be in Indianapolis?"

Again, Vangie's eyes dropped to the floor. "I've been seeing someone. It's not super serious. His name is Travis. Sarah actually fixed me up with him. They did some remodeling last year and Travis's company installed all her new countertops. His boss went to high school with her or something, I don't know. I didn't tell you because I wasn't sure where we were going with it. Travis let me stay with him when I'd come up to visit Jessa. I was going to tell you, I promise. I was just ... I was trying to work things out with Sarah and Ben and I didn't want you to worry."

"Vangie," I said. "You need to stop keeping things from me because you don't want me to worry. I'd say so far it's done you no damn good."

"I'm sorry."

"The bloody shirt they found," I said. "Was it yours? I need to know whose blood they're going to find on it when the labs come back."

Vangie nodded and my heart sank. "It's not what they think. I told you. Jessa's been learning to ride her bike without training wheels. She wanted to show me when I came over. This was before we got into the argument. Looking back on it, I think Ben and Sarah were treating it as a final goodbye or something. Anyway, Ben had shoveled the sidewalk but it was still slippery and she's just learning. Jessa took a fall and scraped her wrists pretty badly when she hit the ground. I got to her first and picked her up. She bled on me. I took her into the kitchen and helped clean her up. That's all."

It sounded plausible. But there was still so much more. It was morbid to think it, but I knew it would be much worse if they found either Ben or Sarah Dale's blood on that shirt.

"And your fingerprints on Sarah's phone?" Jeanie asked.

"Jessa had gotten retakes of her school pictures. Her front teeth finally came in. Sarah had them on her phone and she handed it to me to show me. When I first got there, it was just a nice, normal visit. Then Ben and Sarah sent Jessa to her room and wanted to sit down at the table and talk. That's when they told me they didn't want me around anymore."

"What about that family photo?" I said. "The one the cops say was taken from the house. Vangie, why?"

She put a hand up. "That's a misunderstanding. Sarah gave that to me last year. They had a session with a professional photographer. She had one made for me. Jessa's wearing her favorite shirt in it. I got it for her. There's a little unicorn with a crown on it. It's from this cartoon Jessa likes to watch. They gave it to me. I don't know anything about a copy being taken from the house. I swear. That's all. I didn't take anything from that house. The cops have it wrong."

So Vangie had an explanation for everything. I needed to believe her. "Vangie, is there anyone who can corroborate any of this? I'm going to need to talk to this Travis White."

She shrugged. "Cass, I wasn't even comfortable telling you. Travis is pretty chill but he was still kind of trying to process all the stuff I told at that trial. I mean, I'm not saying he blames me but ... I have a lot of baggage. And like I said, we're not super serious. So, no. I didn't tell him I was having issues with the Dales. He didn't even know I was going over there the other day. He's been working in Chelsea for most of the month."

Great. So Vangie's defense rested on the strength of her own words right now. Though the presumption of innocence was on her side, I knew I'd need a hell of a lot more to get her out of this mess. I may have to track down a killer myself.

"Cass, I'm sorry," Vangie said. "I'm so sorry. I know you think I'm this huge fuck-up."

"No. That's not what I think. At all. I just ..." I stopped myself. I felt a big-sister lecture coming on and I knew that was the last thing Vangie needed. She was scared, vulnerable. In the space of three months, her entire life had been flipped on its side. I was responsible for that. I could have left her alone, living in Indianapolis away from all of us.

"Come on," Jeanie said. "I think we all could use a

break. Cass, let's take a walk. The fresh air will do you good. And Vangie hasn't had five minutes alone since this whole thing started. Let's give her that."

Jeanie pulled my parka off the hook near the door. I took it and shoved my feet into a pair of Joe's old snow boots that he'd left in the mudroom.

"Call Joe again," Vangie pleaded. "I have to know if they found anything."

"I will," I said. "Vangie, I love you. I want to tell you that everything is going to be all right."

"Don't," she said; her expression turned stony. "You can't say that. No one can. And I know what the time means. I know everyone thinks there's no hope for Jessa."

"No one is saying that," I said.

"She's alive," Vangie said. "I just ... I think I would feel it if she weren't. You know?"

I let out a hard breath and tried to muster a smile. God, I just could not imagine what my sister was going through. I'd been frustrated that she hadn't told me more about her issues with the Dales. She made so many bad decisions in the last few days but it was only in hindsight. And as Vangie sat there, her heart breaking and her eyes filled with tears, I understood her. She didn't care about the murder charges. She only cared about Jessa. It was one more thing I felt powerless to change.

Chapter 8

I WALKED OUTSIDE WITH JEANIE. Bitter cold had set in and my teeth chattered. The dock was pulled, but Joe and Matty left one wooden section at the edge of the water. Jeanie and I stood on it, looking out at the frozen lake.

"Well," she said. "What are you thinking?"

"I'm thinking we have some pretty huge problems. It's all going to come down to whether they believe Vangie's story."

"Yep," Jeanie agreed. "But somebody killed those poor people and took that child. That someone is still out there. What's our first move?"

"We shadow the investigation," I said. "I talk to the neighbor who heard their argument and the one who found the bodies. We have to try and start figuring out who else might have had the motive to hurt those people."

"What about her prelim?" Jeanie asked. "You wanna waive it?"

"I don't think so," I said. "Not this time. It's a risk giving the prosecution any insight into our defense strategy, but I have a sinking feeling it might be my best chance to talk to some of the witnesses or at least see how they play in court."

"We're going to need some help," Jeanie said.

She knew where my thoughts led. Jeanie had a private investigator she liked. It might come to that, but first, I had someone else in mind. "I want to talk to Detective Wray from the Delphi P.D.," I said. "Pick his brain on this one."

Wray came with plenty of baggage of his own, but he was smart. Cunning even. And I knew he could look at things with an objective eye.

Jeanie nodded. "Not a bad plan. He's got a good head and I think he'll keep an open mind. Let me see if I can round up a list of friends or family for the victims who might be willing to talk to us."

The wind picked up, making a keening howl. It blew straight through me. God, it was getting so cold. Tonight, it was supposed to get down to ten degrees.

"I just pray to God she's safe," I said. "She wouldn't survive a night in the cold." I pulled my parka tighter around me. I felt perhaps just a little of the despair my sister had. I'd never met my niece. She was part of Vangie's soul. As the wind tore through me, I wondered if I'd ever get the chance to meet her. I had to put on a brave face for Vangie, but knew Jessa's chances dwindled with every passing minute.

"God," I said. "Who the hell could do such a thing? Jeanie, someone has to know something. I need to talk to this boyfriend. Vangie said something about his company doing work on the Dales' remodel. It means he might have had access to the house."

"One thing at a time," Jeanie said. "One foot in front of the other and all that. Let the cops do their job heading up the search. We can only do our job for Vangie."

My phone rang from deep inside my pocket. It was Joe. My heart flipped as I answered. "What?" I couldn't even hide the rising fear in my voice. Please God, let this not be bad news.

"Cass," he said, breathless. "They've got something. Can you meet me?"

Chapter 9

Now I was a liar. I could barely breathe as I gathered
myself to walk back into that house. Joe's words burned
through me. *They've found a little girl matching Jessa's description.
She's at a hospital in Hillsdale.*

As he texted me the address, Jeanie and I decided we
couldn't say anything to Vangie yet. "She'll try to follow you.
You know she will. Then we'll have the added problem of
her breaking her bond conditions. She's already got a strike
against her on that P.P.O. violation."

I gave Jeanie a nod. In a lot of ways, I was asking her to
handle the hardest part of this. She would stay with Vangie
and try to keep her from turning on the local news. I made a
vow to call and tell her what was going on as soon as I got to
that hospital. As we walked back into the house, Vangie had
my laptop open and her face was ashen.

Shit.

"Vangie."

She looked up at me. "My arrest is in the Free Press," she
said. She turned the laptop toward me. Sure enough, her
name was in bold letters across the top of my newsfeed. Star

witness in Drazdowski murder trial now stands accused of double homicide.

I felt a flare of relief that news hadn't broken about the Jane Doe in Hillsdale. Like Jeanie said, it would do her no good to get worked up about that until we knew for sure. But the publicity surrounding the Dale murders would land on all of us hard. There was no help for it.

I took the laptop away from my sister and slid it into my messenger bag. The police had Vangie's cell phone. There was the television, but I felt fairly confident Jeanie could keep that under control.

"I have to leave for a little while," I said, hating the lie I needed to tell. "I'll be back in a few hours. Jeanie's going to keep you company. Try not to worry about the media stuff. It was bound to happen. We'll deal with what we have to and ignore the rest."

Vangie stared out the window, not exactly placated by my words, but the fight had gone out of her. It broke my heart just a little bit more. I prayed I'd have good news for her from Hillsdale.

I heard tires crunch through the snow and saw Matty's truck pull up across the street. Joe was already on the way to the hospital. Matty and I would go together. If Vangie saw him out there, she'd have questions I wasn't ready to answer. I shot a quick look to Jeanie and went quickly out the door to meet my brother.

"What do you know?" I asked Matty as I shut the truck door and he whipped around, heading away from the lake.

"We were working in a grid pattern through Cedar Bend woods. The Ann Arbor cops got a call from the Hillsdale ones. A little girl was brought in to the emergency room there. She's roughly the same age as Jessa and fits the description."

Matty white-knuckled the wheel as he made the turn to

the highway on-ramp. "Matty," I said, my heart pounding. "Is she alive?"

He paused before answering. "Yeah. Cass, I don't know much. Just that they're trying to identify her. But she's hurt badly. Not conscious."

"Oh Jesus," I said. My head pounded. I didn't know what to wish for. Matty picked up speed. Snow pelted the windshield. I know how much he wanted to press the gas. It would do us no good if we got into a wreck on U.S. 12. Mercifully, traffic was light.

"Did you say anything to her?" Matty asked.

"No. Joe and I didn't think it would do her any good. Vangie needs to stay put. I think no power on this earth would have kept her from trying to come with us if she knew. I'll call her from the hospital after we've had a look at this poor kid."

"Joe said they might give us some resistance on that," Matty said. "We're not her legal next of kin."

"You let me worry about that," I said. "Right now, as far as I know, we're the closest thing she's got. Vangie said Ben and Sarah Dale don't really have other family. Ben's got an elderly aunt and uncle but they're down in Boca Raton. With the weather, they're having trouble getting a flight out."

"What a mess," Matty said and I knew he wasn't talking about the roads.

My brother was steady and calm as we made our way west to Hillsdale. I felt suspended in time, praying for a good outcome. Only, I didn't know what that might be. If this was Jessa, how badly had she been hurt? What had she seen? It seemed as though this nightmare grew deeper with each day.

An hour later, we pulled into the parking lot of the Hillsdale Hospital. Part of me didn't want to get out of that truck. Would things be worse an hour from now, or better?

"Come on," Matty said. "Joe's already here. There's his truck."

I gave my little brother a grim nod and the two of us headed into the hospital together. After a few wrong turns, we found the pediatric intensive care unit. As the elevator opened, Joe stood red-faced at the nurses' desk surrounded by three uniformed officers. One of them had his hands on my brother.

"Joe!" I shouted. The last thing I needed was his temper landing him in legal hot water. I had enough on my plate as it was.

Relief flooded through Joe's face as he saw me. "Finally. Cass, tell these boys who we are."

I pulled out my business card. It did no good.

"We've got orders," one of the cops said. He was young, maybe no more than twenty-five. He had a fresh face with rosy cheeks and dark straight hair that he wore slicked back. His nameplate read Denny.

"Officer Denny," I said. "Can you just point me to your sergeant or whoever's in charge here?"

He hesitated, then pointed down the hall. A woman in a blue suit leaned against the wall, talking to one of the doctors. She straightened her posture as she saw me coming toward her. I took a breath and barreled ahead. Joe stayed behind, still surrounded by officers, but Matty followed.

I explained who I was as simply as I could. "We just want to help identify this child," I said. "I need to know if that's my niece in there."

She introduced herself as Detective Laura Gold from Hillsdale County.

"Hold it!" a familiar voice boomed from behind me as Detective Carey caught up with us. "I don't want you anywhere near that child. This is still an ongoing murder investigation and that poor kid may be a material witness."

"Are you serious right now?" I said. "You think I came here to question her or coach her? Christ. I just want to know if it's Jessa. That's all."

"Brett," the woman said. "Let's just handle one thing at a time."

"That baby won't be answering any questions," the doctor said. He was a middle-aged man with a deeply tanned face and wispy brown hair that he wore in a combover.

"What happened?" I asked. "Can you please tell me that much?"

"Dr. O'Dell" was embroidered in blue on the man's lab coat. O'Dell gave a stern look to Carey and Gold. Gold gave a gesture of surrender.

"She was found in an abandoned house a few miles from here. A known crack den," Gold said.

"What's her condition?" I asked. I could hear the sound of my own voice, but it was as if I'd gone on autopilot. I could hear and see, but everything inside of me just ... stopped.

"Serious, but she'll pull through," Dr. O'Dell said. "This child has been abused and neglected for some time. She took a fall. One of the neighbors saw a fire coming from inside the house. He called the police. This little girl was found at the bottom of some broken stairs. Her face is pretty banged up. She's got a concussion and some broken ribs. Her electrolytes are a mess. But like I said, I think she's going to pull through. She hasn't woken up yet. We're trying to bring her body temp up slowly."

"Is it Jessa?" Matty said. The officers down the hall had finally let Joe through. He got to my side, panting, his eyes wild.

"We're not sure," Detective Gold said. "She's got some bruising under her eyes and her color's not good. She's roughly the same age and the basic description matches. We're waiting on her true next of kin." Gold looked at her notepad. "Geri and Martin Dale? Aunt and uncle, I guess. They've got some time-share in Aruba. They're working on trying to get back here."

"Let me see her," I said, my voice shaking. "Please."

"Have you ever even seen your niece before?" Carey asked.

"No. But ... if you'll let me take a picture and get my sister on the phone."

"Brett." Detective Gold stood between Detective Carey and me. "Let her see the kid. Just for a few minutes. She might be able to help."

"Come on." It was Dr. O'Dell who stepped in and took charge. He led me gently by the arm. Joe and Matty didn't wait for permission. They followed. The three of us filed into the small private room at the end of the hall.

Monitors beeped and three nurses tended to the tiny patient in the small bed.

She was pretty, the delicate shape of her face and her rosy, full lips, even with the bruising on her cheeks. Behind me, Matty spoke softly into his phone. He called Vangie the second we started walking down the hall.

I pulled out the 3x5 school picture Vangie had given me of Jessa. The detectives were right. This little girl was about the same age and her hair color matched. Jessa's was a little longer in this picture but it was taken a few months ago. What had struck me most was how much my niece looked like my sister at the same age. I tilted my head to the side. This girl looked like her too but ... I just wasn't sure.

Matty handed me the phone. My sister was nearly hyster-ical on the other end. "You let me see my baby!" she screamed.

"Vangie," I said. "Listen to me. I need you to think. Does Jessa have a birthmark or anything I can look for?"

"I know my baby," she said. "Why didn't you tell me? I know the shape of her hands, her feet, her nails. You're wasting time with this. Is she okay? Tell me the truth. Is she dead?"

"Vangie, I'm not even sure it's her. But yes, this child is going to be okay."

Vangie let out a sob. It took her a few beats, but I heard her breathing become more rhythmic and calmer on the other end of the phone.

"Her foot," she finally said. "Her right foot. She has a little crescent-shaped scar on her big toe. She was playing barefoot on a park slide when she was just a toddler. She cut it."

I moved to the end of the bed and carefully pulled back the pink cotton blanket. The little girl had glittery purple polish on her small toes. But there were no scars on any of them.

"And behind her right knee. She's got a little birthmark. A perfect little brown dot." Vangie quietly sobbed.

I handed the phone back to Matty for a moment as I pulled the blanket further up. "May I?" I said to the doctor. He nodded as I carefully turned the girl's leg so I could see the back of her knee. She had a tiny scab on her calf, but no birthmark like Vangie described. My heart sank and my knees went a little weak. I shook my head no at the doctor and my brothers.

"Vangie," I said, swallowing hard. "This isn't Jessa."

Vangie's sob on the other end of the phone echoed through the room.

My brothers looked at me. No, they looked *to* me, just like they always did. I set the tone. I was always the one in charge. Even though Joe was older by almost a year, I'd been the one to step in and do all the maternal things when we lost our mother. They expected me to make it all right. I *always* made it all right.

I handed Matty's phone back to him. He held it out away from himself as though it were molten. Maybe it was. Air rushed in and the room seemed to darken. I needed a minute. I needed space. I need to get the hell away from all of them.

Chapter 10

I PUSHED through the door and ran down the hall to the stairwell. Slamming my shoulder against that door, I made my temporary escape. There was nowhere to go. I made it down one flight of stairs then sank to the step and buried my face in my hands.

That poor, broken girl. She wasn't Jessa, but she belonged to someone. She'd been abandoned, discarded in the freezing cold. Had the same thing happened to Jessa? My stomach roiled as a worse reality sank in. Ben and Sarah Dale hadn't just been murdered. Theirs had been a brutal, bloody death. Sarah's body at least had been dragged through the house. Had her husband walked in and found her like that? Had it been the last thing he saw before his killer caved in the back of his skull?

The service door at the top of the stairs creaked open and two shadows fell over me. My brothers stood there, watching me fall apart, not knowing what to do about it.

I don't know how long they stood there, but Joe finally came down the stairs and sat in the space on the step beside me. Matty took his lead and sat two steps above us.

"Don't ask me," I said, my voice coming out harsher than I wanted or either of them deserved.

Joe put a hand on my back. I bristled at first. Just that slightest touch threatened to unravel me even more. I let my tears fall.

"We'll find her," Joe said.

I looked at him. "I can't promise Vangie that. I can't promise any of you that. No one can, Joe."

"We'll keep looking," Matty offered. "She can't just have vanished into thin air. Somebody knows something. They have to."

"People vanish like that all the time. Little kids!" My voice didn't sound like my own. It went up an octave. "Pure evil touched that house and took that baby. What I saw ... what happened to them ..."

I couldn't finish. My brothers had been spared the crime scene photos. I would bear the burden of that memory alone for now.

"We'll figure this out," Joe said. "We'll ..."

I snapped. It was so unlike me. "Joe, this is different. This isn't Matty getting picked up for smashing bar stools at Mickey's after a bender. This isn't you and Josie picking custody fights. It's not Dad blowing the money for the electric bill at the race track or even a car accident one of us can't walk away from. This is ... this is the end of the world."

"I don't believe that," Joe said.

"Joe, two people are dead. Murdered in cold blood. They suffered horribly. It wasn't painless. They knew what hit them. And that baby ... if she saw it ... if she's even alive ..."

"Vangie didn't do this!" Matty shouted.

I took a breath. "I know that. But it's bad. Okay? The evidence they have against her is very damning. I can't ... I don't ..."

"Cass, it's okay," Joe said. "We know."

I leaned my head against the wall and looked at my brother. Sweet Joe. My rock. My best friend. His piercing blue eyes hardened as he looked at me.

"I just …" It came out of me like a sigh. "I don't know if I can fix it this time."

And that was it. It was the thing Vangie and my brothers always expected of me and up until now, I knew I could deliver. But this was bigger than me. It was so much worse. As Matty and Joe watched me, I could see the truth finally settle in for them.

"What can we do?" Matty asked. I loved him for it.

I smiled at him and reached out to touch his cheek. "Just … be you. Be steady. I can't handle any more drama and neither can Vangie." He knew what I meant. No matter how bad this got, he'd have to keep his own nose clean and stay away from Mickey's.

"You have to have a plan," Joe said. It took me a beat to realize it wasn't a statement. He'd heard what I said but it hadn't seeped all the way in for him. I closed my eyes and found my breath.

The answer was no. I didn't have a plan. I didn't know how the hell I was going to get my sister clear of these murder charges when she'd kept so many things from me. I didn't know how I could promise her sweet little baby would come back to her safe and whole. Because she wouldn't. No matter what, Jessa would never be the same, if she was even alive at all. I had no plan. No answers. There was no way out.

Still, I found a smile for my older brother and slowly got to my feet. I put a hand out to his. He took it and rose beside me. Matty got up and started back up the stairs.

"Yeah," I said, brushing the hair out of my eyes. "I'll

figure out a plan. We're going to be okay. All of us. I promise."

Joe's eyes flickered with the dark knowledge of the lie I just told. Then he took my hand and we walked up the stairs together.

Chapter 11

BETHANY GERWICK. The little girl in the Hillsdale Hospital had a name. Like Jessa, she was six years old. Unlike Jessa, she wasn't missing and she was no longer in danger. Detective Carey called to fill me in two days later, the day of Ben and Sarah Dale's joint funeral.

Jeanie and I sat across the street from the church in her car with the tinted windows. Vangie wanted to be here. She wanted to pay her respects. Never mind house arrest, the press and mourners would eat her alive.

Mourners lined the streets, waiting for more than six blocks in the bitter cold. Sarah was well loved. A special education teacher in one of the expensive private schools near the University of Michigan main campus. She'd been a twenty-five-year ovarian cancer survivor, contracting the disease in college. It's why she couldn't bear a child of her own. Jessa was their miracle child. She was their savior.

"They'll want blood," Jeanie said.

"Vangie's blood," I whispered back. "And it won't matter that she didn't do this."

A sense of unease settled through me. I didn't know

whether it was better to go in or stay here watching. It felt voyeuristic, but I couldn't help but wonder if Ben and Sarah Dale's real killer was out there somewhere. Was he watching just like I was? Was he in the church?

I'd taken a picture of the Dales' family photo on my phone, the one taken from the crime scene. I pulled it up and enlarged it. They were beautiful. Perfect. They could have easily been the picture frame models and not a real family. Jessa gave a wide smile. She had a slight overbite just like Vangie had at the same age. I traced my finger around her face. It looked like the photographer had made her laugh just before snapping the picture. Happy. Normal. Untouched by any of the horror that was soon to come.

"I wish Vangie had told me," I said.

"She was afraid," Jeanie said.

"Of what? Of me? That I'd disapprove? That I would have told her to get rid of the baby? You know I wouldn't. *She* knows I wouldn't. I would have supported her in this. I would have supported her if she'd wanted to keep Jessa."

"Vangie was in no position to raise a child and neither were you at the time. And stop blaming yourself. There's nothing else you could have done. You're here now. You've always been there for her. You were allowed to look out for yourself and do what you thought was best. Stop beating yourself up for moving to Chicago and staying there. Vangie made her own choices. You can't always fix everything, Cass."

Jessa's sweet face stared up at me from the photo. Her shirt was pink and purple with that silly cartoon unicorn on it. It had a gold crown on its head rimmed with glitter. Jessa wore a little tutu and sat cross-legged between her parents. God, would I ever get the chance to meet her? What had she seen? Was she even alive at all?

"Come on," Jeanie said. "There's nothing more for us to do here. I'm not even sure why we came."

"I don't know," I said. "I just ... I owe them. They loved my niece. Gave her a home and until ten days ago, comfort, warmth, and safety. It's something I should have been able to do."

"Don't start this again," Jeanie said. "You didn't know. As much as it hurts me too, that was Vangie's choice. She has no regrets and you shouldn't either."

I hadn't told Jeanie about my moment of weakness at the hospital the other day. I wished Matty and Joe hadn't seen it. More than at any other time in our lives, they needed me to be strong now. I couldn't afford to fall apart on any of them. I vowed I wouldn't again.

Jeanie put a hand on my back. Her eyes were stern as she looked at me. "You're all right, kid," she said.

I blinked hard. I was done crying. There was work to do.

I looked back at the church. The bells began to ring and the rest of the mourners edged their way in. I took a breath and did a sign of the cross. I prayed for the Dales. I prayed for Jessa. I prayed a little for myself. Beside me, Jeanie crossed herself as well.

It was time to go.

"You ready?" Jeanie asked.

I was. I had to be.

"Yep," I said.

"Good," she said. "Miranda's got the boyfriend coming in."

The boyfriend. Travis White. The guy Vangie had been seeing in Ann Arbor when she came to town to visit Jessa. I didn't know what to expect. He'd been the one to let the cops in and search his place. If he'd refused, I might have at least a glimmer of a chance to keep Vangie's bloody shirt and that family photo of the Dales away from a jury. They would have come in on their warrant anyway, but it would have been something.

I wasn't much company for Jeanie as we drove back to my office. It had stopped snowing and traffic was light. It seemed like everyone was heading *in* to Ann Arbor that day, not away from it. As we pulled around to the back parking lot, Jeanie got a text from Miranda that Travis was already there waiting for us.

"You want me in on this one?" Jeanie asked.

I cut my engine but stared out the window a second longer. "No," I said. "Let me just see if I can get the guy to open up first. You can be a little intimidating on first impression."

Jeanie let out a gruff laugh. Intimidating was a kind word and she knew it. Jeanie was blunt and direct. She also scared the crap out of most men. It made her one of the top family lawyers in the state in her prime.

"Fine," she said. "You know where to find me if you need me. I'm going to see if the full autopsy reports have come back yet." I got out of the car and gave her a wave as she backed out and headed downtown.

I went in the back and passed Miranda's workstation. She rolled her eyes and pointed upstairs. "He's waiting in your office," she said. "Good luck with that one."

"Great. What am I walking into?"

Miranda sat back in her chair. "Well, he's not a fan of your sister anymore. I think some keyboard warriors online have scared him off a little. And ... he's not too bright."

I reached for my mail. "Great."

"How was the service?" Miranda asked.

I put the letters down. They were mostly bills and one letter from a random prisoner seeking legal advice. All lawyers get those. I was pretty sure some inmates just throw darts at pages in the bar journal and write to whoever they land on.

"We didn't go in," I said. "Jeanie talked me out of it. She was afraid someone would recognize me from the news and it would upset the Dales' friends and family. There were a few 'Justice for Jessa' protesters camping out across the street."

"Probably a wise choice," she said. "Things will die down. Once you get Vangie clear of this, I think they'll appreciate that you all have common interests."

I loved that she said *when* I get Vangie clear of this, not *if*. I had my crisis of confidence at the Hillsdale Hospital. I had no room for any more. I straightened my suit jacket and headed upstairs. Hopefully, Travis White could tell me *something* useful. At a minimum, I needed to know how badly his testimony might hurt Vangie.

I opened the door to my office. Travis stood facing the wall, reading my framed certificates. He gave a whistle but didn't turn to face me as I walked in.

"Impressive," he said. "U. of M. Law, Michigan Bar, Illinois, Ohio even? How many times did it take you to pass?"

"Uh ... just the once, thanks," I said. "Mr. White?" I extended my hand. He looked me up and down then shook it.

He was cute in a young Brad Pitt sort of way. The same clear blue eyes, rough smirk, and two days of blond stubble across his jawline. He wore fitted black pants with pointed boots and a crisp gray button-down tucked in only in front. Vangie told me he had aspirations to be some kind of club promoter and first-class bullshit artist. They weren't serious, they were just ... fun ... as she described it.

"Have a seat," I said. "And thanks for coming down. I know it was a bit of a haul for you."

"No problem," Travis said. He was still smirking and I didn't like it.

"Look, I'll get right to it," I said. "I don't want to waste your time, and I'm very sorry you've been dragged into the middle of this thing. I know the police have already questioned you. I've read your statement to them. I just wanted to explore a few things with you relating to the night of the Dales' murder."

He crossed one leg over his knee. "I told the cops everything I know. Sorry, but I'm no alibi for your sister. I wasn't with her on the night of the 8th or the 9th. I was out of town. She was crashing at my place. I got home super early on the morning of the 10th. Like four a.m. early. Vangie was sleeping in my spare bedroom. She'd texted me a few days before saying she was coming into town. We were planning to hook up when I got back."

"When you say hook up ..."

Travis smiled. "Yeah. Hook up. Things are loose with us, you know. Vangie's a cool girl. I mean, I thought she was. She's chill. We're not exclusive. When she comes to Ann Arbor, I like hanging out with her if I don't have anything else going on. For the last year or so, I've been letting her stay at my place when she comes in to visit her kid. That's all that was going on this last time. She texted me on the 6th, said she might be coming in over the weekend. I told her I'd be in and out but that she could come and I'd see her when I saw her. You know?"

"Okay, okay. I get it. But you were home the morning of the 10th when the police showed up looking for her."

Travis picked at his shoe. "Yeah. They showed up banging on the door at like ten, I think it was. I'd only been asleep for a few hours. When I answered the door, I wasn't even sure Vangie was still there. I was kind of groggy. Hungover, actually."

I took notes, but so far, Travis hadn't told me anything I didn't already know. "You let them in? Did they tell you they had a warrant?"

"They said they were looking for Vangie. Like I said, at first I wasn't even sure she was still there. It's not unlike her to split before I wake up and it was late morning already. But I've got no beef with the cops. I figured whatever Vangie had going on, that was her deal. Well, I let them in. Vangie came out of the bedroom. She didn't seem like she knew what the hell was going on either. It was all pretty confusing and happened kind of fast. But at one point, one of them told her she was under arrest. She was really calm. She said right away she wanted to call her sister. She told them you were a lawyer. It was weird to me. I mean, she seemed *too* calm."

"Travis, what do you mean by that?" His statement didn't track with what I heard on the other end of the phone that morning. I didn't know if he realized I was on the phone with her. I decided to keep that to myself. If he was lying, I'd let him walk right into his own trap.

"I mean, if a bunch of cops showed up and said they were arresting *me* for murder, I'd have lost my shit. Not Vangie. At least, not right away. Then one of them asked me if I minded them searching the house. I was all, fuck, no, do whatever you gotta do. This had fuck all to do with me. Well, that's when Vangie started to freak. I mean, *really* freak."

I knew at this point in the timeline, Vangie had called me. I didn't like Travis's take on things at all. He was making it sound like Vangie had something to hide. But I had yet to hear an outright lie. Damn.

"Travis, did you know who the Dales were? I mean, don't you think it makes sense that Vangie would be upset at hearing her daughter's adoptive parents were dead?"

Travis looked back at the wall. God, he would be awful on the witness stand. Forget Brad Pitt, he had a Kato Kaelin slacker vibe that just wouldn't read well at all. "She didn't tell me any of that. I told you. We were chill. I knew she had a kid is all. She never got too specific about the details. I just kind of assumed she had a rich baby daddy in Ann Arbor and she went to go visit when he let her. She didn't ever mention the Dales by name. It was none of my business."

"Okay." I steepled my fingers beneath my chin. "What about before that? Was the morning of the 10th the first time you saw Vangie when she came into town this time?"

"Uh ... no. I told this to the cops. I checked my phone for them and she texted me again saying she was coming in on the 7th. That was that Saturday. She got in about three in the afternoon. I was getting ready to leave. We spent some time together, had a late lunch. Then by five I was out of there. I didn't see her again until I came back on the 10th. That's when all the shit hit the fan."

"Indeed," I said. "So on the 7th, when you *did* see her. Was there anything unusual?"

Travis arched a brow. I got that hollow feeling in the pit of my stomach, as if I were just about to drop down the first hill of a roller coaster.

"She took a phone call. I can't honestly remember if she called someone or if someone called her. But she was arguing with the caller. Like ... loud. Vangie kept saying 'you can't do that, she's my daughter, you can't keep me from seeing her.' And she kind of lost her shit. Went into the back bedroom and started crying. I don't know. It started getting heavy after that."

Travis gave me a look that made me want to reach across the desk and slap him upside the head. *Things got heavy.* As in, it wasn't what Travis White signed up for. My sister was a hook-up to him, nothing more. In fairness, I was pretty sure that's all he was to her, but still, my big sister over-protective-ness flared hard.

"Listen," he said, leaning forward. "I get that she's your sister and all. But you wanna know what I think?"

I bit my lip past the retort, not really. "Sure," I said instead. No matter what else happened, I was stuck with Travis White as a witness. The prosecution would call him. I had to have a strategy for dealing with him. It would start with me knowing every side of his story.

"Vangie was losing her shit that night on the phone. I heard her threaten that person. I don't know this for sure, but I think she was talking to Sarah Dale, her kid's mom."

I held my tongue. We had Vangie's cell phone records as part of the police report. I'd have to check the timeline, but I knew there were calls and texts going back and forth with Sarah Dale all through that day. He was very likely right and Vangie had already told me much of this herself.

"You heard her threaten her how?" I asked.

Travis spread his hands and shrugged. "I'm paraphrasing, but she said some shit like, you'll regret this. You can't keep me from my kid. She said something about how she's stood up to worse and she wasn't going to back down. I'm just sayin' if I were on the other end of that phone, it would have creeped me out."

"Travis," I asked. "Do you know my sister's history? I mean, you must follow the news. You know about the trial she was involved in last year."

Travis shrugged. "Yeah. A little. I know she was messed up from the stuff that happened to her when she was a kid. That's fucked up. I felt bad for her when I found out. I mean, she was always normal with me. Great, actually. She didn't seem like she had any hang-ups from ... you know ... what happened to her."

I gripped the arms of my chair. No hang-ups? Was this creep actually telling me he was impressed my sister was a good lay even though she'd been raped? God, I wanted to do more than smack him upside the head. He seemed to sense something in my expression. Travis held his hands out in a gesture of surrender.

"I'm sorry. Shit. I don't mean to be a dick, or anything. I told you. I thought your sister was a cool chick. I mean, she was. But I'm telling you, she freaked the fuck out on the phone with that woman. She wasn't just pissed. It was ... like serious rage. You know?"

I had to ask him. I would never allow it if he took the witness stand, but here in my office, it mattered. "Travis, do you think my sister actually murdered the Dales?"

Travis looked behind him as if he were concerned someone might listen in. "I think ... I think a bunch of shit adds up. That's all I'm saying. And I'm saying I do feel bad for her. I mean, a little. She had some heavy shit happen to her. She hid it for a really long time. I never would have suspected she had that kind of past. But people snap. You know? It catches up with you. And as bad as I feel for her, I gotta tell the truth. I'm known for my word."

I was pretty much ready to tear the leather right off my chair.

"I appreciate that, Travis," I said through gritted teeth.

"Well, anyway. Yeah. If it was Sarah Dale on the other end of that phone, and I think it was ... Vangie was making sure she knew she was going to do anything she had to to keep her from taking her kid away. That's a fact and that's what I told the cops. It's a damn shame all the way around and I hope Vangie gets the help she needs. But ... yeah ... lady, I think your sister is screwed. And if she's telling you and the cops she didn't do this, well, I think she's probably lying."

"Well, I thank you for your candor," I said. Travis got up to leave. He gave me a wave and a smile as he walked out the door, closing it behind him.

I sat back hard in my chair. Travis White was probably an idiot. But he might just be a convincing idiot if he ever took the stand. His testimony could provide an important nail in my sister's coffin unless I could find a way to discredit him.

Chapter 12

"Please tell me something good," I said to Jeanie. "I'll take literally anything right now."

Jeanie waved off the waitress. At eleven o'clock, it was too late for her to have any more coffee and too early for her to eat lunch. Jeanie was on a chemo maintenance regimen as a precaution after a cancer scare last year. She'd found a way to manage her side effects with a strict diet and liberal use of medicinal pot. In many ways, she was stronger and healthier than I'd ever seen her now.

"Well," she said sliding into the booth opposite me. The leather creaked under her weight. I'd picked a tucked-away corner at Bernadette's Diner in the middle of town. Now that we were here, I regretted the choice. Rumors had just started to die down about my last trial. They were swirling again about my next one. Jeanie paused for a beat too long. My heart sank. She had nothing good to tell me at all.

"My guy didn't turn up anything useful," she said, bluntly as always. "Ben and Sarah Dale were pretty much beloved in their little community. Sarah was more or less a saint. She worked with mostly autistic kids at a private school in Ann Arbor. I've got page after page of witness statements. She saved their kids. Got through to some of the most troubled cases when nobody else could. Ben was quieter, more reserved. The numbers guy. But he was well liked at his accounting firm and up for a promotion. I'm just not coming up with anybody who might have had a motive to hurt them like that."

I wiped the corner of my mouth with my napkin and tossed it on the table. "Except for my sister."

Jeanie gave me a grim nod. "Except for your sister."

I tapped my fingers on the table. I filled her in on my lovely conversation with Travis White. Jeanie's expression stayed hard. I knew she expected as much. "I don't know," I said. "He was just ... hell ... I don't even know how to say it. Shady. Douchey. Whatever."

"Shady," Jeanie repeated. "Shady how? Like you think he might know more or have more to do with what happened than he's letting on?"

I ran my thumb around the rim of my coffee cup, wiping away the lipstick stain. "Maybe. Or maybe it's just wishful thinking on my part. The Dales had money. Lots of it. Travis White is a hustler. He did work on their house. Installed cabinets or countertops, I think Vangie said. He had access. What do we know about their alarm system?"

Jeanie shrugged. "Well, they had one. It didn't go off that night."

"So, whoever was in that house was either let in or the killer knew how to bypass it," I said.

"Damn, that boyfriend would be a natural suspect. The cops grilled him though. He had an alibi," Jeanie said. "He was working in Chelsea the night of the murders."

"Right," I said. "But maybe he gave someone else the information they needed to break in. He could have been working with someone. I need to dig a little deeper into his background."

Jeanie nodded. "Right. But nothing was taken from their house that morning except for what, a family picture?"

"I don't know. Maybe it was a recon mission gone wrong. Like he was there to see what they had so he could come back and clean them out later."

The bell rang at the front of the diner. Jeanie looked over my shoulder. She raised a hand and waved. I looked behind me to see at whom. Detective Eric Wray walked in wearing a bright smile and a new suit. He was handsome, with old-fashioned, rugged charm, dark hair that he wore just a bit too long. He ran a hand through it, slicking it back as he jerked his chin at the waitress and shot her a smile. I could see her blush from here.

"You know," Jeanie said. "It might not be a bad idea to get a second opinion on what we're dealing with here."

I pointed backward with my thumb. "You mean from Eric?"

Jeanie shrugged. "It wouldn't be the worst idea we've ever had."

"Yeah," I said. "I was thinking about that myself." The trouble was, my history with Eric was complicated. And he was a cop. Delphi wasn't Ann Arbor, but I knew he was friendly with and often worked with the detectives in Ann Arbor. I wasn't sure I could trust him. Still, I needed another brain on this case.

The waitress came back and refilled my coffee. In the last few months, I'd trained myself to take it black. I just wanted to simplify my life anywhere I could.

"So talk to him," Jeanie said. "I'll talk to my private investigator and see what else we can find out about Travis White. If it comes to it, you can at least throw some suspicion on him at trial. It's thin, but it's something."

"Right," I said as Eric noticed us in the corner. I took a sip of my coffee. She was right. I should talk to him. But there was something else Jeanie didn't know. That no one would ever know. I knew some of the darkest of Eric Wray's secrets. For that, he owed me.

"Wray can be neutral," Jeanie said. "We need his help. And I like his mind. And uh ... a few other things." I choked on my coffee as she put two fingers in her mouth and let out a piercing whistle that drew the attention of the whole diner. So much for subtlety.

Eric stopped mid-sentence. He was talking to Lowell Ford, owner of Bernadette's. He'd named the diner after his first wife. They'd been divorced for more than forty years and he'd remarried something like five other times, but Lowell knew his brand and stuck with it. Legend had it, it also royally chapped the original Bernadette's ass so Lowell figured it as a win-win.

Eric tapped the counter and said a polite "see ya later" to Lowell as he made his way over to Jeanie and me.

"Have a seat," she said, slapping the one next to her. "Imma let you two chat. I want to catch up on some stuff at the office."

I had no idea what *stuff* she could be talking about, but Jeanie looked determined to leave. Eric raised a skeptical brow and stepped aside to let her pass.

"Please," I said, gesturing to her vacated seat. "I guess we're having lunch together." If this was Jeanie's ham-handed attempt to play matchmaker, she was slipping. My history with Eric was getting more complicated by the second. He'd done some things I wasn't always sure how to feel about. He was technically my client. He was also technically still very much married. That his wife Wendy was in an irreversible coma at a nursing home ten miles away was mostly beside the point.

"Only if Jeanie's buying," he said, smiling. Jeanie was already halfway to the front door.

"On me," I said. "It's a business lunch. I've been meaning to get a hold of you anyway."

Eric's expression turned grave. That secret we shared felt a little like another shoe about to drop. Today though, gravity might be on our side.

"How's it going with your sister?" he asked. Eric was a regular at Bernadette's. He shook an Equal packet while the waitress put a cheese Danish and a fresh cup of coffee in front of him.

I couldn't help but smile. Of course Wray knew exactly how it was going. The man gave off an "aw shucks" small-town-cop vibe, but I knew he missed exactly nothing. As he sweetened his coffee, I knew that's exactly what I needed.

There was just one small problem. I couldn't discuss a word of my sister's case with him without violating the attorney-client privilege. Unless …

I reached into my purse and pulled out the smallest bill I had. I slid a five across the table toward Eric. He paused, then gave me that signature smirk as he picked up and pocketed the bill.

"I don't suppose that's for the coffee," he said. He got my solid gaze by way of an answer. Shrugging, he lifted the coffee to his lips and took a slow sip.

"Consider yourself a paid consultant, Eric." He considered me for a moment, then gave me a knowing nod. From here on out, anything I told him or showed him on Vangie's case could go no further.

"When's your prelim?" he asked.

"Monday morning," I answered. I leaned over and pulled my laptop out of my messenger bag. Firing it up, I pulled up Vangie's digital file and opened the police report. I turned the screen toward Eric and let him read it.

"I'm missing something," I said. "I feel it. I just don't know what."

Eric scanned the report. My guts twisted as I knew what he saw. He advanced the screen with his finger. On the last page, I'd typed up my notes bullet-pointing the major evidence the police had against Vangie.

"Brett Carey's your detective," Eric said, his eyes flicking back and forth as the blue glow of my computer screen shadowed his face.

"You know him?"

"Ann Arbor's not that far," he said. "We've had occasion to cross paths a few times over the years. He's a good guy. He's been doing this forever. Runs a tight case. I mean ... *tight*. Cass, he usually eats defense lawyers for breakfast. You get him on the witness stand he's gonna see your shit coming from a mile away."

"My shit?" I asked. Except I knew exactly what he meant. Brett Carey would be a hard witness to trip up under pressure.

"I gotta be honest, Cass, if somebody I cared about turned up murdered, Brett Carey's the kind of cop I'd want leading the investigation."

"Vangie didn't do this," I said. Actually, I can't believe I said it. It was entirely beside the point. That was me talking like a sister, not a lawyer.

Eric looked back at the computer screen and started thinking aloud. "No signs of forced entry."

"It appears that way."

Eric shook his head. "Hmm. She's positioned weird."

"No, there was a pretty grisly blood trail leading from the dining room into the kitchen. Like she was dragged."

"Husband was hit from behind," Eric said. "She hit him in the back of the head."

"She?" I said.

Eric cleared his throat. "Sorry. The perpetrator."

"Something like that."

He sat back hard in his seat. His expression went through a series of changes as he read through the rest of the file. Eric's pale blue eyes narrowed. He tilted his head to the side as he reviewed the last of the crime scene photos. Then he scanned through the witness statements and remaining documents.

It was killing me to wait for his thoughts. I ordered my fourth cup of coffee. Finally, Eric snapped my laptop closed and let out a sigh.

"It's bad, Cass," he said. "But you already know that."

"And I already know she's innocent. Vangie couldn't have killed those people. It's not in her. She would *never*. And that baby. Eric, she would die for her. You should see her right now. She's destroyed with worry about what happened to Jessa."

"You said you feel like you're missing something," he said. "What? At the scene? Something one of the witnesses told you? Didn't tell you?"

I rested my chin in my palm. "God, I don't know. I really don't. It's just a feeling. It's just ... don't you think ... Sarah's body was staged? Why would someone do that? She was more than dead when she took that head shot. That happened in the dining room. Why go through the trouble of dragging her into the kitchen? I mean, if this was some crime of passion like Carey theorizes, why do that? And the way Ben Dale died. I don't know."

"What about it?"

"I don't know," I said. "I can hardly even let my mind go there, but okay. Let's. So Vangie gets into an argument with Sarah and it ends badly. If she drags Sarah into the other room, it's likely that Ben wasn't even in the house when it happened. I mean, right? Otherwise, wouldn't he have tried to intervene? So, maybe he didn't see it. They found his muddy footprints coming in from the garage. He walked in, saw his wife's body in the kitchen, then gets whacked in the back of the head. There's no element of surprise, right? The killer has to *want* Ben Dale to see his wife dead before he attacks him. Am I nuts?"

Eric waved off a refill on his coffee. "No. Not exactly nuts. I see where you're going with it. But, Cass, there are probably a thousand ways this could have gone down. Maybe the killer thinks he's going to get rid of Sarah's body and Ben walked in when she ... or he ... tried."

"Except Ben was hit from behind. He had no defensive wounds on him."

"Or," Eric said, "the killer is in the process of moving the body, hears the garage door open, hides out of sight and offs him as he walks in. To be honest, I think that's probably exactly what happened."

"I suppose," I said. "It's just ... I don't know. It *feels* wrong to me. I mean, there was a huge sliding glass door off the dining room where the first shooting took place. Why take her in *through* the house? Where was he going to go with her that way? Through the garage and out the front door? The house has a high privacy fence on all sides but behind that is the woods. He's going to dispose of the body by taking it through the garage which opens to the front? It's on a cul-de-sac. The Dales had neighbors on two sides but nobody in back. I don't buy it. Too much risk of being seen by someone."

"Maybe," Eric said. I didn't like his eyes. The scowl hadn't left his face. It felt like he was merely placating me.

"Look," I said. "I'm sorry. I asked for your opinion and here I am getting defensive and trying to explain everything away."

"I understand," he said. "She's your sister. It's just,

maybe you're too close to this."

"I know. But she's innocent."

Eric's hard stare didn't break. "Cass. The Dales' relationship with your sister is problematic. They got an ex parte P.P.O. because of it. Washtenaw County judges hate granting those things unless they've got a pretty ironclad reason."

"Threats are one thing," I said. "This was ... Eric, this ... it was bloody, messy, brutal. You tell me. This doesn't *look* like a crime of passion. This looks planned. Methodical. God. Evil. I feel it. Like in my bones, I feel it. Don't you?"

He didn't disagree.

"What?" I said, feeling my temper rising.

Eric reached for me. He put a hand over mine and the heat from it shocked me a little. "Cass, Vangie's been gone a long time. And she's been through a lot. How well do you really know her anymore?"

I couldn't breathe. I was so angry I could barely see. "No," I said. "Fuck that. No. She's no murderer."

"Cass ..."

"No! Goddammit. You *saw* her on the stand last year. You know what she's lived through and what she's sacrificed. She *loves* that little girl. She fought past so many demons to bring her into this world. So yes, even if I could believe she snapped at the thought of never seeing Jessa again, then what? Where's Jessa? You think she killed her too? How does that even make sense?"

"Cass, it doesn't. You're right. I'm just trying to look at all the angles."

I fought back tears. Dammit, I couldn't give into them now. I didn't have that luxury. "I know," I said. "And that's what I've been doing. Yes, I'm close to this. But that's exactly why I know there's still a killer out there. And God help that little girl if he took her too because we both know what that means."

Eric's face turned ashen. Neither of us wanted to think it, but there it was.

"I'm sorry," he said. "I can't imagine what you must be going through. As your friend, I just want …"

He still had his hand on mine and I slid it away. "Are we friends, Eric? Is that what we are?"

I don't know why it seemed like such a strange thing for him to say. Friends. Maybe we were. God knew they'd been hard to come by since I came back to Delphi. But he had pity in his eyes when he looked at me now. I didn't want it.

I took a twenty out of my purse to cover his breakfast and mine, then flattened it on the table. "Thank you," I said. "I appreciate your perspective."

"Cass …"

I put a hand up as I rose from the table. "It's okay. Really. I just need to get some air."

He nodded. "Will you send me a copy of that?" He pointed to my laptop as I slid it back into my bag. "Give me a real chance to read everything. You caught me on the fly today."

My shoulders dropped. I felt like an ass. "Of course. Eric … thank you. I mean, really. Thank you."

I slid the leather strap over my shoulder as he bit into his cheese Danish. He had a crumb on his mouth and I stopped myself just before reaching out to wipe it away. God, worry and lack of good sleep was throwing me hard off my game. I managed a smile before I turned and walked away.

Behind me, I heard laughter as Eric struck up his conversation with Lowell again. They were easy together. Hell, Eric was easy with everyone. That was part of his charm. He'd called us friends. As the biting air of a Michigan winter hit my face, I knew how badly I'd need to keep the ones I had close.

Chapter 13

MONDAY MORNING, I walked my sister into the Washtenaw County District Courthouse in the heart of downtown Ann Arbor. A group of protesters chanted in front of the building holding picket signs with Ben, Sarah, and Jessa Dale's faces on them. "Justice for Sarah." "Bring Jessa Home!"

I looped my arm through Vangie's. "Keep your head up," I said. "And no matter what they say, keep your mouth shut. That goes for inside too."

"I want to testify," she whispered for about the tenth time. "They need to know I didn't do this!"

"And you're going to have to trust me," I said as we made our way to the elevators. Mercifully, we were the only two going up. It might be the only few moments I had left to talk to her alone. "This is a preliminary examination. The prosecutor just has to prove probable cause that you're the one who committed this crime. Then the judge binds the case over for trial in circuit court. We're early in the game yet, Vangie. There is *nothing* to be gained from having you on that stand right now ... or ever."

"If they just listen to me," she pleaded. She started to

hyperventilate. More than anything, I just needed her to keep her shit together for the next couple of hours while we got through this.

"If they listen to you, they're going to twist you up and ask you questions you don't have good answers for," I said, my voice rising. "You are *not* getting up on that witness stand today. And you are *not* going to say *anything* at any time. I need to know you understand that."

Vangie leaned against the wall as the elevator lurched upward. "They have to let me go. You have to make them understand."

"Vangie." I turned to her and put my hands on her shoulders. "I told you. Unless something earth-shattering happens, which it won't, we're going to lose today. Between your history with the Dales, Jessa's shirt, that family portrait, and the physical evidence at the scene, they have enough to send this thing to a jury. The only thing you could do by getting on the stand is make a bad situation even worse. You need to let me do my job. We'll get through this."

She shook her head. "She's my *baby!*"

"And that's the last time you say that," I said. "That's exactly why they think you did this, Vangie."

The elevator doors opened. We walked into Judge Justin Jensen's courtroom. I said a courteous hello to the assistant prosecutor Rayna Dewitt. I nudged my sister into her seat and pulled my notepad out of my messenger bag.

Jeanie came in through the back. The bailiffs propped the doors open behind her and dozens of people filed in. My motion to keep this hearing closed had been denied last week. For the second time in less than a year, I found myself at the helm of a high-profile murder case where the public wanted blood. This time, it was my sister's blood. I squeezed her hand under the table as we waited for the judge to take the bench.

Jensen had been newly appointed by the governor to fill a vacancy when his predecessor had a heart attack. At thirty-eight, he was currently the youngest judge in the county. Rumor was, he had far higher political aspirations. In this case, that would likely work against me. Justin Jensen wouldn't want to be the one to kick the Dale murder trial before it even got started.

As his bailiff called the case, Jensen stepped out and I motioned for Vangie to stand beside me.

"Are we ready to proceed, counsel?" Jensen said. Not a strand of his thick nut-brown hair was out of place as the judge organized the papers in front of him and looked straight at Rayna.

"The state is ready," she said.

Judge Jensen shot a look to me. "Ready, Your Honor," I said. Vangie shuddered beside me. If I could just keep her quiet through this, I'd call it a victory.

"You may call your first witness," Jensen said.

"The state calls Detective Brett Carey," Rayna called out. Carey was already in the courtroom. He smoothed his tie over his crisp white dress shirt as he weaved his way through the gallery benches and up to the witness stand.

Eric's words reverberated in my brain. If someone he cared about wound up murdered, he wanted someone like Brett Carey on the case.

The bailiff swore Carey in and he made himself comfortable behind the microphone.

This wasn't a trial. There was no jury here. Rayna's job was merely to show the judge the state had probable cause to make Vangie stand trial. The odds of doing that were solidly in her favor. Probable cause is a much lesser burden of proof than what she'd face at trial. She laid a quick foundation, allowing Carey to introduce himself as lead homicide detective in this case, then she got right to the heart of it.

"Detective Carey," she said. "Can you describe for the court what you found on the morning of January 9th of this year?"

Carey leaned forward and spoke clearly into the microphone. "I received a call at approximately 11 a.m. Probable double homicide at 602 Brookside Place, Ann Arbor. When I arrived, the forensic unit had already secured the scene. We found two victims, male and female. Approximately in their late forties. A neighbor positively identified the bodies as Sarah and Benjamin Dale."

"Which neighbor?" Rayna asked.

"Roy and Lisa Speedman. Mrs. Speedman actually found the bodies. She was still on scene, pretty distraught. I went to Mr. Speedman and he made the identification. The Speedmans live three doors down."

"Thank you." Rayna marked several of the crime scene photographs for identification. I had no cause to object so Carey began to go through each one methodically.

"The first victim, Mrs. Dale, was found lying on her back in the kitchen. She had three gunshot wounds. Two in the chest. One in the head. The second victim, Mr. Dale, was found lying face down a few inches from his wife's feet. The back of his skull was crushed."

"No gunshot wounds on Mr. Dale?" Rayna asked.

"No," Carey said. "It appeared he'd been struck with something heavy, possibly the gun used to kill Mrs. Dale."

"Objection," I said. "Calls for speculation." It wasn't the strongest objection, but I meant to keep Rayna and the detective within the lines.

"Sustained," Judge Jensen. "This is prelim, Ms. DeWitt. Proof on manner and means aren't necessary today."

"Yes, Your Honor," Rayna said. "But we do have an affidavit from the medical examiner. It's attached to our reports."

Jensen leafed through his paperwork. "You planning on calling the M.E. this morning?"

"No, sir," Rayna answered. The judge was right. At this stage of the process, she didn't have to prove how the Dales were killed. Just that it was murder and that Vangie was the likely culprit.

"Let's move on," the judge said.

"All right," Rayna continued. "Detective Carey, once you had a positive ID on the victims, what was your next step in the investigation?"

"The immediate concern was finding the Dales' daughter, Jessica. I had uniformed officers canvassing the neighborhood trying to find her. We continued the search in the remainder of the house for any clues."

"Did you find any?"

"To Jessica's whereabouts? No. I'm afraid we didn't."

"We'll come back to that," Rayna said. "Regarding the murder victims, were you able to make an arrest?"

Carey cleared his throat. "I was. Yes. The following morning."

"What were the circumstances leading to that arrest?"

"The preliminary computer forensics on Mrs. Dale's cell came back within a few hours. There were a series of calls from the victim and the defendant in the week prior to the murders. The texts were of an increasingly hostile tone."

"Objection," I said. "The witness isn't qualified to testify about *tone*, Your Honor."

"Sustained," Judge Jensen said. "Please just stick to the facts, Detective."

He was good though. Carey knew damn well that kind of thing wouldn't fly with the judge. But if he said it in front of a jury, they'd accept it as gospel.

"The forensics are appended to my report. May I read from it?"

"Go ahead," Rayna said.

Carey slipped on a pair of reading glasses as he turned to the last pages of his full report. He read the following texts into the record from January third, one week prior to the murders.

Vangie: I need to see Jessa. I understand about Christmas, but I'm coming into town in a few days. Can we work something out?

Sarah: We have things going on. It's not a good time.

Vangie: You keep saying no time is a good time. I know you're mad at me about the trial. I would never do anything to hurt Jessa.

"Three days went by without any response from Sarah Dale. Every other text Vangie sent went unanswered. She texted every few hours over the next four days."

Vangie: Why aren't you answering my calls? Is everything okay?

Vangie: I'm coming into town in two days. Please tell me a good time to stop by. Or maybe I could just take Jessa to lunch or to get a treat.

Vangie: Sarah, please talk to me. I love Jessa. You know that. This is getting ridiculous.

Vangie: You have to let me see my baby. Don't punish her because you're mad at me.

Vangie: Please respond.

Vangie: I've left three voicemails. Please answer me, Sarah.

Vangie: I cannot believe you are trying to shut me out.

Vangie: Do you realize what would happen if the press found out what you're trying to do?

Beside me, Vangie went rigid. She turned to me. "They are taking this all out of context."

"Hush," I whispered. "Not a word."

Detective Carey read the last three texts.

Vangie: She is my daughter. You are violating the agreement we had. Answer your phone the next time I call.

Vangie: Still no response? You have no idea how bad this will make you look. I don't want that but I will not let you take my daughter away from me unfairly.

Vangie: This won't end well if you don't work with me.

Detective Carey put the papers down. "At this point, there was a call from Mrs. Dale to Ms. Leary. That was the night of January 8th. Obviously, we don't know the substance of that call, but it lasted nine minutes."

"Thank you," Rayna said. "Was there anything else that made you suspect the defendant of these crimes?"

"Yes, ma'am," Carey said. It was a nice touch even though he was a good twenty years older than both Rayna DeWitt and me. "It's in the technician's report, but a second set of fingerprints was found on Mrs. Dale's cell phone. They matched the defendant's, Evangeline Leary. Eyewitness testimony put her in the house on the evening of the 9th. Neighbors reported hearing loud voices that evening coming from the Dales' house. They described another female voice in addition to Mrs. Dale's and then Mr. Dale's. There were some strands of hair matching the defendant's along with a partial footprint in the front foyer. The treads matched Ms. Leary's."

"I have a copy of your arrest warrant here," Rayna said. "There is mention of a personal protection order having been entered against Ms. Leary. What can you tell me about that?"

"Once we had confirmation on the identity of the person sending those texts to Sarah Dale, we ran her name through L.E.I.N. The law enforcement information network. That's when the P.P.O. popped up. It was at that point we wrote the arrest warrant and executed it. The order hadn't yet been served on her. It was still with the sheriff's process server but Mr. Dale had apparently given them an address in Ann Arbor where the defendant generally stayed when she was in town."

"That would be Mr. White's residence," Rayna asked. "That's the address listed there on your warrant."

"It is," Carey answered. "We served the warrant at approximately noon on January 10th. We also had a search warrant for the premises but as it is actually owned by Mr. Travis White, we also asked for permission to search the home before we entered. He gave us consent. So, we had both the warrant plus express consent of the homeowner when we went in."

"Then what happened?"

"Miss Leary was in the bathroom. We identified ourselves and she refused to come out. She had her cell phone inside the bathroom with her and she made a call. Incident to her arrest, we searched the bedrooms in Mr. White's home. At that point, we discovered a bloody blouse laying on the floor in plain sight. We collected it. The blood on it matched that of Jessica Dale, the victims' daughter. We also discovered a 5X7 photograph of the Dales among some items in a corner of the bedroom. It was laying beneath Miss Leary's purse. The photograph matched one removed from the Dales' property. In fact, it was the only item taken from the property that we were able to determine.

"At one point, one of our female officers, Janet Wolf, was able to coax Miss Leary from the bathroom. She tried to run. It took three officers to subdue her. She did, however, make it clear that she'd already contacted her lawyer and understood her rights. We respected that and didn't question her. I was concerned with any information she might have about the whereabouts of Jessica Dale."

"Did she say anything about that?"

"No, ma'am," Carey explained.

"Thank you, Detective," Rayna said. "I have nothing further at this time."

"Your witness, Ms. Leary," Judge Jensen said.

"Thank you. Detective Carey," I began. As I gathered my notes, Vangie made an audible gasp. She'd been holding her breath.

I took a moment. This was tricky. There was no jury to impress, no reasonable doubt to raise. The trick to prelim was to get the prosecution to show you their cards without revealing too many of your own. I had a million things I wanted to ask Brett Carey. This was a brutal, bloody, messy murder. And yet, they hadn't found a drop of either Ben or Sarah's blood on my sister. No gun residue on her hands, no murder weapon. As far as the witnesses who claimed to hear the Dales in an argument the night before they were found dead, nobody could say for sure if it was Vangie's voice they heard. But it did me no good to bring this up now. Better to save those holes in the case for a jury if we got that far. Rayna Dewitt was a competent prosecutor. The more she knew about my defense strategy, the better she'd be able to counter-attack.

"Detective," I said. "Was time of death established for the victims?"

"Ma'am, that's a question better answered by the medical examiner's report, but I believe the last witness reported hearing the Dales at around 10 p.m. the night of the 9th. They were discovered at eight a.m. on the 10th. The estimate is that they died between six and eight hours prior to discovery."

"Thank you," I said. "And the murder weapon, that hasn't been found?"

"No, ma'am."

"Are you aware of any firearms registered to either the defendant or Travis White, who she was staying with?"

"No, ma'am. But lack of gun registry doesn't mean she couldn't have acquired one."

"Was there a gun registered to either Ben or Sarah Dale?"

"No," he said. "No guns in the house."

"Detective, regarding the blood found on the blouse at Travis White's residence, do you know for sure if that blouse belonged to Evangeline Leary?"

"No, but Mr. White said he'd seen her wear it before. It's in her size."

"Did you find any of Jessica Dale's blood at the crime scene?"

"What?" Carey reared back a bit. The question surprised him.

"You may refer to your report if you're having trouble remembering."

He did.

"No. The technicians didn't find any blood matching the child's. Just the parents."

The crime scene photos were still up on the monitor over Brett Carey's left shoulder. I walked toward them. I meant to ask him whether he'd found any of Ben or Sarah's blood on my sister or at Travis's residence, but I stopped cold. I tilted my head to the side as I looked at Ben Dale's murdered body. The back of his head was almost completely caved in. I turned and looked at my sister. My heart went hot. Jeanie caught my eye and she sat up a little straighter in her seat. My wheels were turning and she damn well knew it.

I cleared my throat and covered, not wanting to alert either the detective or Rayna DeWitt to anything.

"Detective, have you been able to find any solid leads on the whereabouts of Jessica Dale?"

Carey scowled. He looked to Rayna and back at the judge.

"Objection," Rayna said. "This detective isn't here to

answer questions about an active investigation. That's a separate matter from the two murder charges."

"Sustained," Judge Jensen said. "Please confine your questions to the charges at hand."

There was so little I could do with Brett Carey today. Vangie's eyes filled with tears. I knew she wanted me to make this go away. I couldn't. Not today.

"I have nothing further," I said.

"You may step down," Judge Jensen said. "Let's take a short recess, then the state may call its next witness."

He banged his gavel and I slid back into my seat. I flipped through the screens open on my laptop looking for Ben Dale's autopsy report. Jeanie had come around and slid into the seat next to me.

"What's happening in that brilliant brain of yours?" Jeanie whispered.

I found the item I was looking for. I turned the screen toward Jeanie. Vangie rose out of her seat.

"I need some air," she said. "Or just ... can I go to the bathroom?"

"Of course," I said. "But hurry back. It's just down the hall." I motioned to one of the bailiffs. He gave me a nod and I knew he'd keep an eye on my sister. She didn't need any ill-meaning spectators accosting her today.

Jeanie's eyes went up as she watched Vangie scoot from behind the table and head for the back of the courtroom.

"I'll be damned," Jeanie said. I had my finger on one line of Ben Dale's autopsy report. Jeanie read it. Her eyes went back to Vangie.

"You gonna bring it up?" Jeanie asked.

"Better not," I said. "No use giving Rayna time to explain it away before trial."

"He about the same height, do you think?" Jeanie asked as Vangie stood beside the bailiff. The man was easily six feet tall. My sister was an inch taller than me but still only five foot five.

"Ben Dale was six foot four," I said. "Nearly a foot taller than her. What do you think?"

"I think we better call our own expert before this goes to trial. I mean, it's a little thing just. But maybe it's something. The angle of this wound seems level."

"Exactly," I said.

"So you're thinking it was someone who was either close to Ben Dale's height or standing on a box?"

"Exactly," I said again.

It was a small thing. Tiny, really. But it could be the first real break in the case. For now, I couldn't say a damn thing.

Chapter 14

ERIC WRAY WALKED into the courtroom and tried to take an inconspicuous seat in the back. He nodded to me as I sat huddled with Jeanie. I waved him over. Eric looked left, then right. Nobody else from Delphi was here except us. That said, I knew it wouldn't look good for him if anyone from the Ann Arbor P.D. or sheriff's office saw him talking to me.

He slid into the seat right behind me. "Thanks for coming," I said. "You think you could find me an expert for later?"

Quick as I could, I explained my theory about the angle of Ben Dale's head wound. Eric did the same thing I had and tilted his head, imagining what that blow must have looked like.

"Hard to say," he said. "I mean, she could have thrown something. I don't know."

"There was gun residue in the wound. You know the running theory is he got pistol-whipped with the same gun used to shoot Sarah. I'm just looking for a second opinion. There's no point in getting into it here. All I'd do is raise a question of fact for a jury to decide anyway. But it's more than worth pursuing. Will you help me?"

Eric's eyes flicked to Jeanie. "Yeah," he said. "Let me think on it. I might be able to find somebody. It's thin though, Cass. If this gets to trial you're gonna need ..."

"I know," I said.

Vangie and the bailiff came back into the courtroom. The judge would be just another minute. I mouthed a quick "thank you" to Eric as he left his seat and tried to blend into the background. Rayna saw him and frowned.

When the judge took the bench, Rayna called Travis White to the stand. He walked up to the witness box with a swagger and a smile. A cold chill ran through me. I didn't know this guy but for the brief interview he'd given me, but I had a bad feeling about him.

Five minutes later, Travis turned the case against my sister upside down.

He said all the things he'd told me a few days ago. He and Vangie met online. They saw each other every other month when she came to have her visits with Jessa. It was casual. He thought she was a "cool chick" until last year after she testified in the Larry Drazdowski trial.

"What changed, Mr. White?" Rayna said.

Travis shrugged. The idiot was actually chewing gum.

"I don't know," he said. "It was just a feeling I had. When she came into town, she didn't really want to do anything. She seemed agitated a lot. And then after Christmas she started freaking out big time. She told me her kid's dad wouldn't let her see her anymore. I mean, I didn't know the situation. I mean, not until I read it in the paper about how she got raped and everything and had to give the kid up. That's rough. I wish she'd told me."

"Mr. White," Rayna said. "Did the defendant, Miss Leary, ever express her feelings about the Dales to you?"

"Yeah," Travis said. He leaned far forward, practically kissing the microphone in front of him. "She told me she'd kill those two before she let them take her kid away."

"You're a liar!" Vangie shot up. "He's lying! You piece of shit!"

Jensen banged the gavel. I grabbed Vangie's arm and pulled her back into her seat. "Quiet," I said. "Dammit, not another word out of you."

Vangie turned to me. "I never said that. Not once. Let me take a lie detector!" She was still shouting.

I felt like murdering Travis White myself. And I felt like strapping duct tape over my sister's mouth.

"Mr. White, do you know when Miss Leary made that threat?" Rayna asked.

Travis didn't miss a beat. "On the phone to me. She came in on the 7th of this month. I was out of town but she had a key to my place. I called her that day to tell her when I'd be in. She said she was going over to her kid's parents' house and try to hash it out. That's when she said it. On the phone that time. I mean, I could barely believe it."

"Was she serious?" Rayna asked.

"Objection. Calls for speculation."

"I'll allow it," Jensen said.

Travis shrugged. "I mean, I tried to tell myself she was just kidding around. I mean, who says that? But she was super pissed. And hostile. Like ... really mean. I wasn't down with that. I was going to tell her the next morning that maybe she should find someplace else to stay."

"Thank you, Mr. White," Rayna said. "I have nothing further."

Little white spots wavered in front of my eyes as I reminded myself to breathe. Travis White sat back and dammit if he didn't smirk. There were a couple of reporters in the back of the courtroom and Travis's game became clear. The asshole was using this to get publicity for himself.

"Mr. White," I said. "We've met before, haven't we?"

"Uh. Yeah. You had me come into your office last week."

"That's right," I said. "You never once mentioned this so-called threat my sister allegedly made, did you?"

"Well," he said. "I mean, you're her sister ..."

"Mr. White," I said my voice rising. "Answer the question. True or false. Yes or no. You never once mentioned in that conversation that you heard Evangeline Leary threaten the Dales in that manner, did you?"

"Uh ... it's true I didn't mention it. Yes. But it's true that it happened. Those aren't the same things."

Well, Travis White might be a lying asshole, but he wasn't dumb. I had nothing to gain keeping him up there a second longer than I had to.

"Did you tell anyone about this so-called threat?" I asked. "At the time you supposedly heard it."

"Um ... no."

"And you didn't tell that to the police on the 10th when they came to your house and arrested Ms. Leary, did you?"

"Um ... no. I didn't."

"Mr. White, have you ever been to Ben and Sarah Dale's house yourself?" I shouldn't have asked it. Not here. Not now. But Travis threw me.

"Have I what?"

"Well, isn't it true you met my sister indirectly through the Dales? The company you work for installed countertops at the Dales' residence, didn't they?"

Travis stopped chewing his gum. "Uh ... yeah. Like a year ago or something."

"Did you bother to mention that to the police when they questioned you?"

"They didn't ask," he said.

"Have you been inside the Dales' house?" I asked.

"Lady, you're cracked. Don't try to pin this shit on me. I wasn't even in town when they got shot."

"Your Honor," I said, "Will you please instruct this witness to answer the question posed. He was asked whether he's been inside the home of Ben and Sarah Dale."

"Mr. White, answer the question," Jensen said.

"Yeah," Travis snapped. "Once. We put in quartz countertops. One of the days of the install Vangie was there. We got to talking. That's it. I gave her my number. I didn't know that kid was her kid. She didn't tell me any of that. I found out all that later."

"Thank you," I said. "I have nothing further."

Vangie exploded beside me as Travis White left the stand. She threw herself at him. I acted without thinking, throwing myself at her. I shoved her back hard into her seat. She railed against me as the bailiffs came running.

Pressing my lips against her ear, I said, "If you don't pull yourself together, I'm going to *let* the bailiffs take you back to jail. You got it? This isn't helping. Vangie, this is the opposite of helping!"

"I told you," Travis spat his words. One of the bailiffs had a hold of him and shoved him out of the gallery gate. "Psycho bitch. I hope they lock your ass up for a hundred years."

I was grateful the county banned cell phones in the courthouse. No doubt Vangie's outburst would have made it up on social media within the hour otherwise. I wished one of my brothers were here to sit on her for me. Matty was still working with the search party for Jessa. I insisted Joe go to work. There would be plenty of days in the future when I'd need him by my side. I didn't think today was one of them. This was just supposed to be a formality. Now, my sister had shown the prosecutor and the rest of the courtroom how angry she could get. Never mind the cell phone transcript or Travis's testimony, this would make the *Free Press* headlines.

For her part, Vangie was pretty much foaming at the mouth. One of the deputies got to me. "It's all right," I said. "She's under control." I stared hard at Vangie, hoping my meaning was clear. *You better be under control.*

Vangie's face went white as she saw the deputy looming over her. She gave him a quick nod and folded her hands in her lap.

I straightened my suit jacket and turned back to the judge. One look from him and I knew this was over. What little hope I had of swinging these proceedings in Vangie's direction just vanished. Rayna could pretty much stop things now and the judge would bind Vangie's case over for trial.

"We ready to proceed?" Judge Jensen said. "I trust the defendant understands that another outburst like that and I revoke your bond. Do you know what that means?"

"Yes, Your Honor," Vangie said, meekly. My heart broke for her at the same time I wanted to throttle her. God. She'd been through so much. At the crux of it all, she hadn't slept more than an hour straight since the night Jessa disappeared.

"Call your next witness, Ms. DeWitt," Jensen said.

Chapter 15

RAYNA CALLED Lisa Speedman to the stand. Her testimony was simple, quiet, devastating. On the morning of January 10th, she'd gone to the Dales' because Jessa and Sarah hadn't made it out to the bus stop. She wondered if Jessa was sick because her own daughter, Charlotte, had woken with a stuffed-up nose. She approached the house and found the side service door to the garage wide open. She went inside. She saw Ben and Sarah lying dead in their own blood. It was eight o'clock in the morning.

"Your witness, Ms. Leary," Jensen said.

Lisa Speedman was a small, pretty woman with thin brown hair she wore clipped back. She wrung a handkerchief between her fingers as she waited for my questions.

"Mrs. Speedman," I said. "Do you recognize the defendant?"

She looked up briefly, then back at her hands. "Yes," she said.

"And how do you know her?"

"I've seen her at Sarah's house. She visits every once in a while. Sarah told me she's Jessa's biological mother."

"Okay. And do you know whether Jessa welcomed those visits? Did they seem easy with each other when you saw them together?"

Sarah tilted her head to the side. "Yes. I th-think so. I know Jessa calls her Aunt Vangie. That's what Charlotte says, anyway, my daughter. Jessa had a pair of these pink, glittery high tops that she said her Aunt Vangie bought for her. She loved those shoes."

Lisa Speedman began to sob.

"Thank you," I said. "I have nothing further."

Lisa Speedman stepped down. Rayna DeWitt called one last witness. Holly Kimberly, the Dales' next-door neighbor. Holly recounted how she'd overheard an argument coming from the Dales' home on the night of January 8th.

"Could you hear what was being said?" Rayna asked.

"A little," Holly answered. "It was about Jessa. I heard a woman's voice screaming about her. I couldn't make it all out but a few phrases here and there. Over and over she said, 'You can't take her from me.' I heard Sarah and Ben too, but their voices were more muffled. Like ... like they were trying to keep the situation calm. I was worried about Jessa. As far as I knew, she was inside the house. It was late. Past her bedtime. Still, if the yelling was loud enough for me to hear, surely she could hear it from upstairs in her bedroom."

"Did you do anything?" Rayna asked.

"Well, I thought about going over there to ask if everything was okay. God, if I had. Maybe ... But I'm ashamed to admit it now. I just decided to mind my own business. I'd just never heard yelling like that from Ben and Sarah's place. They're quiet neighbors. Good neighbors."

"Okay. Thank you, Mrs. Kimberly. I just have one last question. Can you state with certainty who the Dales were arguing with?"

"Well, I suppose no. I inferred it. Earlier in the evening,

just after dinnertime, I saw a car pull up. Ms. Leary over there got out of it. I've seen her a few times visiting. She was there that night."

"Thank you, I have no other questions."

It was my turn. "Ms. Kimberly, you said you saw Ms. Leary arrive. Was her car still in the driveway when you heard this arguing?"

"Um ... yes. I mean, I think it was her car. It had one of those rental stickers on it."

"Okay, did you see when she left?"

"No, I'm afraid not. But I left around eleven o'clock that night. My husband works third shift at his factory. His car was in the shop so I drove him in. When I got back at around midnight, I went straight to bed. I didn't hear anything coming from the house."

"Did you notice whether there was a car in the driveway?"

She shrugged. "I can't say. It was dark and I didn't look that way. It might have been there but it might not have. I'm sorry."

"Thank you," I said. "I have nothing further."

"Ms. DeWitt?" Jensen said.

Rayna Dewitt rose. "We have no further witnesses to present, Your Honor. The state respectfully requests this court bind the defendant over for trial in circuit court. We believe we have presented ample evidence that probable cause exists in this case."

"Your motion is taken," Judge Jensen said. "I'll render my opinion first thing in the morning. We're adjourned."

As soon as Judge Jensen disappeared into his chambers, my sister fell apart beside me.

Chapter 16

"COME ON, we can take her out through staff exit. Less likely to run into the crazies out there." Eric Wray was at my side. Vangie had trouble getting to her feet. Her breathing was wrong, erratic. Purple splotches covered her cheeks.

"Thanks," I said. Jeanie had an arm around Vangie. My sister gave a quick nod, indicating she was ready to get the hell out of that courthouse. I gathered my files, my laptop, and stuffed it all into my messenger bag.

The four of us made our way out of the courtroom.

"Hell's too good for you!" Lisa Speedman was just as much a wreck as Vangie was as we entered the hallway. Her husband tried to hold her back but the woman practically foamed at the mouth as she screamed at Vangie. "You're going to rot!"

"Lisa, come on." Mr. Speedman put a gentle arm around his wife's shoulder and tried to lead her away. Two deputies came up to aid him.

Vangie sobbed. "Enough," I said. "Let's get you back to the house. We'll talk."

I followed Eric as he led us to the stairwell. He must have

worked something out with the deputies because the space was clear as we made our way down.

I wanted to tell Vangie that everything would be all right. I'd spent a lifetime telling her that. A hollow space formed in my chest as I realized that I'd been wrong every single time. The unthinkable happened when we lost our mother in a car wreck when Vangie was just four years old. In her eyes, I left her too when she was twelve and I took my high-powered law firm job in Chicago. I wasn't there for her when she was sexually abused and brutalized by her high school track coach and left pregnant. Why on earth would she believe those words from me now?

"I just want to get out of here," Vangie said.

"We are. You don't have to be here tomorrow when the judge reads his decision. I'll take care of it."

"He's going to send me to jail," she said. "Forever."

"No," I answered. "But he's likely going to send you to trial. Let's just work on one thing at a time."

"I don't care," she said. "They can do whatever they want to me. I just want them to find my baby."

I saw something go through Eric's eyes. He tried to hide it from me, but it was too late. I knew what he thought. He was a seasoned detective. He'd handled many missing and abused children cases. It had been over two weeks since Jessa disappeared. Not a single solid lead had turned up except for the blood on Vangie's clothing. Everyone thought Vangie had done something to her. I couldn't tell Vangie yet, but I expected Rayna to bring new charges against her soon. Kidnapping. Child endangerment. Possibly a third murder charge.

"Where's your car?" Eric asked.

"It's in the Ann-Ashley lot. Second floor," I answered. Stone-faced, he gave me a nod.

"If you give me your keys I'll pull it around for you. It's a bad idea for you to walk so much as a block out there right now. There's a group of picketers at the corner."

I took my keys out of my pocket and handed them to him. "Thank you," I said. "You really don't have to do all of this …"

But Eric was already out the door.

Vangie sniffled. I fished a tissue out of my other pocket and handed it to her. "You think he believes me?" she asked.

I wanted to tell her yes. Absolutely. Eric Wray was a friend. But the truth was, I had no idea what Eric thought. For now though, he seemed to be on my side, if not my sister's. It would have to do.

"He's a good egg," Jeanie answered for me. "And he's a good brain to have working on this too."

Vangie nodded. "He's into you, you know that, right?" My sister managed a smile.

"Uh … I don't think … he's just a friend, Vang. A *married* friend. He was helpful on the last case." I couldn't bring myself to say Larry Drazdowski's name. It had been an unspoken rule between us. Vangie wanted to put that part of her past behind her. She didn't think about Jessa as a product of anything evil that had happened to her. She told me that child was the light that came out of her deepest darkness.

There were footsteps above as someone came down behind us. "Come on," Jeanie said. "We shouldn't hang out here too long."

"Whatever you say," Vangie said. "But I know the look when I see one. So, either that guy is into you, or you've got something on him."

She was teasing, sort of. I wanted to be glad Vangie had come around enough to make at least a weak joke. She'd just hit far too close to home. I was about to say something to deflect when a shadow came over us and we were no longer alone.

"Oh, thank God I found you!" A woman stood at the top of the flight of stairs. She had gray, wiry hair and the harsh glare of the light behind her gave off a halo effect.

I moved, putting my body in front of Vangie's. Where the hell were the deputies? I cast a quick glance over my shoulder checking to see if Eric had entered the parking lot.

"Who are you?" Vangie asked. When she tried to move around me I pushed her back.

"I have a thing to say," the woman said as she descended the last few steps.

"I'm sorry," I said. "We've got no comment."

"Oh, I'm not here with the newspaper," she said. As she stepped onto the landing, I studied her face. Though her hair was gray, the woman had scarcely a wrinkle. She wore horn-rimmed reading glasses perched at the edge of her nose. A beaded black chain dangled from them, framing her face.

"Louise?" Jeanie asked. "Shit. I thought you died."

"You know her?" I said.

Louise got bold. She reached out and touched my arm. There was an urgency to her grip. She looked behind her and two red spots appeared on her cheeks. "Not a lot of time," she said. "But I need you to listen."

She wasn't talking to me. She was staring straight at Vangie.

"Your girl," Louise said. "You know she's alive, right? You feel it?"

What the actual hell? I took a step back. Vangie shoved her way around me. Her fingers trembled as she reached for Louise. When I looked at Jeanie, she mouthed one word. "Psychic."

Fuck.

Chapter 17

"What do you know about Jessa?" Vangie asked. She practically shouted it. My sister seemed to have already figured out who or what this Louise was.

"She's alive," Louise said again. "I can feel her. I just wanted to see you for a second to make sure. It helps to have someone close to the person. You know? I can ... I see things. People call it a gift but it's mostly a curse. Jeanie knows. Tell them!" Louise took Vangie by the shoulders. Louise's smile brightened and she took in a great breath of air.

"Louise," Jeanie said. Her tone was light, not condescending but she was being cautious for sure. "Er ... this is Louise Grayson. Yes. She's sort of an Ann Arbor fixture. But ..."

"Shh," Louise said. "I told you. Not a lot of time. I'm actually not supposed to be in this courthouse."

Oh brother. I looked again for Eric with my car.

"Tell me!" Vangie shouted. "Where is my baby?"

"Not another word," I said to Vangie. The last thing I needed was this kook getting called as a witness.

"She's alive. I know that for sure. But she's scared. So scared." Louise took her hands off Vangie and pulled her red knit shawl closer around her. "It's cold where she is. She's safe for now. But ... not for always. I think she's trying to get to you."

"Where?" Tears burst from Vangie's eyes. She grabbed Louise Grayson hard enough to make the woman gasp in pain.

"Vangie!" I shouted.

"Miles," Louise said. "Miles away. But you have to hurry. She won't be safe for long. I feel that too. She's not alone. There's someone ..."

Vangie's knees buckled.

"Enough!" I said. I pulled my sister off Louise and tried to usher her toward the exit. "Ms. Grayson, if you have something worthwhile, tell it to the police. Tell it to Detective Carey. Beyond that, you're not to come near my sister again."

"No!" Vangie said. "I want to hear. I have to know."

"It's a room. Maybe an apartment. Big space. Drafty. There's a light above her head. It swings on a chain. It's not far. Libby? Library? I can't see it all. It's so hard with little ones. They don't have the words they need to make it specific for me."

"Great," I said. "How convenient."

"You don't have to believe me," Louise said. "But she does."

Tires crunched in the snow behind us. Eric pulled up in my black Jeep.

"Let's go," I said, pulling Vangie toward the door. She resisted.

"Where?" she asked. "You have to be able to see where!"

"Vangie, she's a crackpot. She preys on your vulnerabilities."

"Tummy Bear's losing his stuffing." Louise's eyes went wide and filled with tears.

"Oh for shit's sake," I said. Vangie froze. This time, she didn't pull away from me as I led her toward the door.

Chapter 18

ERIC WAS THERE as Vangie folded against me. "Perfect timing," Jeanie said. Louise Grayson backed up the stairs. She held her hand against her mouth and her whole body shook.

"Christ," Eric said. "That you, Louise? Didn't realize you were still alive."

He put a helpful arm around Vangie and guided her outside. Jeanie brought up the rear as we made our way to my waiting car.

"Thanks," I said to Eric over Vangie's shoulder. "I think I can take it from here."

"No," he said. "I'll drive you home. I already called for a squad car to meet us there. They'll take me back. Had a gut feeling the kooks would be out in force today. I thought the Washtenaw County guys had banned her from all the courthouses."

"They have," Jeanie answered as she slid in the backseat beside Vangie. Eric held the passenger side door open for me. I climbed in, yet again grateful for his assistance.

"Don't pay any attention to her," Eric said as we waited

for the security gate to lift and let us out of the parking lot. "Louise means well. And sometimes, she gets things right in a blind-squirrel-finding-a-nut sort of way. Trouble is, she's more nut than squirrel."

"She knows!" Vangie shrieked. "How the hell did she know about Tummy Bear? That's Jessa's. It's this little brown teddy bear she sleeps with. Sarah gave it to her once when she had a stomach ache. That's why she started calling it Tummy Bear. How could she know that?"

"Now, don't go off and get too excited," Jeanie said. "I'm sorry, but Eric's got her number. In the end, Ann Arbor is a pretty small town. She could have gotten that information anywhere. More than likely she's a few degrees of separation from somebody who's friends with the Dales. She's lived here her whole life. It's a racket she's running. Believe me."

Vangie wasn't satisfied. She hugged her knees to her as Eric hit the expressway. I was damn glad I wouldn't have to bring her back here tomorrow, no matter what Judge Jensen decided.

She went silent on me the whole way home. Just as Eric promised, there was a Delphi P.D. patrol car sitting in front of my house when we pulled up. Matty and Joe were there too. I hoped to God they hadn't done any chest thumping with the cop outside. That was the last thing I needed.

I thanked Eric again as we all piled out of the Jeep. Vangie ran into the house, blowing right past my brothers. Matty called after her but it was no use.

"You can clear out now," Joe said. He kept a hard gaze on Eric and the officer behind the wheel. His unspoken message was clear. In his mind, the police were the enemy, even though our sister wasn't even facing charges here in Delphi.

I mouthed an "I'm sorry" to Eric. He clenched his jaw, but kept from saying anything back to Joe. I could practically feel the testosterone level in the air rising. As Eric slid into the patrol car, I put a hand on my brother's chest and shoved him toward the front door.

"How did it go?" he asked as we got inside.

"About as bad as it could," I whispered. "Judge will render his decision in the morning. Can one of you stay here with her during that? I'm not taking her back to court. She did more damage than good for herself today."

I gave them a brief rundown of Vangie's attempted attack on Travis White.

"Do you fucking blame her?" Matty said. For Joe's part, he remained more stoic. "How the hell could you let that asshole get away with that?"

My blood boiled. "Are you kidding me?" I said. "Let him? How exactly do you expect me to stop him?"

Matty was incensed. On an intellectual level, I understood it. He was scared for Vangie. He wanted someone to blame. I was used to being the family punching bag right along with being the family fixer.

"I don't know!" he shouted. "But Jesus. This has gone on long enough. I don't see you making this go away, Cass."

I took a step back, feeling gut-punched. Joe didn't say anything, but his eyes conveyed everything.

Christ. They blamed me. They blamed *me*? I didn't know whether to laugh, cry, lose my shit, or start punching back. Somehow, I managed to do none of those things. Instead, I turned on my heel and walked out on my brothers, leaving them shouting at my back.

Chapter 19

On Tuesday morning at nine a.m., Judge Justin Jensen issued his ruling. He allowed cameras in the courtroom and I knew this would make *MLive* within minutes. I knew the outcome before he even spoke. I'd known it from the beginning. Had warned my sister about it. Still, as the judge read from his written order, each word stabbed into me, leaving me shaken.

"The court determines that a felony has been committed and the state has met its burden. There is probable cause to believe the defendant, Evangeline Leary, perpetrated it. I'm ordering this case bound over to circuit court for trial. You'll receive a new scheduling order and a trial date once it's been reassigned."

"Thank you, Your Honor," Rayna said as she started gathering her papers. There was commotion behind her as reporters clamored to get a statement from her. The bailiffs ushered them outside. If I knew Rayna, she already had her optics planned. She'd give a sober "no comment" other than to say she hoped justice would be served. Then the reporters would try to find me. I already had a plan to sneak out the staff entrance like I'd done the other day.

First, I had to call my sister and break the news to her.

Matty answered my landline. "Hey," I said. "It's the news we expected. Jensen's sending this to trial. Can I talk to Vangie?"

"She won't come to the phone," he said. "She won't even get out of bed. I've tried. Cass, she's completely shut down. And I don't think she gives two shits about what they do to her in court. That psychic you guys ran into has her all turned around."

I sank against the wall. I'd made it to the stairwell without anyone following me. "I know. God. I wish I had something hopeful to tell her."

"Yeah ... well ..." Matty's voice trailed off. As much as I was worried about my sister, I was worried about him too. He got his ninety-day chip from A.A. just last week. He was doing okay for now, but this was tearing him up just like the rest of us.

"I'll be back as soon as I can," I said. "I've got a few things to tend to at the office for other clients. I'll check in with my contact at the Ann Arbor police before I leave town. They're clamming up on me though about Jessa's case."

"I know," he said. "I was not so politely asked not to show up for any more search parties. It's a sham now anyway. It's been almost three weeks, Cass. If ..."

"No," I said. "Let's not deal with ifs right now. Okay? Just ... just keep an eye on Vangie. I don't know. Heat up some soup for her and make her eat it. She's got to hold it together. She's just ... got to."

So did Matty. I couldn't bring myself to say it. If he fell apart on me now, I didn't know if I had the means to pick him back up again. Every ounce of my energy went toward trying to dig Vangie out of this hole. Right then, I felt like I was doing it with nothing more than my bare hands.

"Yeah," Matty said. Then I felt the weight of his silence. I said a quick goodbye and headed out of the courthouse.

Jeanie and Miranda waited for me as I got to the office just after eleven. I'd already texted ahead with Jensen's ruling. I found them both up in the conference room. Jeanie had moved all of Vangie's case material out of my house and back here. I had too many people going in and out to keep things secured at my place. Now, as I walked into the room, Jeanie had huge color photos of our growing witness list taped to a corkboard. As Travis White's dopey face stared back at me, I wanted to throw a knife straight at it.

"How's our girl?" Jeanie asked. She sat at the head of the conference room table. Miranda busied herself straightening some of the pictures on the corkboard. Ever since business picked up after the Drazdowski trial, I'd been able to hire Miranda full time. I used to share her with another law firm that rented space out of this same building. Now it was just us. It made things less complicated, but also far quieter. I liked it that way.

"Our *girl* wouldn't come to the phone," I said. "Matty's with her. I talked Joe out of taking off work today, figuring he's gonna need to save his sick days up for when the real trial starts."

"You really think it's going to come to that?" Miranda asked. She stuck her last push pin in a photo of Detective Carey she'd pulled from the internet. Miranda was more Jeanie's generation than mine. Once upon a time, she'd been a close friend of my mother's before she died. She wore a silk blouse today with a flouncy bow in front. I loved her style and hoped I could hold up half as well as when I was her age.

"Well, a plea deal is out of the question," I said. "Even if the state was offering one. I don't know, it's all just ..."

"Overwhelming," Jeanie finished for me. She got up and went to the bookshelf. Ever since she'd taken the office across the hall, she started adding little touches here and there. She moved a volume of *Proof of Facts* to reveal a bottle of scotch. She kept the shot glasses behind one of the volumes of *Michigan Compiled Laws*. I only kept those things there for show anyway.

She poured two glasses when Miranda waved off a third. Jeanie slid mine over to me.

"Might as well," she said. "It's going to be a long day."

I twirled the amber liquid in my glass. "I don't know," I said. "It's not even noon, Jeanie. This is straight out of Joe Sr.'s playbook."

My father, Joe Leary, had been an epic town drunk. In a lot of ways, that's the reason Jeanie Mills came into my life in the first place. The court had appointed her guardian ad litem for my younger brother and sister after about the fourth time the state tried to take them away from my dad.

"I would have figured he'd have turned up by now," Jeanie said, sipping her scotch. "What with all the heat you and Vangie got in the news this last year. Old Joe's bound to think there's money in it somewhere for him."

"Unless he finally up and died on us," I said, sipping my drink. Though I really didn't believe it. I always figured I'd feel a tremor in the force the day my father died. "I've got enough trouble brewing with just the family I do have. Joey and Matty are pissed I'm not doing more to make this all go away."

"You've got to be kidding me," Miranda chimed in. "Not doing enough? What exactly do they expect you to do?"

I did take a drink at that. It felt good going down. Almost too good. Oh, I had plenty of Joe Sr.'s DNA flowing through my veins.

"Well, thanks for saying that, at least," I answered. "It all just seems so ... hopeless to everyone right now."

"Including you?" Jeanie asked. She leaned forward to pour me another shot. I let her, but I didn't touch it. If I did a second one, I'd be pretty much on my way. As tempting as it was, I wanted to keep a clearer head.

"I just need ... I need like a day where I don't have to think about my fucked-up family and all the trouble Vangie's in. Or I need some good news about that little girl."

The landline rang at Miranda's desk. She cocked her head and gave me a smile. "Don't get your hopes up," I said. "It's probably even more bad news."

Miranda left us as Jeanie finished her second shot. She could hold the stuff far better than I could. It would take at least two more of those just to get her warm. I'd watched Jeanie drink men twice her size under the table at Mickey's.

"How can I help?" she asked.

"You already are. But ... I don't know ... find me a witness. Find me a murderer. Or, I'd settle for a time machine. So I could go back and talk some sense into my sister before she let things escalate with the Dales. As it stands right now, she appears to be the only person on the planet with a motive to do them harm. Rayna put on the bare minimum of what she needed to prove probable cause. She has far bigger guns than that. The jury is going to hear from the Dales' lawyer, the one who helped them draft their P.P.O."

Jeanie fingered the label on the bottle of scotch. She hesitated, then put the stopper back in it. "And he's going to paint a pretty bleak picture of how scared they were of Vangie," Jeanie said. "Dammit. I thought she had more sense than that."

That second shot of scotch called to me. I stared at it.

"Cass." Jeanie leaned forward. "I hate to bring this up.

Hell, I hate to even ask this. But ... have you thought about your *own* bigger guns?"

Miranda had already shut the door to the conference room when she left. I could hear her lilting laughter coming from downstairs as she managed whatever client had called.

I took the scotch.

Jeanie crossed her arms as she rested them on the table. "Honey, you never talk about it. And I would never think to even ask you about it if it weren't for dire straits. You were gone a long time in Chicago. I don't believe rumors and I don't believe everything I read online. But I know your ex-client Killian Thorne didn't just get rich exporting car parts. I may be small town, but I know his brother's law firm doesn't just handle real estate closings for him. You were part of that."

"Jeanie, don't," I said. I didn't want to lie to her. I didn't want to evade her either. Plus, she already knew. Jeanie Mills had one of the shrewdest minds I knew. Thirteen years ago, when I graduated from law school, she begged me not to even take an interview with the Thorne Law Group. But the money was just too good. I suppose devil's bargains are always like that. So, I took it and then spent the next decade and more working my way up to partner. I could admit it to myself if I couldn't quite say it out loud to her. I'd been a mob lawyer.

"He helped you last year," Jeanie said. "When you needed Vangie to testify, it was Thorne you called to find her, wasn't it?"

I fingered the shot glass, thinking hard about taking a third. "It wasn't one of my finer moments. But I thought the ends justified the means."

Now I wasn't sure. What if I'd never had Vangie dragged back to town? If I hadn't made her testify and expose Coach D for who he really was? Then she could have lived her life quietly like she wanted. She wouldn't have run foul of Ben and Sarah Dale. Maybe there never would have been a personal protection order.

If only …

"Don't do that," Jeanie said, already knowing my mind. "Don't blame yourself for any of it. That's not why I brought it up. And I'm not asking you to spill secrets or client confidences. I can put two and two together well enough. You didn't come back home to Delphi because you wanted it exactly. You did it because you had no other choice. I'm glad for that. I missed you. I bring it up because maybe …"

I turned to her. "You think maybe my contacts back in Chicago can help with this?"

Jeanie shrugged. "I don't know. I think real darkness came into Ben and Sarah Dale's lives and ended them. Sometimes you can't fight that kind of thing without going dark yourself. I know it's a long shot. But if there's even a chance that little girl is still out there somewhere, maybe …"

"I know," I said, my voice rising higher than I wanted it to. The truth was, I'd thought about it. Killian Thorne already owned a pound or more of my flesh for helping me last year. What could I ask him for now? Could he really help me find that precious baby? Or, if the worst happened and she was convicted, now that he'd found my sister, could I ask him to help her disappear again?

"I don't know," Jeanie said. "Just forget it. I don't know what I'm saying. I'm desperate. That's what. I just wish there was something I could do."

I reached for her, putting my hand over hers. She had a devilish twinkle in her eye that made me smile. I loved her like family and she'd been there for me plenty more than my own had been at times.

"It's okay," I said. "And yes, I've thought about it. With Killian, things are complicated. I'm not even sure I'd know what to ask him for if it came to it. As bleak as things are getting, I don't think we're there yet in any case. I'm not planning to give up. Probable cause is one thing. Reasonable doubt is something else."

"Right," Jeanie said. "I've got faith in you, kid. I always have. Don't let your screwy brothers get you thinking you're not doing enough. You've been amazing. And I've always known you to be at your best when you're backed into a corner. So, let's get to work."

I wanted to hug her. I hadn't realized how badly I'd needed just that little bit of a pep talk. Jeanie believed in me. At some of the darker times in my life, that had saved me. I just hoped it would save my sister now.

Jeanie went to the corkboard and started arranging the witness photos again. She had a call into the medical examiner's office. He'd agreed to meet with me tomorrow afternoon. It was time to poke holes in Rayna DeWitt's case. It was time to see if I could catch the real killer.

I felt lighter as I started laying out the evidence again. There was something there. There had to be.

Working made me feel better, more in control. I lost track of time as Jeanie and I talked out the biggest strengths of Rayna's case. I didn't hear Miranda come back into the room at first. When I finally looked up, her expression caught me.

"What?"

"Your brother's on line one," Miranda said. "He said he's been trying to call on your cell."

I meant to ask her what on earth he needed. Miranda seemed to already know. Car doors slammed out front. I went to the window. Two police cruisers parked at odd angles in front of the door. A third, unmarked car pulled in behind them.

"Vangie," Miranda said. "Your brother ..."

I moved in slow motion, reaching for the phone. I don't even remember saying hello.

"Cass." It was Joe on the other end. His tone was low and flat. "Cass, you need to get back home. It's Vangie. She's ... gone."

My heart fell to the floor as four uniformed police officers burst into the room.

Chapter 20

My heel slid on the slick hospital floor. I touched the wall to steady myself. My vision tunneled and I took a second to catch my breath. I'd been here before so many times. So many phone calls that brought me racing to this place. My mother never came out.

Once again, the presence of uniformed police officers marked my destination. I heard Joe's voice, yelling. I made my way past the nurses' station to one of the exam rooms. They were more or less glass cubicles with the huge nurse's desk at the center.

My breath left me in a whoosh as I saw my little brother Matty sitting on the edge of the gurney, a bloodied cloth pressed to his head.

He looked up at me, his eyes cold and stern. Delphi detective George Knapp stood beside him, writing notes in a book.

"He's not giving a statement," I said, brushing my way past Knapp. He was a good guy. At least, that's what Eric always said. Tall, well over six feet. He was the most experienced detective with the Delphi Police Department. Still, he was standing between my brother and me.

"Ms. Leary ..." Knapp started. I shot him a look. I was a sister. I was a lawyer. Matty was done talking to anyone but me for the time being.

"I'm going to need a minute," I said. Knapp closed his book. He said something to the uniformed officers behind him. Probably a caution not to let any of us leave without telling him.

"Can you walk?" I asked Matty. He pulled the cloth away from his head. My brother had an angry welt just above his eye. It was still bleeding a little, but from my untrained eye, didn't look like it would even need stitches.

I turned to one of the nurses at the station. "Is there someplace I can take him that's more private?" I asked. She stepped around the desk and pulled the huge glass double doors together, walling us off. I mouthed a "thank you" then whipped around to face Matty.

"What the hell happened?" I asked.

"She took off," he said. "I was on the couch taking a nap. I heard the front door open. Vangie was about to head outside. I told her not to. She warned me not to get in the way. Then she cold-cocked me and took off running, I guess. When I came to, I was on the floor and that ankle monitor was out in the snow, blinking. Pair of garden shears right next to it. I was about to call the cops."

Joe loomed behind Matty, still as a statue with his arms crossed in front of him. I looked from one brother to the other. Pressing my thumb and forefinger against the bridge of my nose, I tried to figure out where to even start with them.

"Bullshit," I finally said. I kept my voice in a low whisper. The doors were closed, but there was no telling if they were soundproof.

"You calling me a liar?" Matty asked.

"Yeah," I said. "That's exactly what I'm doing. I know damn well Vangie wouldn't hit you. And I'm pretty sure if she really wanted to make a run for it, you'd help her. Did you?"

Matty glowered at me. Still, Joe said nothing.

"I don't believe this," I said. "What did you tell the police?"

"I told them just what I told you."

"Matty," I said. "They're at my house. They have a search warrant. Jeanie's there to manage it, but Jesus. How? When they find her ..."

"And I told you, she took off on her own."

I went to my brother, ignoring his scowl as I got a better look at the wound above his eye. The welt formed a nearly straight, perfect line. Either she hit him with a ruler or my brother had just cracked his head on the edge of a table ... or the overhang on my granite kitchen countertops. I felt the urge to bash him with something equally heavy just then.

"What did she hit you with?" I asked.

Matty's jaw dropped. He couldn't answer.

"Matty, I swear to God."

He circled his fingers around my wrist, pulling my hand away from his head. "I told you. She took off. I wasn't part of it."

"You better not be," I said.

"I told you," Matty said. "I was about to call the cops. On my own sister. That damn tether must have malfunctioned or something. I thought it was supposed to send some kind of signal."

I started to pace at the end of the bed. On one pass, I stopped in front of Joe. "Are you just going to stand there?"

"What do you want me to do?"

"I don't know!" I yelled. "Matty, they're going to try to

get a subpoena to search your phone. You were staying with her. What will they find?"

"They've got nothing on me. I told you. This wasn't me."

I pointed a finger straight at his face. "You sure they're not going to find some videos on how to cut an ankle tether in your search history?"

Matty blinked. It was all the answer I needed.

"Son of a bitch," I muttered.

"You think she's guilty," Joe said, his voice a monotone.

"What?"

"Admit it. From the very beginning, you've doubted Vangie's story."

I threw my hands up. I couldn't believe what I was hearing. "Are you kidding me with this? Right now, it doesn't exactly matter. She's violated her bond conditions. They *will* find her. And when they do, she's going to have new charges tacked on. She's going to jail, Joe. For real. I can't make that go away."

I could feel the judgment in his eyes. There was a part of me that could still see it all almost from a distance. He was worried. Terrified, actually. We were both still working through the guilt of not protecting our baby sister from a sexual predator when she was just a kid. She'd borne that secret and the repercussions of it all by herself. It clouded his reason, made him lash out at the only person he could. Me. And yet, I pretty much wanted to rip his face off then and there.

"We have to find her," I said, taking a different approach. "Matty, there is three inches of snow on the ground. They found footprints heading down the street and then nothing. She got in a car. She's with somebody."

"I don't know," he said. "But I'm not going to sit here and pretend I don't want her to disappear for a while."

I went to him, placing my hands on his shoulders. I

looked him straight in the eye. My brother was a man. Twenty-six years old. He had enough of the look of our mother with his clear blue eyes and light brown hair. A cowlick stuck up in the back and when he was a kid I could never get it to lay flat. He wore it cropped short now, but there was still that little traitorous swirl.

"Matty," I said. "You have to tell me what you know. I meant what I said about the cops. They *will* search your browsing history. If you let Vangie use your phone, they'll figure that out too. You're not scot-free yourself. You've got a DUI and two disorderlies on your record. If they charge you with aiding and abetting, they won't go easy on you. I can't make it go away."

He clenched his jaw. "I told you what happened."

I searched his face. Matty couldn't lie to me. He tried so many times when he was a little kid and a teenager. He'd get these two little red blotches on his cheeks from holding his breath when he tried.

Are you smoking? Did you take my car? Tell me you didn't steal Mr. Porter's geometry test.

He hung with the wrong crowd. Hell, the Leary family *was* the wrong crowd. Eastside trash. Troublemakers. No jury would ever believe he hadn't helped Vangie skip. My brother took a breath and his cheeks reddened.

Chapter 21

MATTY WAS LYING. Only, I couldn't hear him say it. This was getting harder and harder for me to control. I suppose it was an illusion to think I'd ever had control at all. I kissed my brother's head again and let him go. The nurse came back in with a wheelchair. "Sorry," she said. "Doc wants to get a head CT. As soon as that's clear, you'll be free to go."

"Thank you," I said. Detective Knapp waited on the other side of the glass. He was deep in conversation with another officer, their foreheads nearly touching.

"They'll leave you alone until after your tests are done," I said to Matty. "Probably. Don't give a statement or answer any other questions unless I'm with you. Tell them you know your rights."

"I know what to say," Matty said. Of course he did. I turned and went to him. Sighing, I planted a kiss on his forehead, just above the welt. God help me. I loved him. I'd take a bullet for that boy and he knew it.

"Come on," I said to Joe. I thought he might resist, but he followed me out of Matty's room as the nurse got him situated in the chair. I held a finger up, gesturing to Knapp. He'd want my statement. He'd get it soon enough.

Joe and I walked down to the lobby. It wasn't exactly private, but nobody followed us. We picked a quiet corner and sat on one of the couches.

"How bad is this going to get?" Joe asked.

I met his eyes. My brother was only twenty-two months older than me. I moved back to Delphi less than a year ago. In that time, I think he'd aged a decade.

"They're going to catch her," I said. "That's a foregone conclusion. She took some cash I keep in my nightstand. I asked Jeanie to check when she met the cops over at my place. It's about three hundred bucks. It's not enough to help her disappear. I predict they'll have her in custody again within the next twenty-four to forty-eight hours. And then she's going to sit in jail for months. Maybe years. And that's *if* we get an acquittal on the Dale murders."

"She's out there looking for Jessa," Joe said. "And no, I had nothing to do with what she did, so don't even ask."

I couldn't help it. That made me smile. I put a hand on my brother's knee. "I wasn't going to. I know you didn't."

He dropped his head, covering it with his hand. My heart stopped as my big strong brother started to silently cry.

"I wish I had," he said, looking up at me, his eyes red-rimmed. "Dammit, I wish I'd have been brave enough to help her days ago. She loves that little girl with everything in her. She doesn't care about the murder charges or what they do to her. If it were my baby. If it were Emma out there hurt, probably dead ... I can't even ..."

"I know," I said.

"No," he said. "You don't. Not all the way. You don't have a kid."

His words felt like a sock to the stomach. I reared back. "You're kidding me, right? I *do* have kids. I've had two of them since I was fourteen years old. Including you, some-times three. You know I've been more of a mother to Vangie than anyone. This is killing me too. But we have to find her, Joe. If you know something ... if you can get Matty to tell you something ... we have to act on it."

He cocked his head to the side. "You want Matty to rat out our sister?"

"Dammit," I said, my voice rising. I hated the accusation in his tone. "I am *trying* to save her. I know you're all pissed at me about the prelim. You think I've got some magic beans or get-out-of-jail-free card that I should have used to make this all go away. Well, it doesn't work that way. I don't have that kind of power. This is real. This is serious. And I'm doing the best I can."

To his credit, Joe looked stunned. His face hardened. He went silent as people walked by on their way out of the hospital. Then he whispered so softly I could barely hear him. "And I'm telling you, if it comes to it, I'm not going to turn on my sister."

"Great," I said. "Well, you want to throw my lack of chil-dren in my face? Let me throw it back at you. You're a father, Joe. You're Katy and Emma's sole source of income right now. You get in the way of the investigation on this, they'll throw your ass in jail too. If Vangie reaches out to you, you have to tell me."

Something changed in his face. It was just a flicker. I couldn't always read Joe the same way I could Matty or the way he could read me. But my blood ran a little colder. For the first time since I came back to Delphi, I felt truly alone. Turning from Joe, I rose to my feet.

"Ms. Leary?" Detective Knapp came around the corner. His tone let me know I'd put him off as long as I could.

Chapter 22

I MADE it back home three hours later. Matty's CT scan came back normal. Rather than coming back with me, he chose to disappear. One silent glance from Joe and I knew he'd stick close to keep Matty out of trouble. Well, there was one potential fire that wouldn't ignite. At least not tonight.

Jeanie's car was still parked in front of my house but the Delphi P.D. was gone. As I walked in, I heard Jeanie swearing up a storm and banging around upstairs.

I had a headache. A big one. At just past eight o'clock, it was already pitch black outside. Snow began to fall again. The weatherman predicted we'd have another four inches by morning.

Jeanie heard me come in and barreled down the stairs. "Cops made a mess of your guest room," Jeanie said. "I just got it put right."

"Thank you. Anything else I should know? Did they find anything?"

Jeanie froze on the last step. I leaned against the door, exhaustion flooding through me.

"Not really," she said. "She never had a phone when she was here, did she?"

I shook my head. "No. But God knows what she and Matty talked about. He got through his statement all right. It's just …"

"If he hadn't brained himself in the head, I'd be doing it for him," Jeanie said, fuming. She plopped down on the couch and put her feet up on the coffee table. I pulled a bottle of wine from the fridge and brought two glasses.

"Got anything stronger?" she asked.

"I was hiding this in the lettuce crisper. As far as I know, Matty's resisted temptation since he's been staying here but …"

Jeanie took the offered wine.

"Well, shit," she said. "He still sticking to the story that Vangie knocked him out cold?"

The wine was cold and good going down. But, like Jeanie, I could have used something stronger. "Yes," I said.

"What the hell is she thinking?" Jeanie shook her head. "We can't fix this. She's going to do time."

"I know. I just don't think she cares. She's out of her mind, Jeanie. That kook at the courthouse sent her over the edge. She believes Jessa's out there somewhere alone, looking for her."

"Poor kid," Jeanie said. She reached for the wine bottle. "Both of them. So now what?"

"Now"—I clinked glasses with her—"we wait. They're going to find her. She's only got the couple hundred bucks she took from my drawer. Her picture is plastered all over the place. Everyone in town knows what she looks like anyway and they all think she's a killer. She's gone off the reservation, Jeanie. Who knows what she's capable of."

"Dammit," she said.

"Exactly."

The neighbor's dog started to bark. Tires crunched on the snow outside and headlights flooded the window.

"Son of a bitch," Jeanie said. "I thought I got rid of everybody."

I set my wine glass on the table. Eric Wray stood on the porch, his face hard. His knocking so forceful it shook the windows. He barely waited for me to open the door before he barged right in.

"Sure," I said. "Come right on in. Your timing is perfect."

"Don't," he said. Eric lifted his hand and made a claw of it, shaking the air as if he wanted to do the same to my neck. He saw Jeanie and his shoulders dropped. She rose.

"Listen," she said. "I'm beat. I'm going to head on out before the roads ice over again. We'll get back at it all first thing in the morning. Thanks for the wine." She gave a grim smile to Eric and sashayed past him for the front door.

She started her car and drove away before Eric collected himself to say something to me. "Cass," he said. "I need you to tell me the truth. Right now. Did you have anything to do with Vangie running?"

I crossed my arms in front of me. "I already gave a statement to your partner. Unless you came with another warrant …"

"Dammit!" he shouted. "I didn't come here as … this isn't." He started to pace. It took him almost a full minute before he collected himself.

"Cass," he said. "I'm not here on the department's behalf. Though I damn well should be. You realize I had to give a statement too?"

"Why?"

"Enough people know we're friends. Knapp's just covering all his bases. He's doing exactly what I would have done in his place. Cass, this puts me in a hell of a position."

"Again I say, why?" I sat back down on the couch and poured myself a second glass of wine.

"People know I was talking to you about the case," he answered.

"So what? My sister's been charged in Washtenaw County, not here. You don't have a conflict of interest. And I never forced you to talk to me, Eric. I don't get why this is a problem for you. I'm honestly sorry it is, but I've also got too much other crap on my plate right now to ..."

"Did you help her?" he asked, exasperated. "Jesus. Matty's telling some ridiculous story about Vangie knocking him out. It's a farce. Everybody knows it. Lucky for him they can't prove it. Yet. I know how protective you are of your brothers and sister. I get it."

I rose to my feet. "And I told you, I gave my statement to George Knapp. I don't have anything else to add. I don't know where my sister is."

"Right," he said. "And if you did, I'd be the last person you'd tell."

"Eric, you're out of line right now," I said. "If you're so worried about guilt by association with me, what are you doing here?"

His face fell. My question seriously seemed to throw him. Hurt him. He took a step back. "Cass, I'm worried about you. I'm not sure you get how close you are to disaster."

"And you think you're here to save me from it?" I didn't like the tone of my voice. On some other level, I could see what Eric was doing. He really was trying to be a friend. He'd called it though. This was a family matter. I couldn't afford to let anyone else in.

"Yes, dammit," he said, his face getting more red.

"Tell me something," I asked, taking a step toward him. "Do you think my sister murdered those people?"

A beat passed. Then another. Eric stayed stock still but

for the steady pulse of the vein running along his jaw. It was all the answer I needed.

"Cass," he said. But the moment was already gone.

"Eric, thanks for checking up on me. And thanks for everything you've done so far to help."

"I haven't done anything," he said. "I just want you to listen to me. If they find something. I mean, anything. They're going to come after you and your brother for helping Vangie escape."

"Don't worry about me," I said. "I know the difference between the light and the dark side."

It was a cheap shot. Eric flinched. I knew his deepest secret. My duty and my oath would keep me from ever revealing it. Even without those, I might have kept it. I just never thought I'd throw it back at him so quickly.

"Do you?" he asked. "Because I don't know. This feels different."

"How can you honestly think Vangie did this? You saw those crime scene photos. What happened to Ben and Sarah was brutal. Sadistic almost. Vangie isn't like ... she's not like us. Even with everything she's been through, she still has a pure soul. I've seen it in the way she talks about her daughter. She'd do anything for her."

The second I said those words, I wanted to take them back. Eric's face changed again. God, I had no idea why it mattered to me so much that he believed she was innocent. It just did.

"Look," he said. "I didn't come here to debate what happened to the Dales. As far as that goes, I said I'd help you if I could. I meant it. I still mean it. I just ... I'd just hate to see you go down in the process."

"Thank you," I said. "You did what you came for. Consider me duly warned."

My words didn't satisfy him. I didn't expect them to. I

meant to show him out. Thank him again for trying to be my friend. But my ringing phone stopped me from saying anything else. I looked back where I'd left it on the coffee table. I didn't recognize the number that came up.

"I'll wait," he said.

I picked up the phone and walked outside. The snow had started falling again.

"Cass?" It was Vangie. My heart thumped right into my throat. I went rigid, afraid to turn and let Eric see my face.

"Hi, there," I said, trying to make my voice light. "Thanks for calling me back. It's kind of a bad time though."

"Is someone else there?" Vangie asked. She sounded so far away and breathless. I wanted to run to the end of the street and demand to know where she was. I never turned. I barely even breathed. But Eric walked outside next to me. I pressed the phone tighter to my ear, scared to death he could hear my sister through the phone.

"If you call my secretary, Miranda, she can set something up."

"Okay," she said. "I know you're pissed. I know you want me to say I'm sorry but I can't. They're not doing anything. Jessa's out here somewhere. I'll find her myself."

"That's not such a good idea. I really wish you'd set something up so we can talk in person. There's a lot of misinformation on the internet. Every case is different." I barely recognized my own voice. Eric was staring straight at me. He had something else to say. I plastered on a fake smile and held up a finger, gesturing "one minute."

"I'm okay," she said.

"I'll just catch you later," Eric said. Thank God, he turned and started walking to his car. I had to get more information from Vangie. I had to get her off my damn phone. There was at least an outside chance the police would subpoena my phone records as well as Matty's.

"Where are you?" I whispered into the phone as soon as I was certain Eric was far enough away.

"I'm safe," she said. "For now. I'm just ... I'm scared, Cass."

"I know. Oh honey, I know. But this is no good. They're going to find you. You know that." With every second that went by, my own position became more precarious. This was aiding and abetting.

"I don't know what to do!" Vangie started to cry and it broke me. She was five years old again in my heart.

"It's going to be okay," I heard myself say and hated the lie.

"I went by Ben and Sarah's house," she said.

"Jesus Christ," I whispered. In Vangie's current state, I was gravely worried she might get hurt when the cops caught up with her. I worried she might not care.

"Honey," I said. "I need you to tell me where you are. I'll come get you."

"I have to go," she said. "I don't want them to be able to trace the call."

I looked skyward. I didn't have the heart to tell her it didn't work like it did in the movies. The second she called my phone she was traceable.

"Who are you with?" I asked. "Honey, I know somebody had to be helping you. Did you get in someone's car? Vangie, they're at risk now too."

I didn't say the other thing at the forefront of my mind. Now I was at risk too. I'd stepped to the brink just like Eric knew I would.

Vangie was full-on crying now. "I just want it all to stop. I want to go back in time and change it all. I never would have let Jessa out of my sight. I shouldn't have let Sarah try to bully me."

"Vangie, where are you?" I said, getting angrier. I'd never

heard Vangie like this before. Never mind the cops, I worried she might be suicidal.

A car door slammed. I turned away from the sound. But it was too late. Eric came back up the driveway. He stopped short, all color draining from his face. He'd heard my last words. I pulled the phone away from my ear.

"Don't," I mouthed to Eric. He shook his head no.

"Give me the phone, Cass," he said.

"Cass?" Vangie's voice came through loud and clear, even without the speaker.

It was then I noticed Eric held his own cell phone just away from his ear. His eyes flickered. He too was breathless.

"What is it?" I said.

"Cass," he said. "A call came in from the Toledo Police. They found a little girl. They're pretty sure it's Jessa Dale. She's just been admitted to Toledo Hospital."

The call dropped. Vangie wasn't there anymore. My knees gave out and I sank to the porch step.

Chapter 23

I DON'T KNOW what he did. I don't know what he said. But Eric Wray talked us past a doctor, three nurses, and the detectives on scene as soon as we got to the hospital down in Toledo.

Vangie hadn't called back. When I redialed the number on my phone, it kept dropping. She'd probably been smart enough to call me from a burner phone and dumped it into a toilet or something when she finished.

I stood outside a closed door to a private hospital room on the pediatric floor. Eric had a hand on my lower back as we listened to the doctor. His name was Dixon. He was calm. Smiling. He kept looking at the Toledo detective standing behind us. Next to him, two social workers crammed into our little huddle to hear the words that stopped my heart.

"She's okay," Dr. Dixon said. "Stable. We've got her on IV fluids and we're getting her electrolytes under control. She's a bit dehydrated. She's got an old scrape on her elbow that's healing well. But other than that, there are no serious injuries."

I started to breathe again. "I need to see her," I said. "So we can be sure."

"Ms. Leary," the Toledo detective said. Her name was Mary Braden. "Have you ever even seen this child before?" She'd been on the phone with Brett Carey for most of the time I'd been here. He was on his way down. There was a pretty good chance I'd never get in that room once he got here. Once again, I marveled at Eric. He was risking a lot by helping me but here he was.

I turned to Dr. Dixon. "She has a birthmark behind her right knee. And a crescent-shaped scar on her right big toe. Did you check for that?"

Dixon looked at Braden. He gave her a quick nod. "Yeah," he finally answered. "All that checks out."

Eric took me aside. My heart raced. "Tell me again?" I asked him. "They found her where?"

"She was found in an abandoned apartment downtown. There was an older woman taking care of her. Mrs. Florence. Mary Braden says she's kind of a downtown fixture. Eccentric. Fairly addled. But she's essentially harmless. They don't have a clue how this kid got mixed up with her. She was wearing a red windbreaker when they found her but no other coat. Adult sized. It's got a business logo. Tiller Manufacturing. Carey says there's a neighbor two doors down from the Dales that works there. He's being brought in for questioning."

"You think this neighbor had something to do with the murders?" I asked. I could barely process any of it. I just wanted to get behind that door and see Jessa. It was her. I felt it in my bones.

"No one knows anything yet. The little girl hasn't said a word."

"I need to caution you," Dr. Dixon said. "She's been traumatized. There's no sign of any physical abuse. But she's frightened. I'll allow you in there for just a few seconds. You have a picture of your niece?"

I nodded, sliding the 3x5 photo Vangie gave me out of my coat pocket.

"Okay," the doctor said. "Just you then. Too many adults she's not familiar with could frighten her even more."

"I understand," I said. Dixon gestured for me to come forward. The others stood back except for the two social workers. The doctor opened the door.

I didn't need the photograph. I didn't need to know about any scars or birthmarks. The second I laid eyes on that sweet, tiny girl sitting in that big hospital bed, I knew she was Vangie's daughter. Jessa had wide blue eyes framed with thick long lashes. She sat with her knees drawn up and a tattered brown teddy bear clutched under her arm. Tummy Bear. One of the nurses sat beside her and smoothed Jessa's blonde hair out of her eyes.

"Hi, there," I said, smiling. "My name is Cass."

Jessa looked straight at me, her expression blank. She wasn't scared. She wasn't sad. She just seemed ... gone. It took everything in me not to run to her and gather her into my arms. She looked so much like my sister it gutted me.

"It's her," I whispered back to the doctor. "Tell them it's her. There's no doubt."

I felt a hand on my shoulder. "That's fine, Ms. Leary." It was Detective Mary Braden. She'd gotten her marching orders from Carey, no doubt. They didn't want me saying anything to Jessa about Vangie. They actually worried I'd try to question this baby. I just wanted to take her in my arms and tell her everything would be all right. Just like I'd done for Vangie all those years ago.

"I'll be back," I said. "I'm glad to see you're feeling better, Jessa. These people are going to take care of you. You don't have to be scared. Okay?"

Jessa looked at the nurse beside her. Then she turned and looked at me. Her bottom lip quivered but she didn't cry. She gave me a little nod then hugged Tummy Bear even tighter to her.

I left the room. One of the social workers took me aside. She introduced herself as Kelly Malloy. She worked for the county. She was pretty and young with straight black hair and perfect make-up.

"What happens now?" I asked.

"The doctors are going to run a few more tests. I'm going to stay with her for every step of that. I won't leave her side. She may be discharged as soon as tomorrow. After that, we'll work on a placement plan."

My brain felt like it was coated in molasses. A placement plan. God, I'd heard those words so many times before.

"Foster care," I said. "You're thinking of foster care placement."

"Well, we ... she has no immediate family."

"She has me," I said. I pulled out my business card. "I know this is an unusual situation ..."

"Ms. Leary," Kelly said. "You're right. This is all highly unusual. In the eyes of the law, you're not even related to Jessica."

"I understand the law," I said, pointing to my card. "But you and I both know putting Jessa in the system after all of this is the worst-case scenario. I'm not going to let that happen. All I ask at this point is that you keep me informed before any decisions like that are made."

My head started spinning. This was finally a problem I knew how to solve today. Behind us, two female orderlies went into Jessa's room.

"My understanding is they're taking her down for an x-ray," Kelly said. "Her elbow was pretty banged up."

Her elbow. My mind ticked off the things Vangie had

told me. The day before she went missing, Jessa had wanted to show her how she'd learned to ride a bike without training wheels. She fell, landing hard on her elbow. The blood from the scrape got all over my sister's shirt. The one she wore home. The one the police found when they executed their warrant on Travis White's home.

"Cass." Eric came to me. He'd been carrying on an intense conversation with Detective Braden. The elevator doors opened and Brett Carey stepped off. He took one look at me and his face hardened.

"Son of a bitch," he muttered, charging forward. "You gotta be kidding me. Who let her in here?"

Mary Braden's jaw dropped. She looked at Eric and her face went white. He'd gone out on a limb for me and probably called in some favor with the T.P.D. Now it would come back to bite him in the ass. I was grateful, but not sorry. That was my niece in there, dammit.

Carey started barking orders, his voice rising. The hospital walls were thin. My anger bubbled over and I put a hand on him.

"You can be as pissed at me as you want to be," I said. "I have a right to be here. And you better calm your shit right now. That little girl in there has been through enough. She doesn't need you scaring the hell out of her because you're pissed about procedure."

"Procedure?" His eyes widened. "Procedure? Jesus. She's a material witness to an open murder case."

"Brett, hang on," Eric said, getting between us.

"This you?" Brett shouted. "I don't give two shits what you do in Delphi. But when you start pissing all over *my* cases, we've got a problem. Get your head out of your dick, Wray."

Eric moved with the force of an avalanche. He squared

off with Brett Carey. They stood nose to nose, faces red, fists clenched.

It was Kelly Malloy who defused that particular testosterone bomb. She put a hand on Brett Carey's shoulder and gave him a good shove. Wide-eyed, he stepped back.

"Look," she said. "I don't care what this is about. You boys can work it out on your own time. Right now, I've got a little kid in there who needs to be cared for."

"I need to question her," Brett said.

"No way!" I shouted. "Not now."

"For all I know," he said, "you've already tainted her statement. At a minimum, I'll have your license over this."

"Are you threatening me?" I said.

"Only if I said it right," he answered.

"Enough!" Kelly said. "All of you. Detective Carey, that child is not in any condition for questioning. She's not even medically cleared yet. Once that happens, we'll figure something out. But nobody goes near her without me or a member of my staff at her side. She's fragile."

"I need to know everything she's said so far," Brett said. "Who's been talking to her?"

"No one." Dr. Dixon joined the fray. "She's been talking to no one. She hasn't said a single word since we picked her up. You can question Hattie Florence. She's waiting downstairs. You might not get much out of her, but she's been taking care of this little one for weeks from what I can tell. Start there."

Brett Carey's shoulders dropped. Mercifully, Dixon and Malloy managed to quench the dynamite inside that man better than Eric or I could. Though it killed me, for now, I had to trust the two of them to take care of Jessa.

"Fine," Brett said. "I'll go talk to her. In the meantime, these two don't go anywhere near that little girl." He gestured to Mary Braden.

"We'll put an officer outside her door," Mary assured him. She shot a murderous look at Eric. I imagined he had a reckoning of sorts with her coming later. For now, he jerked his chin toward me. There was another, smaller waiting room down the hall. I was at least reasonably sure Kelly Malloy could handle Carey. So I went with him, keeping Jessa's door within sight.

"Thank you," I said to Eric once we were out of their earshot. "I guess you burned some bridges for me today."

"You let me worry about that," he said. "Chances are, Mary Braden will need something from me soon enough. She'll save face with Brett Carey and stay pissed at me for a few weeks. It's worth it."

"Well, thank you," I said. "What else did you find out?"

Eric gave me a sideways glance. He'd already done one huge favor getting me in here. But I knew the man. There was more he had to tell.

"It's not much," he said. "You heard what they said about the jacket Jessa was wearing. There was also some blood on her clothes. They'll test all of that to see if it belongs to her or to ..."

"Her parents," I said. God. What had happened to that sweet baby? What on earth had she seen? The urge to run to her and get her away from all of this burned in me. I felt helpless.

"She's safe now," Eric said, sensing where my thoughts ran. "She's not physically hurt. This is good news, Cass. The best there is."

I exhaled. "I know. Christ. I need to call my brothers. In all the chaos I didn't even think ..."

Behind us, I heard Kelly Malloy's soothing voice as Jessa's door opened. I turned. She was sitting in an adult-sized wheelchair looking so small and frail. She squeezed that little pink bear tightly against her chest. Kelly kept a hand on

Jessa's shoulder as a nurse pushed the chair toward the elevators. Carey hung back with Detective Braden.

"I should go with them," I said to Eric. "I really don't care what Carey has to say about it. She's my niece."

"Cass," Eric started. Then he saw the look on my face and held his hands up in surrender.

"You should go," I said. "I've dragged you through enough for one day. Thank you. I really mean that."

He let out a sigh instead of a "You're welcome." I hoped it didn't mean he regretted it. For now, my focus had to be on Jessa. I started toward the elevators. They may not let me board, but I could at least find out what floor radiology was.

The elevator doors opened and time seemed to stop. I heard a mangled cry that seared my heart.

Vangie stepped out.

Carey looked up. He shouted.

Vangie took a faltering step, then another. She sank to her knees in front of Jessa's wheelchair, tears spilling down her face.

Then Jessa stood up. She made a noise. Not a cry. Not a shout. It was primal, like a wounded animal. She flung herself into my sister's arms, dropping the pink bear to the ground. Vangie scooped her up and kissed Jessa's cheek as her little girl cried into her shoulder. Jessa wrapped her arms around Vangie's neck and squeezed her tight as the police moved in.

Chapter 24

KELLY MALLOY TOOK one look at Vangie and Jessa together and pulled every string she could to get her released to me temporarily. We had one thing going in our favor. Vangie was still listed as the preferred guardian in Ben and Sarah's will. Though she was off to jail, I was the next best thing. It might not ultimately hold up in court, but it was enough for Malloy to go on today. She rightly knew it would be up to the Wood-bridge County Probate Court to sort out and it would keep Jessa out of foster care for now.

Jeanie met me at the hospital the next morning. Jessa sat in the same big wheelchair. I bought her a new brown bear from the gift shop. She held it in her lap, her young face haunted and blank.

"Well, hey, there," Jeanie said as she pulled up her pants at the knee and crouched in front of Jessa. As a family lawyer, Jeanie had decades of experience dealing with young children in emotional upheaval. She struck just the right tone.

"You must be Jessa." Jessa looked at Jeanie, but didn't

utter a sound. She'd still said not one word since the police found her.

"Jessa," I said. "This is Miss Mills. She's a friend of mine. She's going to drive us to the lake house I was telling you about."

Jessa clutched the bear closer. The police had taken her "Tummy Bear" as evidence. One of the nurses noticed a faint blood stain on its right foot.

Kelly came down the hall. She gave me a nod. I made a quick introduction between her and Jeanie.

"Jessa?" Kelly said. "I'm going to talk to your Aunt Cass here for a few seconds. We'll just be over there by that big fake tree. You'll be able to see us the whole time. Miss Mills will make sure you have everything you need."

Jessa nodded. For now, it was the only communication she was capable of. She'd wailed as the police took Vangie. For her part, Vangie had played it so much smarter and cooler than I would have predicted. Instead of fighting against the officers, she became calm. At once, my sister had become keenly aware of Jessa's distress. She told her daughter she had to go with the police to answer some questions. She introduced me to Jessa again. She promised Jessa that I would make sure she stayed safe. Whatever bond they had, Jessa seemed to trust my sister enough to listen. I can't say she was happy to be with me, but Jessa was resigned to it. Somehow, that broke my heart even more.

"The sooner you get out of Toledo, the better," Kelly said. "Once you get Jessa settled at your place, you'll need to file formal paperwork in Woodbridge County."

"I'm aware," I said. "And thank you. I know you've gone out on more than a limb with this one."

Kelly cast a nervous glance over her shoulder at Jessa and Jeanie. Jeanie was busy tying Jessa's shoe.

"I just know what I saw. Your sister is the only family that baby has left."

"No," I said. "She's got me. And she's got two uncles who are anxious to meet her."

Kelly nodded. "Be careful on that. She seems to get more agitated around men. I don't know what that means. But just go slow. You've got that referral your friend gave you?"

"I do," I said. I was taking Jessa to a child psychologist who specialized in trauma later in the week.

"Good. Dr. Spencer is good with people. She was a mentor of mine. In the meantime, your friend is good with her."

I turned to look. Jeanie had produced another small stuffed bear from her purse. Jessa reached for it. It was no Tummy Bear, but she was responding.

"Thank you," I said. "I know how unusual this case is."

"It's more than unusual," she said. "I just can't see how putting Jessa in foster care would serve her. Since no one has come forward from either Ben or Sarah Dale's family to claim her, she just fits through about every jurisdictional crack there is. Her parents were domiciled in Washtenaw County. Her next legal guardian is in jail for the time being. Then there's you."

"And I'm the only one who's asking," I said.

"Right. Well, you may have a fight on your hands when it comes to the prosecutor's office in Ann Arbor."

"You let me worry about that," I said. "I just want to get Jessa somewhere safe and warm."

"Me too," Kelly said. "Good luck, Cass. You're going to need it."

I thanked her again and went to Jeanie and Jessa. "You ready to get out of here, kiddo?" I asked. Jessa hesitated for a second. She looked at Kelly, then back at me. Finally, she let out a breath and nodded.

She was so little to be so brave. Jessa slid out of the wheelchair. She looked down at the new red tennis shoes I bought for her. I panicked a little and bought three pairs, not knowing which ones she'd like. Jessa picked these. They had sequins on the side and lit up when she walked. Jessa reached for me. My heart shattered as I took her hand in mine and we walked out the hospital doors.

"SHE'S SOMETHING," Jeanie said. We'd managed to get Jessa to eat a slice of pepperoni pizza from Zanetti's at the corner. She ate it on the couch, right in front of the double doors looking out at the lake. Some of my neighbors had cleared a circle in front of our houses. It was dark now, but earlier, a few of the neighborhood kids had gone out ice skating. Jessa sat mesmerized as she ate her pizza.

It was a good distraction. Kelly cautioned me against letting Jessa watch television or do anything online. Until we had a clearer picture of what Jessa had been through, she didn't want to risk triggering anything in her. We had an appointment with Dr. Spencer at one o'clock tomorrow afternoon. First thing in the morning, I was due at Rayna DeWitt's office to discuss the new charges filed against Vangie. She also had evidence to share after the Toledo Police filed their report on Jessa's recovery.

By eight o'clock, Jessa fell asleep on the couch. I'd set up the guest room for her, but didn't want to move her.

"I'll just sleep on the other couch," I whispered to Jeanie. "I don't want to risk her waking up in the middle of the night and not knowing where she is."

"Good call," Jeanie said. "I'll take the guest room at the top of the stairs."

"Jeanie, you don't have to stay here. I can't ask you to do that."

"You didn't ask. I'm offering. You can't be here every second of the day and still do your job for Vangie. On that note, how's she holding up?"

I let out a heavy sigh. Vangie had been extradited back to Washtenaw County earlier this afternoon. There she would sit in the county jail until she faced trial for Ben and Sarah's murder, unless I could figure out a way to get the charges dropped against her before that.

"I don't know," I said. "Joe and Matty went up with her. She knows not to say a word until I have a chance to talk to her. I'm heading there right after I deal with the prosecutor's office."

Jessa squirmed on the couch. She didn't wake, but she tucked her little legs under her body and her thumb found its way to her mouth. She was so tiny. Vangie had been like that. Small but fierce. And like Vangie, she'd been through far too much in her young life.

"Do you think she saw it?" Jeanie asked.

I didn't have to ask her what she meant. It had been on my mind too. I'd get the results of all the forensic tests on Jessa's clothes soon. But the fact remained, she'd been in the house when her parents were murdered. If she'd seen their killer, she would hold the key to freeing Vangie.

Except trauma had rendered Jessa silent.

Chapter 25

NEW SNOW FELL OVERNIGHT. Woodbridge, Washtenaw, Lenawee, Hillsdale, and Monroe Counties were under a blizzard warning. I gave myself nearly two hours to make it back to Ann Arbor. Jessa was still sleeping under Jeanie's watchful eye.

As I made my way up the stairs to Rayna DeWitt's office, I passed Detective Carey heading down. He froze when he saw me, red-faced.

"You're somethin' else, lady," he said.

"Good morning to you, Detective," I answered, not wanting to give him anything. Carey threw nothing short of a fit when he heard I was bringing Jessa home with me.

"How is she?" he asked, taking a beat; his eyes softened. No matter what else happened, I knew this man was genuinely concerned for Jessa's well-being. He and his department had been searching for her for over three long weeks. Though no one would say it out loud, most of them had given Jessa up for dead.

"Exhausted," I said, grateful to share a brief truce. "Traumatized. But physically healthy and whole. She fell asleep watching the snow falling on Finn Lake. It made her happy."

He turned his head but not before I saw his eyes mist.

By his nature, this man was my adversary. He'd put together the case that might very well get my sister convicted of two murders. But Jessa was just a baby. Brett Carey was human. A father and grandfather. I knew he brought this case home with him every night. It was the kind that would likely stick with him to the grave. Except I knew he had it wrong. I did something I knew I shouldn't have. I got personal.

"Carey," I said. "You saw what happened at that elevator. Vangie didn't kill the Dales. She loves that little girl. And she loves her right back. You know your theory doesn't make sense."

Carey's face hardened. "I know the evidence. And you have no idea whether Jessa even saw what happened that night. Rayna's got my report and the forensics upstairs. I'll let her tell you."

"So, you're just going to ignore what you saw?"

Carey lifted a hand. He clutched the air then curled his fist to his side. "I care what Jessa saw and that hasn't been determined yet. She needs to be questioned by someone qualified. If I find out you've done anything to tamper with her testimony …"

"Okay," I said. "We're done here."

"Consider it a warning, Cass," he said. "I'll make sure you never practice law again."

I pushed past him and went upstairs. He was still standing on the landing, staring up at me with anger in his eyes as I opened the door. Rayna's office was at the end of the hall. She was already waiting for me in the doorway as I left Brett Carey fuming behind me.

Rayna said a pleasant hello as she ushered me into her

office. She had a thick manila envelope on her desk with my name on it.

"The labs came back," she said. "I've made copies of all the reports and the new charging documents are inside." She handed me the envelope.

I fingered the metal tab. Rayna gestured to the chair in front of her desk. I really just wanted to take the report and start the long drive back to Finn Lake.

"You could have emailed all of this to me," I said. "Why'd you ask me to come in?"

"Why did you say yes?" she answered.

"Fair enough," I said. "I ran into Detective Carey in the stairwell. I don't suppose he filled you in on what happened when my niece saw my sister for the first time?"

Rayna gave me a dismissive wave. "Cass, we go way back, don't we? I won't waste your time bullshitting. Please believe me when I tell you how deeply glad I am that your niece is safe. I can't imagine how tough this has been on you and your family."

"Thank you," I said, and meant it.

"I've heard from the T.P.D.," Rayna said. "They're pretty close to wrapping up their investigation on how she came to be found there."

"What? Why the hell are they talking to you?"

Rayna smiled. "You're not the only one who can pull strings down there. Anyway, it dovetails with my case. The jacket she was wearing matched one belonging to the Dales' neighbor two doors down. His name is Matt Hadley. His statement is in the report. He's passed a lie detector. His garage door was unlocked the night of the murders. We think Jessa may have run there and hidden in the backseat of his work car. He's a salesman for Tiller Manufacturing. He commutes to Toledo. He left at around five a.m. on the morning of January 9th. He went straight to work. He keeps that jacket in the second backseat of his car along with some blankets. We think Jessa was hiding under them and stayed quiet. The guy likes to blare 80s hair bands pretty loud when he's driving. He didn't hear her."

"Jesus. Your theory is Jessa hid in this guy's back seat and he drove to work not knowing she was there?"

"A few strands of hair matching Jessa's were found on the carpet under blankets he keeps for when they travel with their husky. Anyway, the Tiller office building is two blocks from the apartments where Jessa was found. Hettie Florence said in her statement she found Jessa wandering near the entrance to the public parking lot across from the Tiller building."

"Good God," I said. I squeezed my eyes shut trying to imagine the sheer luck of it all. What if no one had found her? What if she'd gotten hit by a car? What if someone far worse than Hettie Florence had found her?

"It's just a lucky thing Jessa didn't wind up in the hands of someone far worse. The Tiller office building and those apartments aren't in the greatest part of town. Hettie Florence is just a kindly, crazy old lady who doesn't trust the police. She thought she was doing a good deed taking care of Jessa and not turning her in. She doesn't have a television or even a cell phone. She didn't see the Amber Alerts and I doubt she would have really known what it all meant in any case."

"Yeah," I said, my thoughts wandering. "Lucky thing. She spent three weeks living in filth. Alone. Terrified. Wearing the same clothes she had on when her parents ..."

Rayna clamped her mouth shut. "Hey. Oh. Cass, I'm sorry. That came off as insensitive."

"Look," I said. "I appreciate your taking the time to meet with me. But like you said. This whole thing has been pretty hard on my family. I need to get back to them." I started to rise.

"Cass," Rayna said, my name coming out in short staccato.

"I'm willing to talk about a plea deal," she said.

"You're what?" I sank back into my chair.

"Second degree," she said. "Times two. I won't lie to you. Your sister will still spend most of her life in prison, but at least she'll have a *chance* at parole. If she goes down for first degree on even one of those murders, she'll die behind bars for certain."

"Why now?" I asked. "Carey seems to think your case is stronger than ever?"

Rayna let out a breath but she didn't blink. "Think about it," she said.

"You want to give me the spoiler alert?" I said, waving the envelope. "What are the forensics going to say? Clearly it's something you don't like or we wouldn't be having this conversation."

Rayna steepled her fingers under her chin as she leaned back in her burgundy leather chair. "The blood on Jessa's clothing and her teddy bear is a mixture of Ben and Sarah Dale's. We already knew she was at the crime scene ... but ... There's a splatter pattern on the front of the pajamas she had on. The blood belongs to her father. Look, we don't have an expert opinion on this yet. I need to do a lot more testing. Of course, you'll get all the test results. She was standing close enough to get sprayed."

I felt ash in my mouth as I tried to breathe. God.

"She has to be questioned by a professional. Soon," Rayna said. "But no matter what, that child is a material witness. Think about the evidence we *do* have, Cass. Your sister is going down for this. But if she pleads out, she can spare that little kid from having to potentially testify. You don't want that. If she loves her, I can't imagine Evangeline wants that."

I got up out of my chair. My fingers trembled as I gripped the envelope. I'd have to read it. Every cold, grim detail of the physical evidence from Jessa's clothes. There could be no doubt. She was a witness. She was standing close enough to her father to have his blood sprayed all over her the moment he died.

Jessa may hold the key to saving my sister. But the price might be too high for that fragile little girl to pay.

Chapter 26

VANGIE SAT ACROSS FROM ME, tugging at the collar of her orange jumpsuit. She was shackled. Her eyes were dark and hollow.

"Don't tell me it's going to be okay this time," she said. I didn't.

"Jessa is safe," I said. "You didn't dream that. She's been through a lot, but she's physically okay."

A weight lifted off my sister's shoulders.

"She's really okay?" she asked.

"Yes. She really is." I took a breath. I had to tell Vangie what we knew so far. She had to hear it and she had to be strong.

"She isn't speaking," I said. "We're working with professionals. But Vangie. I think Jessa knows who killed her parents. Or rather, she knows who didn't. Anyone who saw how she reacted to you when you came off that elevator could never believe she saw you hurt them."

"But she can't say it," Vangie said, assessing the situation correctly.

"Not so far, no."

I hesitated before telling her the hard part. I was still trying to wish it weren't true. "Vangie." I reached for her, putting a hand over Vangie's. "She had blood on her clothes. I can spare you the details, but the scientists are pretty sure she was in a position to see exactly what happened to at least her father."

Vangie trembled and she closed her eyes. "Cass, you have to get me out of here. I have to see her. She needs to know I'm going to take care of her."

I straightened. "Vangie, look at me. Open your eyes." She did.

I squeezed her hand tighter. "I can't get you out of here unless we get an acquittal. No judge will ever set bail for you again. That's on you."

"Cass ... I had to ..."

"Stop. You made this so much worse. My job is now one hundred times harder. But I'm going to keep doing it. I need you to start helping me. Vangie, think. Is there *anyone* else who might have had a beef with Ben and Sarah? Was there anyone new in their lives?"

"New? What do you mean?"

I sat back. "I don't know. The cops are adamant that there was no forced entry to the house. Were the Dales in the habit of leaving their doors unlocked?"

"No," Vangie said. "Ben was kind of a nut about that. He had a security system and everything. Top of the line. The way he talked about it, you'd think he worked for the company."

"Right," I answered. "Okay." It was the thing that bothered me the most about this whole scenario. How the hell had the killer gotten into that house without breaking in and setting off the alarms?

So far, Travis White was turning into a dead end. He had an alibi. We had the names of the two other men who installed the Dales' countertops with him. One now lived in Arizona. The other was in the army reserves and had been deployed out of the country two weeks before the murder.

"Cass," Vangie said. "I'm sorry. About this." She lifted her wrists, making the chains rattle. "I just ... I couldn't stop. I wanted to try and find my baby." Tears rolled down her cheeks. I was still furious with Vangie. But here we were. I couldn't undo what she'd done. We could only move forward.

"I know," I said. "You need to understand something from here on out." I felt my tone grow flat. There was a thing I had to say to my sister. I would never abandon her. But I also wouldn't help her keep digging this hole she was in.

"You may not like some of the things I have to ask you to do," I said. "I know you. You've been impulsive your whole life. It's never done you any good. If you can't do what I tell you now ... then ..."

"I know," Vangie said, still crying. "I know. I'm so sorry, Cass."

"No more being sorry. That's not helping us either."

"Tell me what to do?"

"For now," I said. "Absolutely nothing. You follow the rules in here. Don't make waves. Survive. Don't talk to *anyone* about why you're here. Don't talk about Jessa. None of it. Don't make friends but don't make enemies either."

"I keep to myself," she said. "That won't be hard."

"I love you," I said. Vangie blinked. I hadn't realized how badly she needed to hear it. "Good."

"Will you take care of her? I know it's a lot to ask. You didn't sign on for any of this. But ... she doesn't have anyone else. I've made such a mess of this. I should be there for Jessa."

"Don't," I said. "No more crying. We don't have time for

that. I need you to hold it together, Vangie. For yourself and for Jessa."

"Promise me," she said.

"I'll take care of her," I finally answered. "You know you don't even have to ask. I'm filing a petition in probate court tomorrow. I'm going to ask to be appointed her temporary guardian. It's a formality. Since Jessa has no other family, it's either me or the state. The prosecution's not happy about it. But they have no real legal standing to interfere."

Vangie wiped her tears. "Thank you. Oh God. If I know she's safe. That she's taken care of. I can handle anything in here. I promise. I won't fuck up again."

There was a soft knock on the door. I was only given fifteen minutes with my sister. She had to go back to her cell.

"I'm going to hold you to that, little sister," I said, rising. She looked so small and scared as I took a step toward the door. I blew Vangie a kiss as the guard held the door open for me.

I hated leaving her here. The look in her eyes gutted me. She believed I was the only chance she had of ever getting out. The air left me as I realized I was.

Her only chance. And I might be Jessa's only chance now too.

Chapter 27

Jessa had her first appointment with the child psychologist later that afternoon. I took her to Dr. Collette Spencer's office in nearby Chelsea. In a few days, Rayna DeWitt wanted her own psychologist to interview her.

Collette Spencer looked like she'd come straight out of grandmother central casting. Heavy-set, she wore a pretty blue shirt-dress and a string of white pearls. Her half-moon glasses perched on the end of her nose and she had soft gray hair pulled into a messy bun.

Jessa clung to me, pressing her body against my legs as we walked into Dr. Spencer's outer waiting room. Dr. Spencer was waiting for us, sitting in one of the chairs. Her smile lit her whole face as we approached.

"Hi, there," she said. She had a storybook in her lap open to the middle. It was as if we'd just walked in on her as she sat in her comfy chair reading by the gas-lit fireplace beside her. The whole scene was warm, inviting, the opposite of clinical. So far, it seemed to have the desired effect. Though Jessa didn't exactly run up to Dr. Spencer, she was calm and curious by my side.

"Jessa," I said. "This is Mrs. Spencer." She'd instructed me on the phone to leave the doctor title off. She wisely understood my poor niece had been through enough doctors in the past few days.

"Hello, Jessa," Dr. Spencer said. She closed the book in her lap but made no move toward Jessa. "I'm super glad you came to visit me today. It's pretty cold out there. I love your pink boots. Are those new?"

Jessa looked down at her feet. My brother Joe and his wife Katy had made a late-night run to Walmart to get clothes for Jessa. The boots were fuzzy and warm and Jessa slid them on right away, wanting to wear them even indoors. She squeezed my hand but stuck out a leg, giving Dr. Spencer a better look.

"So pretty," she said. "Have you had a chance to play in the snow with them yet? I heard your friend Cass here gets to live on a lake. That sounds amazing."

Not so much as even a nod from Jessa, but she'd moved a little away from my thigh. Dr. Spencer kept on like that, making small talk. Jessa and I moved to a couch beside Dr. Spencer. After a few minutes, she started reading from the book on her lap. It was a Christmas story about a less famous reindeer. Jessa sat with rapt attention, but still, she never spoke or smiled.

Collette Spencer took her time building a rapport with Jessa. She told me not to expect much at this first session. If she could get Jessa to happily spend some time with her, she'd call that a victory. After about thirty minutes, Dr. Spencer sat beside Jessa. Jessa held a different book and she let the doctor turn the pages. It was at this point that Dr. Spencer gestured to me over Jessa's head. I was to wait in the next room if Jessa was comfortable with that.

"Jessa," I said. "I've got to go and make a phone call. You

can sit and hang out with Mrs. Spencer for a bit yet if that's okay."

Jessa's feet came just to the end of the couch. She had yet to take her puffy blue coat off. She smoothed her hair away from her face. She looked from Dr. Spencer then back to me. Her face was neutral as she nodded. Victory.

"I'll be back in a few minutes," I said. With an encouraging nod from the doctor, I left the two of them alone together. I went down the hall to a larger waiting room that served all the offices in the building. It was empty so I took a seat. The television was tuned to the noon, local news.

I checked my phone. There were two missed calls from Joe. I called him back.

"How did it go?" he asked.

"Still going," I said. "We're here and Jessa let me leave the room so that's huge. I was told not to expect much today. Did you see Vangie?"

"Yeah," he answered. "Just got back. She seemed okay. I mean, as okay as she can be. She's anxious to hear how this appointment goes."

"I've got a hearing next week on my full guardianship petition. I'd like you to be there for that. Katy and Emma too. We need to put up a united family front. You might even be called as a witness."

"I thought you said it was just a formality," he said.

"It is," I answered. "But it's still going to require some hoop jumping. I want to be prepared."

"I'll be there," he said. "And it's just all temporary anyway. As soon as Vangie gets out, she can be with her daughter."

I resisted the urge to remind him *if* Vangie gets out. The words died on my lips though as the television in the corner caught my eye. Jessa's school picture flashed on the screen. I pulled the phone away from my face. The tagline under Jessa's photo read, "Child Witness to Grisly Murder Found Safe."

A young male reporter stood in front of the Dales' house in Ann Arbor. "Ben and Sarah Dale were found brutally murdered in their Ann Arbor home earlier this year. The frantic search for their missing daughter has finally come to an end as little Jessica Dale was found safe in Toledo, Ohio. No one knows how she came to be there. The question remains, what really happened in this home on the night of January 9th? A source close to the investigation tells me that little Jessa is likely the only witness to the brutal murder of her parents. She was found wearing clothes splattered with her father's dried blood. In a horrible twist, little Jessica's birth mother stands charged with the crime. Join me tonight for an in-depth look at the crime that has rocked this quiet little cul-de-sac and what we know so far."

"Cass?" Joe was still on the line. I brought the phone back up to my ear.

"Jesus," I said. "Are you near your computer? Go online and see what they're saying about the Dale murders."

"Yeah," Joe answered. I held my breath as I waited through the clicking noises on the other end of the phone. It took him about thirty seconds but I already knew the answer from the way Joe started breathing.

"Shit," he said. "Is this true? All kinds of headlines about how Jessa was living in bloodstained clothes for weeks. I think I'm going to be sick."

I pressed the back of my head against the wall. "They're leaking it. Son of a bitch. The cops or the prosecutor is leaking this stuff to the news."

"Cass, is it true?"

I hesitated. Part of me wanted to protect my brother

from the worst parts of this case. The news and maybe the police were now making that impossible.

"Yeah," I said. "It's true."

Before I could tell him any more, Dr. Spencer found me. She had finished with Jessa for the day and it was time to talk.

Chapter 28

JESSA WAS content to quietly play with a dollhouse in the corner in the room adjoining Dr. Spencer's office proper. We watched her from a two-way mirror.

"She's a very sweet child," Dr. Spencer said.

"Did she say anything to you?" I asked.

Dr. Spencer sat with her legs crossed, her chair turned toward the mirror. Jessa was busy rearranging the tiny furniture in the dollhouse dining room.

"No," Dr. Spencer answered. "She's completely non-verbal. Where are we on getting copies of her school records?"

I had very little to go on. Sarah Dale had shared a few progress reports by phone with Vangie. She also had a handful of pictures Jessa had drawn and a Thanksgiving poem she'd written three months ago.

"From everything we know, Jessa was just a normal, happy kid up until now."

"You have to be patient," Spencer said. "I know it's hard. But this child has been through trauma we can't even imagine. Her silence is a coping mechanism. A defense. We have to be very careful how we come at her. She has to feel truly safe again. And she might not for a very long time."

"Dr. Spencer," I said. "The thing is, Jessa saw something. I have every reason to believe she witnessed her parents' murder. She may be able to identify who killed them. Or ... at least who didn't."

Collette Spencer slid her glasses from the bridge of her nose. "I understand. I told you on the phone how unusual I thought this whole thing was. That precious baby may be the only person who can possibly exonerate your sister."

"Yes. But you have to know that neither I *nor* my sister would ever suggest doing something that would hamper Jessa's well-being or progress. No matter what."

"I'm glad to hear that."

"If you'd seen how she was when she saw Vangie ... if anyone had any lingering doubts about whether she committed those murders ..."

"Ms. Leary," Dr. Spencer said. "Let me stop you right there. This is a very complicated case. When you're dealing with a child that young and the level of emotional trauma at issue ... things aren't always as straightforward as we'd like them to be. Now, I have no idea what's happened with your sister. For Jessa's sake, I truly hope she's innocent. But Jessa has a bond with your sister. Just because she seemed relieved, even overjoyed to see her as you described, that doesn't mean she's innocent."

My face fell. "That doesn't make any sense. If Jessa were afraid of Vangie, she never would have ..."

"She might have," Spencer continued. "That's what I'm telling you. You may very well have read the situation correctly. It's just ... children process trauma in a million different ways. It's possible Jessa is in denial about what she saw. It's possible seeing your sister ... a familiar ... otherwise loving presence in her life ... it may be that her need for that love outweighed any memory of other things she'd seen. Please understand, I'm *not* saying I think your sister's guilty. I have no opinion on that yet. When I agreed to take this case, we set those ground rules. I'm not here to help you with your defense. I'm here to help Jessa and Jessa alone."

"Thank you," I said. "That's all I ask. And I do value your opinion and guidance with this."

"When is your custody hearing?" she asked.

"Next week. I've been granted guardianship on an emergency basis. Otherwise she would have been put in foster care, possibly even down in Lucas County where she was found. I go for temporary full guardianship in Woodbridge County at the next hearing."

Dr. Spencer nodded. "Obviously, I can't make a full recommendation until I have a chance to work with Jessa and you more. For now, I think you're doing the right things. I'm willing to say that. Let's have you bring Jessa back every other day the rest of this week. I'll write a preliminary letter by Monday. You understand it will be my honest, professional opinion thus far."

"I understand," I said, leaning over the desk to shake her hand. "That's all I ask. In the meantime, is there anything I should do or not do where Jessa's concerned?"

Dr. Spencer smiled. "The sooner she can get into a more or less predictable routine, the better. Let's hold off putting her back in school for at least a week or two. I'm not so much worried about any academic issues at this point. But I do want her to feel comfortable socializing with her peers again. For now, focus on small steps. Meals at the same time. A set bedtime. I don't know what your home life is, but I'd be cautious about having too many new people in and out."

"The trouble is, everyone is new to her right now. But I think I know what you mean. So far, she's with me, Jeanie

Mills, who you already know. She's one of the people who recommended you to me."

Dr. Spencer's smile didn't fade. If anything, it widened. "Yes. Jeanie and I go way back. If I'm being honest, she's the reason I'm willing to move heaven and earth for you and that child if it comes to it. Let's just say I've known Jeanie Mills to be an excellent judge of character."

"So have I. There are also my two brothers, Joe and Matty. They already adore Jessa. We're all on the same page about wanting to protect her as best we can."

"Good," Dr. Spencer said, rising. "So let's keep our appointments to an hour every other day. Two o'clock. It will take me some time to build trust with Jessa. I told you not to expect quick miracles. Slow and steady. She's got a lot of things to work through."

"Thank you again," I said.

Jessa came to me readily when we walked into the playroom. I squatted down to her eye level and offered her my hand. She grabbed it, holding it maybe just a little less tightly as we made our way out of the office and back to the car.

Chapter 29

Joe and Matty were waiting for us at the house when we got back. The news stories about Jessa triggered both of their alpha-male protectiveness. They had ready smiles for our little niece, but good instincts. They kept their distance. Matty turned on one of the cartoon channels and Jessa climbed on the couch next to him. The hint of tears made his eyes glisten. He seemed to understand how big a step even that was for her.

I had a call to return from Jeanie as Joe busied himself ordering gourmet pizzas from the parlor down the street. Jessa wouldn't tell us her favorite, so my brother overcompensated and ordered enough to feed about ten people.

"I got nowhere," Jeanie said when I asked her about the leaks. "Rayna's office is in turmoil over it. She's asked for an internal investigation at the police department. They're claiming it wasn't any of their people. They used an outside firm to handle the forensics and they're looking into loose lips there. At the same time, enough people think *we're* responsible for blabbing Jessa's business all over town."

"Jeanie," I said. "This is a disaster. That poor kid is under enough pressure. It's everything I can do to keep her away from the internet and the local news."

"I know. I know. Vangie's freaking out too. I popped in to see her this afternoon. I'm worried about her, Cass. She's depressed. She feels helpless."

I sighed as I closed my eyes. "She is. That's the real problem."

"Cass, I just need to warn you. This stuff in the news about Jessa, it could come back to bite you at the custody hearing next week. Some of the comments under the online news stories are pretty scathing. There are some who think you're trying to exploit that kid and turn her testimony."

"Well, I'm doing everything humanly possible *not* to. Collette Spencer is a good person. You were right about her. I swear I'll do everything she says."

Jeanie made a defeated, almost grunt-like noise. "We need a break, dammit. A big one. Every lead we've tracked down led nowhere. The Dales were saints in that community. Vangie's the only person they had any kind of beef with. If this was random ... and it had to be ... it makes no sense there were no signs of a break-in. Nothing taken. No suspicious characters lurking around. Nobody else in the entire neighborhood noticed anything. No *other* break-ins anywhere close in the last six weeks or more. It just doesn't make sense, Cass. None of it."

"I know," I said.

"Where are the shed keys?" Joe called out. "I want to take a snowblower to the ice. Clear a rink. I brought some of Emma's old skates."

"That's a great idea," I said, shielding my hand over the phone.

"I'll talk to you in the morning," Jeanie said. "We could both use a good night's sleep and fresh brains. I want to look over the evidence with you again. We're missing something."

"I feel it too," I said. "Joe's got the day off and so does Emma. She's always been great with little kids so I'm going to take a chance and leave Jessa with them if she seems amenable to it. I just don't want to go too far."

"You're good. Miranda's cleared your calendar this week. We should go over the game plan for your probate hearing on Tuesday too."

Happy to have a plan and a purpose, I hung up with Jeanie. While Joe worked on the patch of ice in front of the house, Matty was already showing Jessa the pair of skates he brought her. She was definitely interested. She stuck a leg out and let Matty start putting them on her feet. I gave Matty a thumbs up.

I enjoyed watching them together. In a lot of ways, my little brother Matty was just a big, goofy kid himself. It felt like just yesterday when he was Jessa's age. We'd just lost our mother and we came here to Grandpa Leary's house. He'd cleared a makeshift rink on the lake just like the one Joe was making now. Joe held Matty's hand as he toddled out on the ice. I had Vangie on my hip. She'd just been four years old. We didn't have skates to fit her so she stood on my feet as I skated in slow circles and made her laugh.

"Have you ever skated before?" Matty asked once he had Jessa's laces tied. She chewed her lip. No smile. No frown.

"Well," Matty said. "I'll show you how. Would you like to try?"

Jessa reached for Matty's hand by way of an answer. Matty caught my eye and we both froze for an instant, afraid to give in to any big emotions or frighten Jessa. Instead, Matty held his arms out and Jessa went into them. He lifted her high and walked out the double doors. Joe had just finished clearing the circle. He waved and smiled as Jessa and Matty trudged through the snow to greet him.

I went to the window. My heart nearly bursting, I

watched Matty set Jessa on the ground. She clutched his hand for support. Joe leaned down and spread his arms wide, giving her a target to skate to.

She did. Her legs were wobbly. Matty never let go of her hand. She took the first slow, tentative, trusting steps toward Joe. I found myself wishing Vangie could see this. I did the next best thing and brought my phone up, intending to record what I could.

My phone rang just as I pushed the red button. I didn't recognize the number.

"Cass Leary speaking," I said.

"Ms. Leary." It was a male voice. Gravelly. Distant.

"Yes?"

"It's a noble thing you're trying to do," he said.

"Excuse me? To whom am I speaking?"

"Would you care to comment on the reports regarding your ... uh ... niece?"

I pulled the phone away and looked at the number again. It was a 517 area code. "I'm sorry," I said. "What news organization are you calling from again?"

"Citizen outreach," he said. It meant nothing. "She's such a lovely child. Pretty smile. Little unicorn princess."

"Who is this?" I realized this would likely be the first of many crackpot calls I might get now that Jessa's story had hit the internet. Unicorn princess?

"Such a shame."

"Look," I said. "I have no comment. Please don't call this number again."

He started to hum. Something about it made my blood run cold. His voice had a lilting, disconnected quality. The melody seemed familiar but it took a moment for my brain to catch up with my ears. He started singing the words just as it did.

"Hush, little baby, don't say a word ..."

"Who are you?" I shouted. I pressed a palm to the window. Jessa was safe. Matty held one of her hands while Joe the other. Together, they glided across the ice with her. As they turned and I could see her face, Jessa was smiling. Dear God in heaven. She was smiling!

"Don't say a word ..." the caller sang the line again.

"I said, don't call here again!" My heart thundered in my chest. It was just some whacko. My name, my cell phone number, anyone could find it online in the Bar Directory in about ten seconds.

"Sleep tight, little unicorn," he said. Then the phone went dead.

Chapter 30

THAT NIGHT and the whole next day, I couldn't shake the call. I tried to explain to Jeanie why it had me rattled.

"It was just ... that song. 'Hush Little Baby.' It felt threatening."

We sat in the conference room. Miranda had kept us in a steady supply of coffee and donuts. She poked in and out to give us her take on the evidence reports splayed out on the table. Sipping her own coffee, she picked up the new photos we'd received of Jessa's clothing.

"It makes me want to commit murder myself," she said. "And she's saying nothing about it now?"

"She's saying nothing about anything," I answered. I'd briefly filled them in on Dr. Spencer's thoughts.

"Well," Jeanie said. "I don't care what she says. I just don't believe there's any way in hell Jessa would have run to Vangie like that if she'd seen her murder her parents three weeks before. It's admissible. You have to use it at trial."

"I can get it in through Detective Carey himself. He was standing closest to her when those elevator doors opened. He saw the whole thing," I said.

"Well." Miranda took a seat. "Except, then Jessa's own therapist is going to get up there and testify about how it might not mean anything."

"You gotta hope the jury thinks like we do," Jeanie said. "Or that Jessa finds her voice before then."

"She's out of the equation," I said. "I can't think any other way. That's the one thing Vangie and I are in total agreement on. I will not use Jessa if it will damage her in any way. She's not taking the stand in open court even *if* she has total recall of what happened that night. We'll find another way if we get to that point."

I stood up and circled the conference room table yet again. I ticked off the things we had in our favor. "No murder weapon. We have more than reasonable doubt on how Vangie's fingerprints got on Sarah's phone. Regardless of what the neighbors have to say, Vangie was a known visitor at the Dale home. That's to our advantage."

"Except the part about there being no forced entry," Miranda offered. In these strategy sessions, she played the perfect devil's advocate.

I sat down at the head of the table. My head pounded inside my skull. After the mysterious phone call, I hadn't gotten much sleep. Certain phrases just stuck in my head. There were the "Hush, Little Baby" lyrics, yes, but also something else.

"Cons are still the cons," Jeanie said. "The jury isn't going to like Jessa's blood on Vangie's clothes."

"Except the only injury on her when the police found her was a scraped elbow. That's consistent with Vangie's story about her falling off her bike the day before. No matter what else happened, the killer did *not* hurt Jessa. That's a known fact now."

I picked through the scattered photographs and reports on the table. I was still waiting for an analysis from my own forensics guy about the nature of Ben Dale's wound. "She's tiny," I said, thinking aloud. But Miranda and Jeanie had worked with me long enough to pick up my verbal shorthand and know my train of thought.

I stood up. "They want a jury to believe that Vangie is tall enough to hit Ben Dale square in the back of the head. The angle of the wound, at least to my eye, looks like it was a downward strike. Vangie isn't tall enough for that."

"How soon are they going to let us visit the crime scene with your expert?" Jeanie asked.

"Two weeks," I answered. "But I've combed through those photos. There's just no way the killer was standing any other way but on level ground. There's no step-up. Nothing. It's a thing. It has to be."

"Well," Jeanie said. "You'll have your forensics soon enough. Good call leaving that little tidbit out of the preliminary examination. That's the kind of thing Rayna DeWitt will find somehow to explain away given enough lead time."

I picked up the photos of some of the other evidence. I had a copy of Ben Dale's petition for his personal protection order. Attached to it were screenshots of Vangie's texts to Sarah. I set them down and picked up the other screenshots of Sarah's Facebook wall.

"I still can't believe they got a P.P.O. based on that stuff," Miranda said.

"I can," Jeanie said. "This situation has been unique from the start. You wanna know the truth? I think the judge didn't like that Jessa got brought up in the Drazdowski murder trial. The Dales had connections. I think they may have called in a favor."

"Can you prove that?" I asked. "It's not much, but maybe it'll help."

Jeanie shrugged. She didn't have to say what was on her mind. Getting one county judge to let in evidence that a colleague had been unduly influenced may be a non-starter. It might land me in more hot water than it would help Vangie. Still, I wasn't going to overlook any leads, no matter how small.

"The Dales' lawyer isn't talking," Jeanie said. "At least not to us. I'm real worried about what she's going to do to us in front of a jury."

"I'm worried about all of it," I said. "There has just *got* to be something I'm missing. I know Vangie didn't do this. No matter what Spencer says, Jessa knows Vangie didn't do this. There's someone out there. Someone knows something. I feel like it's right in front of me, only I can't find it."

I set the screenshots down and picked up a copy of the family photo found in Vangie's things. Jessa's sweet face smiled back at me. Sarah had dressed her in purple. Vangie said it was her favorite color. She had a purple bow in her hair and that frilly purple shirt with the cartoon character on the front.

I sat up so hard I nearly toppled the chair over.

"Miranda," I said. She was sitting closest to me. "Look at Jessa's shirt in this picture."

Miranda was a grandmother. She had three granddaughters. One of them was Jessa's age. She took the picture and squinted at it. "Unicorn," she said. "Princess Beula. Or maybe it's Princess Petula. I can't keep 'em straight. I think it's Beula. She's got the crooked crown. It's on the preschool cartoon channel. Ugh. They sing this song that ..."

"Unicorn princess," I said.

"Come again?" Jeanie asked.

"Unicorn princess," I said louder. "That's what he said. The creep who called me yesterday. He kept referring to Jessa as a unicorn princess."

"Jesus," Jeanie said. "They're going to have every shred of evidence leaked to the press before we get to trial."

I stared at the photo. Something didn't feel right about Jeanie's explanation but I couldn't place what. I set it down. "Rayna sent over a stipulation for a gag order. We're in agreement on that."

"Fat lot of good that'll do," Jeanie said. "This particular unicorn is already out of the barn."

I ran my fingers over the picture again. Unicorn princess.

Miranda had walked to the window. The bell on the front door downstairs had rung. "Your man's here," she said, teasing.

I let out a sigh, knowing exactly who she meant. "Will you stop with that? He's not my man."

"Detective Wray?" Jeanie called out. "Come on up. We could use another brain."

"I've gotta go through the mail," Miranda said, winking at me. "You good on coffee?"

"My kidneys are swimming, thanks," I said.

Eric Wray's heavy footsteps shook the stairs as he made his way up. He was wearing a suit and had his badge around his neck.

"You ladies decent?" he asked.

"Tell him what you told me," Jeanie said. "Cass had a weird call last night."

Eric's brow furrowed. Describing it all out loud again made me sound crazy. Especially now as I got to the unicorn princess part. But if Eric thought I was grasping at straws, his expression stayed serious. He looked through the documents and photos on the table. He'd done it with me before. He didn't say anything for almost a full minute. He just pored over the pictures as I held my breath.

"I don't know," he finally said. "I don't like it. It's probably nothing. Do you still have the phone number?"

I pulled my phone out of my bag. I clicked on recent calls

and wrote down the number from last night. I slid the paper over to Eric.

"I'll look into it," he said. "Chances are it's nothing. Every case I've ever worked that got media attention also came with whackos like that calling in."

"Sure," I said. "It's just ... I don't know. I don't remember any story posting information about that family photo."

"It was in Sarah Dale's Facebook feed," Jeanie said. "That's how the cops figured out what picture was taken from the house in the first place."

"She's right," Eric said.

"Except Sarah's profile was taken down weeks ago," I said.

"Her name hit the news first," Eric offered. "People are nuts. I think you're right to be cautious and I'm right to look into that phone number, but I can almost guarantee it's going to be nothing."

"Thanks just the same. It's just ... with all the stories about this case, I've never once seen that particular picture on the news. We need to check. If that piece of evidence isn't out there, how the hell did this guy know about it?"

"I said I can *almost* guarantee it's some crackpot. Still a good idea to watch your back. I'll talk to the Woodbridge County guys and see if they'll put a couple of extra patrols around the lake."

"I appreciate that," I said. Jeanie was up and moving.

"Talk later," she said. "I'm going to finish up some paperwork and head out. What time did you tell Jessa you'd be home?"

I looked at my phone again. I'd promised to work just a half day. I planned to be home to eat lunch with her. Joe and Emma were there today. It was eleven thirty already.

"Thanks for the reminder," I said. "Dr. Spencer told me she needs a set routine as much as anything else right now."

Nodding, Jeanie gave a little wave and disappeared down the stairs. I turned to Eric.

"Thanks again for your thoughts and for calling the sheriff. I can do it myself too. I don't want you to feel like you have to call in favors for me."

"I don't mind," he said. "But there is something I wanted to talk to you about. You're not going to like it. I just gotta say it."

"Eric, I know. Okay? You're a cop. We look at things in different ways. It's why your help has been so great. But if you're going to ask me to entertain the possibility that my sister actually did this again ..."

He put a hand up. "No. That's not what I'm going to say. What I'm *going* to say is this. I'm worried you're too close to this. Rayna DeWitt is tough. Brett Carey is even tougher. They'll find a way to use the fact you're Vangie's sister against you. I'm just ... I'm wondering if maybe you should call in another lawyer."

"I have another lawyer," I said. "Jeanie's co-counsel."

"Right," he said. "And she's great. But Jeanie's a family lawyer. And now you've got a material witness living in your house. If I know anything about Rayna, she's probably trying to figure out a way to make that blow up in your face. I think if she had standing to challenge your guardianship, she would."

Eric wasn't saying anything I hadn't already turned over in my head a million times. "Eric," I said. "I appreciate that. I really do. And it may come to that."

"Will you at least maybe consider consulting with an unbiased defense lawyer? I can give you a name or two."

"You? Seasoned detective? Recommending the enemy?" I was teasing. A little.

"Yeah," he said. "I'm full of surprises."

A shadow crossed his face. Once again, I was reminded

of just how far Eric Wray could go when pushed. I hoped he would always be on my side.

"Okay," I said. "I'm open to help from wherever it comes."

"Anytime," he said, smiling.

Miranda came back into the room. She held a packet of documents in her hands and her expression turned grave. I leaned back hard in my chair.

"Don't," I said. "I don't think I can handle another piece of bad news."

Miranda looked from Eric to me. "I'm sorry. Dammit. Cass, I really am. This just came from the Woodbridge County Friend of the Court. They've amended their recommendation to the probate court judge."

"What?"

Miranda set the documents in front of me and stepped away from them as if they were radioactive. "Someone's filed an objection to your guardianship petition. Another family member. The F.O.C. no longer thinks it's in Jessa's best interests to live with you. If you want to get custody, you're in for a fight, honey."

Chapter 31

"I NEED you to let me do what I do best," Jeanie said. We stood in the tiny law library of the Woodbridge County Courthouse. She had my shoulders in a vice grip. I was sweating.

"This is an ambush," I said, heart racing.

It was bad enough the caseworker assigned to Jessa's file had gone south on me. A week ago, this custody hearing was just a formality. Now it was a full-blown trial. I peered into the hallway again. Woodbridge County had exactly one full-time juvenile probate judge. The library was across the hall from his chambers. Further down, I could see the clerk's window. Bill Walden, the county's longest practicing family law attorney, stood in front of it.

"This could still be okay if you keep your cool," Jeanie said. This wasn't supposed to happen. I was supposed to walk in for this hearing, let the judge swear me in, and basically read my guardianship petition into the record.

"What do you know?" I turned to Jeanie.

She finally let go of me. "Walden's filed a pro hac vice motion on behalf of some fancy Florida lawyer named Lud

Donnelly. He's a big gun. I won't lie to you. But this is my town, not his. Donnelly's been brought in on behalf of Geri and Martin Dale, Ben Dale's aunt and uncle. I know Judge Epperle. He's not going to be impressed by a flashy smile and fancy suit from out of town. He'll keep things focused on what's in Jessa's best interests and that's that."

I started to pace. I'd seen Geri and Martin Dale exactly once outside the church at Ben and Sarah's funeral. I whipped around. "This is insane. The Dales are like seventy-something years old. They can't seriously be thinking of bringing a traumatized six-year-old into their lives."

"Be that as it may," Jeanie said. "They're legally Jessa's next of kin."

"They've never even *met* Jessa, as far as I know. I think Vangie said something about them coming to visit once when she was an infant. This will destroy her. That poor kid is *just* starting to come out of her shell a little."

"And we'll get a chance to point all of that out. You know how this goes. If you march in there all blustery and indignant, it won't look good. You have to let me do my job. You're the client now, not the lawyer."

And that was the crux of it. It would kill me to sit back and let someone else take the wheel. But I knew Jeanie was right. How many times had I said those exact words to a client? Let me do my job. Jeanie was good. The best. She'd kept my family together when every odd in the world was stacked against us. I had to trust her now to do the same thing for Jessa.

"They're ready for you." Judge Epperle's bailiff, Tara Cordray, poked her head into the room. She was striking with white-blonde hair cropped short. Jeanie told me she'd just finished a tour in Afghanistan and was halfway through law school. I had my eye on her to clerk for me in a year or so.

"Thanks," Jeanie said. She gave me a wide-eyed look of resolve then followed Tara into the hallway.

The elder Dales were already in the courtroom. They sat at the table next to Lud Donnelly. I knew a million lawyers like Donnelly back in Chicago. Hell, I'd *been* a lawyer like Lud Donnelly back in Chicago. He was calm, cool, self-assured. His tailored suit probably cost more than a half a year's house payments for most of the people in Delphi. He leaned in and whispered something to Martin Dale that got a laugh out of him. Lud turned and watched us walk in. The man was handsome, mid-forties with a two-hundred-dollar haircut and manicure. He looked wildly out of place here. Bill Waldon in his cheap seersucker suit sat behind him. It would have been comical if I didn't feel like I was fighting for Jessa's life.

Judge Epperle took the bench. He was the second-longest-serving judge in the county. I'd yet to appear before him, but Jeanie insisted he was fair and could cut through bullshit with ease. I hoped so. This whole thing felt like one giant pile of it.

"All right," Epperle said. "I've read through the petition, objections, and F.O.C. recommendation. Ms. Leary, are you prepared to present evidence?"

"I am," I said, starting to rise. Jeanie put a hand on my sleeve. She got to her feet first. "Your Honor, I'm appearing on behalf of Ms. Leary."

"Right," Epperle said. "Yes. Ms. Mills. It's your petition. You may present your first witness."

"Your Honor." Donnelly rose. "I believe we still need to clarify the petitioner's burden of proof. I'm Lud Donnelly, appearing on behalf of the respondents, Martin and Geraldine Dale. We don't believe the minor child has an established custodial environment. As such, the petitioner's burden of proof is clear and convincing evidence."

I gritted my teeth. It was a procedural maneuver, but one that would make the mountain we had to climb that much higher.

Epperle nodded. "I agree we need to clarify that burden. However, let's get on with the presentation of proofs. You can make your argument later after I've heard everything. Ms. Mills, you're up."

"Thank you. I'd like to call Cassiopeia Leary to the stand."

I rose and walked around the table. Tara Cordray stayed stone-faced as she had me take my oath. I stepped into the witness box and straightened my skirt. Jeanie was all business as she walked around to the podium.

"Ms. Leary," she said. "Can you please explain your relationship to the minor child?"

"She is my niece. My younger sister, Evangeline, is her birth mother. She has been staying with me on Finn Lake since she was released from Toledo Hospital."

"How has that been going?"

I'd been watching Jeanie Mills in court since I was a teenager. For as tough as she was, she had an easy, almost casual demeanor when questioning witnesses. She kept things conversational. It worked miracles in front of juries. But this case wouldn't be decided by a jury. One man held Jessa's fate in his hands. I turned and looked at Judge Epperle.

He was completely bald and took to wearing his thick reading glasses on his forehead. It lent him an almost cartoonish appearance.

"It's a process," I said. "Jessa is very fragile. She's been through a lot. I'm taking her to a therapist, Dr. Collette Spencer, three times a week. Her curriculum vitae is attached to our supplemental petition. Jessa's in the early stages of her recovery, but you'll see from Dr. Spencer's preliminary report, she's encouraged."

"When you say fragile," Jeanie said. "What exactly do you mean?"

"This child was severely traumatized. We don't know what she saw, but regardless of any of that, she lost her parents. She ran for her life. She spent over two weeks living in a strange place in a strange city. She's been frightened to death by doctors and police officers ever since. But she survived it. She hasn't spoken a word since we found her, but I believe she's beginning to trust me."

"How do you know that?" Jeanie asked.

"When Jessa first came to stay with me, I couldn't get her to look at me. She would barely eat. Now, even though she won't talk yet, she's starting to do more normal, little kid things. She's eating and sleeping on a normal schedule. She's interested in watching cartoons. She likes the lake. Just the other night, my brothers cleared a rink for her and she went ice skating. She's smiling again. She also seems to like Dr. Spencer. I've seen her play there. Like a normal kid. It's little by little and it's early, but Jessa's coming out of her shell. She's made some very important steps. That needs to continue. Again, you've got Dr. Spencer's report, but keeping Jessa in a steady, secure, safe routine is critical right now."

"Thank you," Jeanie said. "And what about now? You're here in court, who is with Jessa?"

"Family," I said. "I mentioned my brothers, Joe and Matthew. They've been a constant presence at the house. When I'm not there, one of them is. Right now, Joe is there with my other niece, Emma. She's seventeen. Jessa seems to like her."

Jeanie asked a few other follow-up questions. The rest would come from Dr. Spencer's report. Had it not been for the Dales and the F.O.C. turnaround, this would already be over.

As soon as Jeanie sat down, Lud Donnelly rose and came to the podium. "Good morning, Ms. Leary," he said, smiling. "Just so we're clear, who's been charged with the murder of Jessica's parents?"

I leaned forward without a pause. "My sister, Evangeline, has been charged."

"How's that going?" he asked, mirroring Jeanie's questioning. His snide tone heated my blood. This fucker. Jeanie rose to object.

"I'm sure you know that's wildly inappropriate for you to ask," I said.

"You think so?" Donnelly said. "She's your sister. If she hadn't jumped her bond, where would your sister be living right now?"

I looked at Jeanie, then the judge. I had no choice but to answer. "Vangie was staying with me."

Donnelly rifled through some papers. "You say your brothers are her secondary caregivers after you? You mentioned Matthew. Matthew Leary. Your Honor, may I approach the witness?"

"You may," Epperle said. On his way, Donnelly handed a sheet of paper to Jeanie. He gave a copy of it to me. I gritted my teeth. It was Matty's rap sheet.

"Do you recognize that?" he asked.

"Objection," Jeanie said, but we both knew it was hopeless.

Judge Epperle had a third copy of the rap sheet. He lowered his glasses to his nose. "Go ahead, Mr. Donnelly."

"Can you read into the record what you're looking at?"

I took a breath. "My brother has had issues in the past. He has a D.U.I. from five years ago. A drunk and disorderly from two years ago. He's also just got his ninety-day chip from A.A. He's in recovery."

"Right," Donnelly said. "How's his home life?"

"Excuse me?"

"Your brother Matthew's home life. How is it?"

"Objection, relevance," Jeanie said.

"Your Honor, Ms. Leary has made it clear who Jessica stays with when she's not around. The stability of that arrangement is the heart of this matter."

"Sustained."

"My brother and his wife are currently separated."

"Why's that?"

"You'd have to ask them," I said.

Donnelly nodded. "Sounds like a good idea. Let's move on. Surely you've seen the personal protection order that was entered against your sister prior to the murder of Sarah and Ben Dale, haven't you?"

"Objection," Jeanie said. "This is completely irrelevant. We aren't trying the Dale murders here. Evangeline Leary isn't even a party to this litigation."

"Your Honor," Donnelly said. "The petitioner has used Ben and Sarah Dale's will in her argument. A year ago, they named Evangeline Leary as their daughter's guardian in the event anything happened to them. I'd put it to the court that their feelings changed. Given a chance, I believe they would have changed their estate planning documents. We can't unfortunately call the Dales as witnesses and ask their prefer- ence now. But the things they said in support of their P.P.O. are the next best thing."

"Overruled for now," Epperle said. "We're going to focus on the custodial situation as it exists now, Mr. Donnelly."

"Fair enough, Your Honor." Lud Donnelly pivoted on his heel.

"Ms. Leary, what do you do for a living?"

"I am a general practice attorney, here in Delphi, Mr. Donnelly. I believe the court already knows that."

"And where did you practice immediately before you came back to Delphi?"

My heart sank. I should have seen this coming. I looked to Jeanie for cover, but knew she could provide none. Lud Donnelly was asking the exact questions I would have if I were in his shoes. The bastard.

"I was a partner at the Thorne Law Group in Chicago."

"Impressive firm," he said. "My firm has dealt with them a time or two. You specialized in white collar criminal defense, didn't you?"

"That's a fairly simplistic, *Hollywood* description of it. I did some criminal defense work, yes, for our corporate clients."

"Your corporate clients. The Thorne Law Group. Can you tell me who the senior partner is?"

I shot a look at Jeanie. She gave me a slight nod. She was going to let the guy have a little bit of leeway. I knew her strategy was to pretend like this was no big deal. It wasn't. Or at least it shouldn't have been.

"Mr. Donnelly, to the extent you're asking me to testify about past clients, you know that won't fly."

"You've represented Killian Thorne," he said.

"Is that a question or a statement?"

"It's a question. Did you or did you not represent Killian Thorne in a RICO case beginning three years ago?"

"My court appearances are a matter of public record."

"Objection," Jeanie said. "Does Mr. Donnelly even have a point with any of this?"

Judge Epperle's glasses were perched back on his forehead. "I surely hope so. I suggest you get to it."

"Of course, Your Honor," Donnelly said. "You were a mob lawyer, weren't you, Ms. Leary?"

"Objection!"

I crossed my legs. My blood heated and I stared hard at Lud Donnelly.

"Overruled," the judge ruled. "I'd like to hear your answer."

"I can't answer that," I said. "I've never represented a *mob*, whatever that means."

"It means Killian Thorne is the head of one of the largest criminal organizations in the country. He's been the subject of federal criminal investigations no less than six times in the last ten years. Isn't that true, Ms. Leary?"

"To the extent you are asking me about legal issues surrounding a former client, you know I can't answer that. If you're asking me to confirm gossip and innuendo about a former client, I won't do that either."

"Objection," Jeanie said.

"You're objecting to your client's answer?" Lud Donnelly had the smuggest look on his face.

"No, I'm objecting to this line of questioning. Again. In its entirety. It's irrelevant. It's protected by attorney-client privilege. It calls for speculation. What else do you want, Your Honor?"

Epperle scowled.

"I'll rephrase," Donnelly said. Jesus. He was walking all over this judge.

"Ms. Leary, have you ever been approached by the F.B.I. regarding Killian Thorne or any client you represented at the Thorne Group?"

"Objection!"

"Your Honor," Donnelly said. "We're here to establish what is in Jessica Dale's best interests. I don't think anyone here will argue that she is a six-year-old child who has been through a life's worth of trauma in the last month. Ms. Leary's associations are absolutely relevant here. I am prepared to show that she has existing, deep connections to men and organizations that have been the subject of several far-reaching federal criminal investigations."

"If you're asking her to rat out former clients in a custody hearing, that's not going to happen in my court-room, Mr. Donnelly."

Score one for the judge. Donnelly looked truly flustered. He stammered, took two steps away from the podium, then squared his shoulders and started again.

"Ms. Leary, have you ever associated with known felons?"

"Have I ..." It was my turn to stammer. "What do you mean, associate?"

"To your knowledge, has Killian Thorne ever been charged with a felony?"

I gripped the arms of my chair. "Yes. But you're a lawyer, aren't you, Mr. Donnelly? Surely you know the difference between a charge and a conviction. Mr. Thorne has never been convicted of a felony."

"Isn't it true that you've been romantically involved with Killian Thorne in the last year?"

I felt raw, exposed. My brother Matty had just entered the courtroom. He sat in the back, his eyes narrowing. I hadn't told him this. I hadn't told anyone this. What the hell else did Lud Donnelly know? How did he know it?

I could almost feel Killian's presence in the room. I'd never talked about him publicly. I'd barely talked about him privately. Now, here I was, being forced to testify about one of the most intimate aspects of my life in front of my own brother and the entire town. And I had brought it all on myself. This wasn't about me. This was about protecting Jessa. I just prayed that she wouldn't end up paying for any of my past sins.

I took a breath.

"I have," I said, keeping my voice even and clear. "But I

have not seen Mr. Thorne in almost a year. Not since I moved back to Delphi. There is no association. I don't know where else you plan to go with this, but Mr. Thorne is not a felon in any event. He has never been convicted of anything, as I said."

"Well, it appears in addition to the other ... um ... services you've provided for Killian Thorne, that just makes you a good lawyer."

Jeanie vaulted to her feet. If I had been close enough I would have grabbed her arm and pulled her back into her seat. As it was, I thought for sure she would dive across the table and go for Lud Donnelly's throat. The man had basically just called me a whore in open court. Matty rose at the same time, red murder in his eyes.

"You son of a bitch!" Matty yelled. "You gonna let him keep going with this?" Judge Epperle banged his gavel. The elder Mrs. Dale fanned her face and leaned against her husband's shoulder.

"You're on very thin ice, Mr. Donnelly!" Judge Epperle's voice boomed through the room. "Move on. That man in the back of the room, I'd like him escorted out."

Good lord. He hadn't yet realized "that man" was my brother, the one I'd just testified to leaving Jessa with. I didn't blame Matty for being angry for me. But he wasn't helping one damn bit at the moment.

"Ms. Leary," Donnelly said. God, the smug look on his face made my blood boil. "Do you believe Jessica witnessed her parents' murder?"

I curled my fists, digging my nails into my palms. "I don't know," I said, giving as truthful an answer as I could.

"Well, bear with me then. Would you at least admit that there is a possibility that Jessica witnessed those murders?"

"Of course," I answered. "I've said that."

"And you're defending your sister against the murder

charges. So, you've filed a petition for sole custody of potentially the only eyewitness to a murder that your *sister* is accused of perpetrating?"

"Yes," I said. It was the truth. It was what it was.

"Ms. Leary," Donnelly said. "Did you or did you not publicly expose Jessica Dale's paternity to further your own ends?"

"Excuse me?" I looked at the judge. Jeanie was still standing.

"You may answer," Epperle said.

"I take issue with the phrasing of the question," I said. "I've done nothing in my own self-interest where that child is concerned."

"Okay, let me ask this another way. Isn't it true that you used Jessica's paternity as part of the legal defense of your client in the Larry Drazdowski murder trial last year?"

"Again, I take issue with your characterization."

"And how exactly would you characterize that revelation?"

"I'd say it's far more complicated than can be explained here. But yes, Jessica's paternity was brought up during a case I tried last year."

"And what is the nature of her paternity?"

"Objection," Jeanie said. "This isn't a paternity case. There's absolutely no dispute about Jessica's birth parents. This isn't relevant. The only thing that's relevant is right here, right now, what is in this child's best interests for custody."

"Agreed," Judge Epperle said. "I see no reason to …"

"Your Honor," Donnelly said. "I'm getting to it. But I would pose the argument that Ms. Leary has been using this child for her own ends from the very beginning. She allowed her sister to publicly reveal that this child was conceived by rape. She did not ask the Dales for permission to do that. She did not warn them ahead of time so they could prepare that it was coming. That story was plastered all over the internet. People in Delphi are still gossiping about it. And yet, Ms. Leary thinks it serves Jessica's best interests to *live* here? Moreover, her sister stands accused of murdering Jessica's parents. That alone should illustrate why living with her is *not* in this poor child's best interests. Jessica may even be called as a witness in that trial."

"You're arguing, Mr. Donnelly. You should be questioning your witness."

It didn't matter. The damage was done and it was devastating. Donnelly turned to me.

"Ms. Leary, you didn't warn the Dales about your sister's testimony in the Drazdowski trial, did you?"

"No, I did not. But I didn't know the extent of what she would say until she said it."

"And isn't it true that was the crux of the trouble between your sister and the Dales? The trouble that led to the personal protection order?"

This was a disaster. Another spectator had quietly entered the courtroom. It was Rayna DeWitt. If I wasn't careful, I could walk right into the trap of being forced to testify about things that could be used against Vangie in her criminal trial. This was an absolute, unmitigated mess. I was being forced to choose between Jessa's best interests against my sister's.

"I ... I believe it was a misunderstanding. I believe my sister and the Dales would have worked it out in time. But yes, that's what started it."

It was almost as if I existed in two places. There was the part of me sitting in that witness chair testifying. Then there was another part of me, the seasoned defense lawyer who knew exactly how I would use this testimony if I were the prosecutor.

"And do you now believe that Jessica may be a material witness in your sister's murder trial?"

"I can't answer that," I said. "What you're asking is protected by privilege." Though I knew that was all the answer he needed. The judge could fill in the blanks himself.

"Thank you," Donnelly said. "I have no more questions."

Jeanie came to the podium. "Cass," she said. "How do you feel about Jessa?"

I blinked hard. "I ... she's ... she's one of my babies. She's family. I'm falling in love with her and I think she's starting to love me."

"Thank you."

Judge Epperle adjourned for lunch. As I stepped down from the witness box, I felt as if I'd left a piece of my soul there. Jeanie could do some damage when she cross-examined the Dales, but Lud Donnelly may just have made the kill shot.

Chapter 32

JEANIE CALLED GERALDINE DALE NEXT. The woman was tiny, dignified, wearing a forest-green suit with a lace collar. She had pure white hair cut into a sleek bob. But she looked every inch of her seventy years, as did her husband. That was Jeanie's biggest weapon against them and right now it felt very thin.

Jeanie established some background. The Dales lived near Boca Raton but they traveled for half the year to their condo in Aruba and cruises they liked to take. Both retired, Martin Dale had amassed a small fortune in the banking industry. He'd gotten out just before the last recession, his golden parachute intact. They were childless, active members of their church and the Homeowner's Association where they lived.

"Mrs. Dale," Jeanie said. "How often did you and your husband visit your nephew, Ben?"

"Every other year or so. He and Sarah used to vacation with us before they got the baby. It got harder for them after that."

"And how many times have you visited Jessica?"

This was really the heart of it all. Jessa had no relationship with these people. "We came once," Geraldine answered. "A year ago last Christmas. I took Jessica and her mother on a shopping trip. I bought her some little outfits. They have just the cutest things for little girls."

"Thank you. Mrs. Dale, how is your health?"

Geri Dale blinked. She looked at her lawyer. Lud gave her a small nod. "My health? Oh, I've got my aches and pains. But I get around just fine. I walk five miles a day. I swim laps. Marty joins me. We have an indoor pool at the rec center down the block from where we live. Jessa will love it. I have an orange tree in the backyard. We have a fence. We've been talking about buying her a little dog. She'd want for nothing."

"What about Mr. Dale's health?" Jeanie continued. She'd been put in the position of having to examine these witnesses without the benefit of prior discovery. But this was technically an evidentiary hearing, not a full-blown trial. I just prayed she could get some hits off without sustaining any more damage to our case.

Again, Mrs. Dale looked to Lud Donnelly. Jeanie caught it. "Ma'am," she said. "Your lawyer can't answer these questions for you. All you need to worry about is telling the truth here."

"Marty's fine," Geri snapped. "He had a heart attack when he was sixty. It slowed him down some, but he's healthy as can be."

Jeanie got testimony about the medications they collectively took. My heart sank. We were working with what we had. But the judge would be weighing cholesterol medication in with my mob-lawyer past and my sister's murder trial.

Lud Donnelly made quick work of the Dales on cross. At the conclusion of Mrs. Dale's testimony, he asked her, "Geri, can you tell the court in your own words why you think Jessica would be better off with you and your husband?"

She smiled. "Judge, I won't sit up here and tell you this is where I thought my life would end up. I'm seventy years old. We tried for children when we were younger. It never worked out. But we are that little girl's only family. Her only legal family. I know Ms. Leary thinks she's doing right by her sister's child. Well, we're trying to do right by our nephew's child too. She doesn't belong here. There are too many demons for that precious child here in Michigan. She deserves to grow up away from all the scandal and rumor and trauma. Here, she's surrounded by it. I'm not a young woman anymore, but I'm healthy. We can provide a safe, stable home for that baby filled with love and support. She'll have the best of everything. She'll have privacy. And she can grow up with the people who loved and remember her parents. It's what's best for her. I think if she searches inside of herself, Ms. Leary will come to understand that too."

Geri Dale stepped down.

Judge Epperle brought his glasses down and looked hard at all of us. "All right. I've got reports from Dr. Spencer and the amended F.O.C. recommendation. Is there any other written evidence either side would like to present?"

"Your Honor," Lud Donnelly said. "We'd like the opportunity to have Jessica interviewed by our own therapist."

"Well, I've never known Collette Spencer to be for sale. I'm concerned about bringing too many strange adults into this child's life. But I'll take that under advisement. In the meantime, I want to set up a reasonable visitation schedule. Ms. Leary, when's Jessica's next appointment with Dr. Spencer?"

"It's tomorrow at two, but Your Honor ..."

"Fine," Judge Epperle interrupted. "You get with opposing counsel after we adjourn. I want the Dales to meet with you there. Work it out with Dr. Spencer, but I want Jessica to have time with her aunt and uncle. I'll have a decision on your petition within fourteen days." He banged the gavel and ended the hearing.

Jeanie understood the look on my face. "Go," she said. I hugged her and left her to deal with the particulars of the exchange with the Dales. Under no circumstances was I going to allow them to take Jessa anywhere without me. I felt certain that Collette Spencer would agree that could erode what little trust we'd built.

I made my way to the back of the courtroom. Matty blocked my exit. "Don't," I whispered. "I have to see Vangie. She needs to know what's going on."

"Cass, have we screwed this up for her? My drinking, your ... past ..."

"Don't," I said it again. "It's not going to do any good. For now, just get back to the lake house. Spend some time with Jessa. Tell her I'll be home by dinnertime. Stay there with her."

"What do you want me to tell her about the Dales?" he asked.

I looked down the hall. They had already left the courtroom and stood in a huddle near the stairwell. Lois Reese walked out. She was the Friend of the Court caseworker who'd turned on me. She seemed startled to find them both standing there as she opened the door.

Jeanie came out of the courtroom. Lud was all smiles and charm as he held the door for her. He spied his clients and I watched his eyes. I don't know what I was looking for, but I felt something in the air. I waited for him to walk out of earshot and turned to Jeanie.

"Listen," I said. "It's probably nothing. But do you think you can have your super-secret investigator sniff around a little?"

"What for?"

I looked over my shoulder at the Dales. They'd been joined by Donnelly. Lois Reese gave him a polite but faltering smile, then slipped back into the stairwell.

"You don't think …" Jeanie started.

"I don't know what I think. I just don't want to leave any stones unturned."

"Hmmm. And you're thinking something Florida ugly might crawl out of one of those rocks?"

"Er … maybe." Matty's posture shifted as he tracked my line of thought.

"You think they paid that bitch off?" he asked.

"Lower your voice. And you let me worry about that stuff right now. Just do what I said. Stay with Jessa. She likes you."

Matty wasn't happy with my brush-off, but I knew he was just as eager to get back to Vangie's daughter as I was. Except I had to face her first. God. What the hell was I going to say?

"I've got a call into Dr. Spencer's office," Jeanie said. "The Dales will meet you there a half an hour before Jessa's appointment. They're asking for a half hour with her after or maybe even during Jessa's session. To start anyway. At least for now, they're putting their trust in Spencer. That's the good news."

"Right," I said. "It'll give me something encouraging to tell Vangie."

Jeanie squeezed my arm in support. I took a steadying breath. I had an hour-long drive to Ann Arbor. Plenty of time to figure out what the hell else I could say to her that wouldn't make her lose hope.

Chapter 33

I GOT EVEN MORE time once I got to the jail. There'd been a mix-up and my visit request hadn't been logged.

"Family visitation is on Fridays," one of the clerks tried to explain.

"I'm not just family. I'm Evangeline's lawyer."

She went back to her computer screen. "Why didn't you say so?"

I resisted the urge to tell her I had. Multiple times. Instead, I kept a polite smile on my face as the minutes ticked by.

"Just have a seat in the family waiting room," she said. "There's nobody in there right now on account of it's not Friday. This will take me twenty minutes or so to straighten out. You have plans?"

"My plan is to meet with my client. I'll wait." I sent a quick text to Joe to let him know not to hold dinner. I still planned to make it back in time. I'd just have to cut things even shorter with Vangie.

The family waiting room had furniture from I think the

seventies in it, chairs with burnt orange upholstery and dark wood paneling. Somewhere, some designer must have thought it was homey. They failed. I could close my eyes and know I was in a correctional facility. The place smelled of disinfectant, body odor, and despair.

An old, boxy television set sat perched on a shelf above me. It was tuned to cable news so I got treated with a barrage of slanted political coverage. I couldn't reach the thing to turn it off.

Twenty minutes went by. Then another. I watched the same four news stories replay. The clerk assured me it would just be another "couple of minutes." Though I'd been in no hurry to deliver bad news, this was getting ridiculous.

"We have some grisly news out of Milwaukee this afternoon. Police have identified the bodies of the Whitefish Bay couple found murdered in their beds as Steven and Amanda Kent. Sources say they were likely killed the night before last. There were no signs of forced entry or theft and investigators have yet to zero in on a motive for the killing."

My gaze went straight to the TV set. A photograph appeared on the screen of the murder victims, Steven and Amanda Kent. It was one of those cheesy department-store portraits with a fake farmhouse background. They were young, white, attractive. I couldn't stop looking at them. I searched for the remote control, wanting to freeze the picture and rewind. Certain words repeated in my head.

No signs of forced entry. No motive.

But the report ended and the reporter cut back to the news desk. The anchor gave a grim-faced response then launched into yet another report on the congressional gridlock.

I pulled out the notes app on my phone and typed in the victims' names and Whitefish Bay. It was a long shot. I was grasping at the thinnest of straws. But maybe …

"We can take you back now, Ms. Leary," the clerk said. She at least had the decency to look embarrassed. I slid my phone in my purse and headed for the steel double doors that would lead me to my sister.

Chapter 34

I DID my level best to keep Vangie's spirits up. She slumped into her seat on the other side of the table. In the last week, she looked like she'd lost twenty pounds and aged as many years.

"You can't let them take her," Vangie said. "Jessa doesn't know Marty and Geri. It's all complete bullshit anyway. Sarah couldn't stand them. She said they were impossible. Always trying to show Ben up with all the stuff they could afford. Ben and Sarah had money too, but Marty Dale is a multi-millionaire. I'm telling you right now, if they can find a way to buy that judge or Jessa, they will."

I didn't want to tell her what I suspected about Lois Reese, the F.O.C. caseworker. It was based on nothing more than a casual look of discomfort when she saw me in the hall.

"We're looking at every angle," I said. "I promise. I wish I could stay here longer, but I promised Jessa I'd be home for dinner. She's hanging out with Emma and Joey today. Emma's so cute with her."

Vangie gave me the first real smile I'd seen from her in

weeks. "She's amazing, isn't she? I told you. Jessa's ... despite everything ... she's special. She was put in my life for a reason. I might regret everything about how she was conceived, but I don't regret her. Not for a second."

"I know." I reached across the table and gathered my sister's hands in mine.

"Just keep her safe," Vangie said. "I can take anything in here as long as I know that."

"I will. Matty's heading up here on Friday. You call me if there's anything you need."

"I love you," Vangie said. I hadn't realized how badly I needed to hear it from her. I leaned in and gave her a kiss on the cheek then gestured for the guard. It was time for me to go.

LATER THAT NIGHT Jessa curled up next to me on the couch. Joe said she'd been content all day. She and Emma baked cookies, then they went out on the ice. They built a lopsided snowman in the backyard. Jessa smiled when Emma decided to name him Slushie.

"Don't look now," Joe whispered. "I think she's sleeping."

Sure enough, Jessa grew heavier against my arm. It was nearly nine o'clock. "You think you can carry her upstairs?" I said.

Joe was already on it. He slid his strong arms under our tiny niece and lifted her easily. Jessa's blonde hair fell against his leg. Joe shot me a wink and carefully walked Jessa up to bed. I went to the kitchen and poured myself a glass of wine.

Moving back to the couch, I slid my laptop out of my messenger bag and fired it up. It was the first time I'd had more than two minutes to myself all day. I hit my news slider, looking for another story on the murder in Whitefish Bay.

The one I found yielded no more information than what I'd seen on cable news this afternoon.

Whitefish Bay was an affluent suburb of Milwaukee. The article listed their address. I pulled up a map and clicked on the street view. It was a pretty, two-story house on a wooded cul-de-sac. I hovered my mouse, rotating the image.

"What're you looking at?" Joe came back downstairs.

"Nothing. Straws," I said.

He tilted his head to the side, giving me that confused dog expression. He took the seat beside me.

"Is that Ben and Sarah Dale's house?" he asked.

"No, but it looks like it could be, doesn't it?"

"You shopping for grander digs than this?" Joe teased.

"No, I'm just ... I don't know what I am." I closed my laptop.

"She's down for the count," he said. "She sleeps just like Emma. You could pretty much hang her up by her feet and she wouldn't wake up."

"Speaking of, where'd she escape to?"

Joe let out a hard sigh. "She's got a study date."

"Well, thanks for bringing her today. She might just be my secret weapon when all is said and done."

"So," Joe said. "You wanna tell me what the hell happened today?"

I gave him side-eye. "You wanna pretend you don't already know? That Matty didn't call you the second he got out of that courtroom?"

Joe made a gesture of surrender, hands up. Then he grew serious. "Tell me the truth, are we going to lose her?"

For a moment, I wasn't sure if he meant Vangie or Jessa. I wished I had a better answer for both.

"The truth is, I don't know. This lawyer they brought with them, he did real damage. Jeanie's good, but she can't hide the facts. Our family has ... issues."

"Killian Thorne again," Joe said. Last year, we'd argued plenty about my prior business associations. I'd used them to help find Vangie in the first place. Now it seemed yet again I couldn't outrun my past.

"It's more than that. The stuff I've done *looks* bad if the judge wants to go that way."

"Yeah," Joe said. "But I know damn well you'd never do anything to hurt Jessa. I don't care who these people are. Jessa is a Leary. She's ours. I'm sorry for what happened to Ben and Sarah Dale. I'm just not sorry for wanting to keep her. She belongs with us, Cass."

I rested my head on his shoulder. "I know. And I'm trying."

We stayed that way for a few minutes, completely silent, staring out at the dark expanse of the frozen lake. Finally, Joe took a breath and asked me the question I knew had been most on his mind.

"Matty said you testified that you and Killian Thorne were ... involved."

It was starting to snow again. Tiny flakes spun and danced before settling on the lake. Light. Harmless. In a few hours, Matty's ice rink would be completely covered over again.

Killian had been the secret I kept from my family for all those years I lived in Chicago. He was dangerous. He was powerful. And there was a time I believed he was the love of my life.

"Yes," I said. "It got complicated. He was my client. Later, he was more. But I've left all of that behind me. You already know that. That part of my life is over."

"Is it?" Joe turned in his seat to face me. "You used that guy's connections to find Vangie and bring her back to Delphi. He had her here in a matter of hours when we hadn't heard from her in years."

"Joe, what are you really asking me? Do I regret getting involved with him? Honestly? I don't think so."

Joe ran a hand over his brow. "No ... it's ... Jesus. I can't believe I'm about to ask this. Shit. We're in trouble, Cass. About as deep as we've ever been. Vangie's going to go down for those murders. I feel it in my guts. And Jessa? People like the Dales win when they come up against people like us."

I sat up. Fire tore through my veins. "No, Joe. I'm not done fighting. I don't plan on stopping. I love you. You know me better than probably anyone. But you don't know everything I'm capable of. I'm very, *very* good at what I do. This isn't over. Not for Vangie and not for Jessa."

Joe stood up. He took three steps toward the double doors then turned around and came back. He sat on the coffee table and leveled a hard stare at me.

"I'm not making myself clear. Cass, I know you're different than you were before you left Delphi the first time. You're stronger. Hell, maybe even smarter. What I'm saying is ... do it."

"Do what?"

He gripped the edge of the table. "Call Thorne. Call in whatever favors you can. If we have to fight dirty, if that's the only way we get Vangie out of this, I want you to do it. I was worried about you when you came back. It bothers the hell out of me that you got mixed up with people like that. I know asking makes me a hypocrite but I don't care. Whatever it takes. We have to protect Vangie and Jessa. We have to keep this family together."

The air grew thick between us. Poor, sweet Joe. He didn't even really know what he was asking me. He wanted me to what? Have Killian's men take out Marty and Geri Dale? Jessa's caseworker? Bust Vangie out of jail and help her go on the lam again? The thing was, if I thought for a second any of those things had a chance of saving her ...

I took Joe's hands in mine. "I love you. But no. That's not the way we win. Even if it was, you're underestimating the level of influence I have with my former bosses. I can't tell you everything. But what I will tell you will be the truth. I have no favors left to call in." I couldn't bring myself to tell him the greater truth. I'd barely escaped the Thorne Group with my life. There was no going back.

Joe dropped his head. "I'm sorry. I shouldn't even have brought it up. It's just …"

"Forget it," I said. "You don't owe me an explanation. Plus, I meant what I said. I'm not done fighting and you haven't seen yet what I can do. Vangie hasn't been convicted of anything. Let's hold on to that. Let's worry about getting Jessa through all of this. That's our biggest fight right now."

My phone rang on the table just behind Joe. It made him jump. Then he gave me a sheepish grin as he handed it to me. Not before he glanced at it and read the caller ID at the same time I did. Joe's lips pursed as I took the phone away from him. I walked past him and out on the front porch, bracing myself against the cold.

"Eric," I said. "Please tell me you have good news."

Eric Wray let out a little laugh. "Yeah. I heard you had a pretty rough day. You okay?"

"I'm fine. It's just … it's been a long one."

"Well, I don't have much to tell you. I'm sorry. I ran the phone number you gave me. Has he called back since?"

I pulled the phone away from my ear. I'd barely had two seconds to check my messages all day. But there was nothing. Just texts back and forth between Joe, Miranda, Jeanie, Matty, and me. No missed calls.

"No," I said. "Our mysterious Lullaby Guy has yet to make a repeat performance."

"He probably won't then," Eric said. "I told you. Anytime you have a case that gets even the slightest news coverage, it draws the crackpots. Anyway, the number came up as a dead end. Came back to a burner phone. You know, one of those prepaid phones you can pick up at the grocery store. Probably some crackhead or God knows who."

"I don't know," I said. "Or somebody who knows how not to be tracked. Eric, he knew about the photograph. The unicorn princess. That just can't be a coincidence."

"Right, and Sarah Dale's Facebook feed is exactly how the Ann Arbor cops connected that photo to Vangie. It's out there."

"Really?" I said. "Her account's been deactivated since the day after her body was found. It just seems way too farfetched."

"I know you want this to be something else. So do I. I just don't have anything solid to go on."

I bit my lip, hesitating to tell him the rest of what I was thinking. It was one thing to work it through in my head. It was another thing to say it out loud.

"Eric, there was a double homicide in Whitefish Bay, Wisconsin. It's been all over the news. Steven and Amanda Kent were the victims. Christ. I know how looney this sounds but I pulled up their address on a street view map. They lived on a cul-de-sac just like Ben and Sarah."

"Cass, Whitefish Bay is like three hundred and fifty miles away."

"I know. I know. I get this is more than grasping at straws. But they haven't arrested anyone yet for it. There was no forced entry. I'm just wondering if there's any way we could find out whether there were any other similarities to the Dale murders. You know? Something they would have kept from the news reports."

Eric sighed. "I don't know anybody in Whitefish Bay."

"Come on. You know somebody who knows somebody. I know how this works. You're a cop."

"You're killing me," he said, but I could tell he was smiling.

"And you owe me. Remember?"

I meant to keep my tone light, but Eric made a tiny noise. A little grunt. I was skirting the line of pissing him off. Too bad.

"I'll try to look into it," he said. "I'll admit there are very superficial, wide-as-a-canyon, similarities. Just ... don't get your hopes up."

"I won't. And thank you."

"Right," he said. "But then you're going to owe me. Big."

Something about the tone in his voice brought a blush to my cheeks. Or maybe it was just the frigid air. Or the beginnings of frostbite.

Chapter 35

"YOU SURE ABOUT THIS?" Jeanie asked. We sat in her car just outside of Dr. Collette Spencer's office. I had Jessa bundled up in the back seat. She clung to her new little brown bear and watched the snow falling outside the window. I didn't want to say too much in front of her, but once we got out of the car and met the Dales and their lawyer Lud Donnelly, I wouldn't be able to unring this particular bell.

"I'm sure," I said, keeping my voice bright. "I have no idea if that subpoena will yield anything. But if my hunch is right, maybe it will make them nervous and shake something loose before the judge's final ruling. He said both sides could amend their document list if anything new came to light."

Jeanie held a thin file folder in her hands. In it, we'd prepared a subpoena duces tecum and document request. I wanted details on the Dales' finances. It was a fishing expedition. But if there was even a sliver of a chance that they'd bribed Lois Reese to change her findings, I meant to bait the hook.

"Well," Jeanie said, "the odds of either of them being

dumb enough to write a personal check or make some kind of direct transfer …"

"I know," I said. Behind us, Jessa had started to unbuckle her seatbelt. I reached over the back seat to help her. She gave me a tiny little smile that melted me. A week ago, she might not have let me this close to her.

"We're going to have fun today," I said. "Mrs. Spencer said she has some new games to play. And some friends of mine have come here to hang out with you. If you want."

I had to choke past the word "friends." Though I knew the Dales were more than within their rights to challenge my guardianship, it was hard not to see them as the enemy. But this wasn't about me. This was about what was best for Jessa. I hoped Judge Epperle would rule my way. If he didn't, I had to do everything in my power to make sure any transition for Jessa stayed as smooth as possible.

Lud Donnelly was waiting in the lobby as we walked inside. He wore a dark wool coat and a business suit. He made a big smile at Jessa and started to walk toward her. She darted behind me and made a small, fearful noise.

"Back off!" I mouthed the words.

Jeanie came around us. "And this is exactly why this arrangement is a terrible idea," she whispered. "You talk a big talk in court, Donnelly. But you have no idea what that kid's been through."

Donnelly kept his smile plastered in place as Jeanie shoved her file folder in his hands. "Some homework for you," she said.

Donnelly's face fell just a little as he quickly scanned the contents. His eyes hardened as he looked up at me.

Collette Spencer opened her office door and beamed at Jessa. She came out from behind me and took the doctor's offered hand. "So glad to see you today," Dr. Spencer said to Jessa. "You look so pretty in that purple coat. My secretary just baked some chocolate chip cookies. You wanna help me eat them?"

Jessa answered by walking with Dr. Spencer. Spencer shot us a glance over her shoulder. "Did your aunt tell you I have some friends I'd like you to meet? Actually, you've met them before, but you probably don't remember. You were just a baby …"

Her voice trailed as she led Jessa through her inner office door. My heart squeezed with the urge to just take her and run straight out of the building. As soon as the door shut, Lud Donnelly turned on us.

"You're desperate," he said. "And you'll have my motion to quash by the end of the day."

"What are you afraid of?" I asked, taking a step toward Lud Donnelly. "You want the court to hear all about my background? Your clients are fair game. Unless … they have something to hide."

"You might want to reread the statute," Jeanie said. "I mean, I know you're from Florida and all, but there's nothing in that subpoena that isn't proper discovery. File your motion if you must, but you'll lose."

"If you do anything to sabotage my clients' relationship with Jessica … I'll …"

"That's the point, Mr. Donnelly," I said. "They have no relationship with her."

"And neither did you two weeks ago. Christ. Your sister is going to be convicted of murder. You're going to lose that case. You think Judge Epperle—*any* judge—is going to think it's in that child's best interest to be raised by her sister?"

Jeanie had a hand on me as my anger rose. I knew what she'd say. There was no point fighting with this guy here. It's what he wanted. So I said nothing and hated myself for it. It was lucky that neither Matty or Joe were here. I'd have to hold Matty back from decking him.

Lud pulled out his phone. Two clicks and he turned it toward me. "Did you see this?" he asked, practically shoving the thing in my face.

He had it open to a news site. The first two headlines dealt with the current congressional investigation and yesterday's stock market. Beneath that, the local news headline made the blood drain from my head.

Accused Murderer's Defense Lawyer Tries to Adopt Child Victim and Only Witness

I resisted the urge to grab his phone from him.

"That's just the first one," he said. "This is popping up all over the state. You checked your inbox lately? It's probably blowing up. Because the comments below this story will blow your hair back. You're not too popular around town, Ms. Leary."

No sooner had he said it before my phone buzzed in my purse. He wanted to watch me take the call. I shot a look to Jeanie and stepped away. It was Joe. I walked outside to answer.

"Jesus, Cass," he said. "Have you been online yet?"

"No. I'm at Dr. Spencer's with Jessa." As we spoke, three texts came in from Miranda. I pulled the phone away long enough to look at the gist of her messages. She'd had some angry visitors at the office.

"Is Matty still at my house?" I asked. It was one thing if people showed up to harass me at the office. It was quite another if they followed me home. The trouble was, it was Delphi. If these were locals, I wasn't too hard to find.

"I think so," he said. "I'll head over myself after work. I don't like this. I didn't want to tell you, but some people were hassling Emma at work and at school yesterday. Can you call your friend at the Delphi P.D.? It's like the Drazdowski trial all over again. "

Except it was worse and we both knew it. "You mean Eric? What for?"

"Or maybe you and Jessa could just bunk at my house for a few days. I just don't like you being by yourself at the lake. At least let me call my guy about installing a security system. I've been up your ass long enough about that."

This was a train wreck. Lud Donnelly would probably file an emergency motion to get Jessa removed from my house at the same time as his motion to quash. Lord. It's exactly what I'd do in his place.

"We'll talk when I'm done here," I said. "Joe, I'm sorry about Emma. Is she okay?"

"Emma knows how to take care of herself. She's like her aunt." From the tone of his voice, I knew he was smiling. It helped a little.

"We'll get through this," I said. "Somehow. I've gotta go."

I clicked off and went back to Jeanie's side. She had just finished unloading on Donnelly.

"We'll expect your response," Jeanie said.

With that, she brushed past Lud Donnelly and we went into Dr. Spencer's waiting room. Her office door was open just enough to give me a view of Jessa clinging to her as Marty and Geri Dale sat stiff and smiling on the doctor's leather couch.

Chapter 36

THREE DAYS LATER, Lud Donnelly filed his emergency motion to have Jessa removed from my home. Along with it, he responded to my subpoena with reams of financial documents for Jeanie and me to make sense of.

"When's the hearing?" I asked Jeanie. We sat in the conference room. Now half of the table was taken up with discovery on Jessa's guardianship case. I'd brought in a second table to hold the trial materials for Vangie's murder defense. It gave me the sensation of being buried alive.

"Two days," she said. "How's Jessa holding up?"

"Matty's taken her for ice skating lessons over at the Briarfield Arena. I gave him my credit card so he can get her new skates. She seemed happy about it. Or at least …"

"She still hasn't spoken a single word?" Jeanie asked. She already knew the answer. I shook my head anyway.

"Dr. Spencer said not to get discouraged. Even with that, she's seen good progress in just the three weeks since she started treating her."

Jeanie reached over and grabbed the news story I'd printed out about the Whitefish Bay murders. Though she hadn't discounted my idea outright, I knew the look in her eyes when I tried to explain. It was just like Eric's when I ran it by him.

"No break in this case either?" she asked.

"Eric said he'd look into it. But so far, no."

She put the papers down. Right now, Jeanie looked like I felt. She had dark circles beneath her eyes and was still wearing the same clothes as yesterday. We'd pulled an all-nighter writing up a response to Lud Donnelly's custody motion.

"No more calls from your mysterious Lullaby Guy?" she asked.

"No. I know. You all think I'm crazy for even thinking twice about that. Hell, Miranda's had about twenty hateful voicemails just today. Everybody thinks I'm trying to coach Jessa to help my sister get away with murder. I don't know. Maybe they're right. Maybe I'm nuts to think keeping Jessa is good for her."

It was the first time I'd said something like that out loud. I didn't really feel it. I was just ... exhausted.

Jeanie came to me. She gathered my hands in hers. "Hey. This is me you're talking to. I know your heart, Cass. I know how much you love Vangie and Matty and Joe. I know how hard you fought to keep them whole after your mom's acci-dent and your dad's ... well ... trouble. If it weren't for you, Matty and Vangie would have disappeared into the system. For good."

"I can't take credit for that," I said. "That was all you, Jeanie."

She let out a sigh. "Like hell. And anyway, I've seen the way you look at that little girl. You're falling in love with her. So am I. She's special. She's a miracle. And she's in our lives for a reason. She's a gift. And I don't believe for a second she's better off with Marty and Geri Dale. I'm not going to lie. You, Joe, Matty, Vangie, you're all a hot mess. But Jessa's one of you. She's a Leary. She belongs with us. So what we're going to do is, we're going to keep fighting. It's what we're good at. Remember?"

I hugged her. Hard.

"Right."

Miranda buzzed in on the landline. "Cass, you've got a call on line one. I know you didn't want to be disturbed, but he says he's from Whitefish Bay and you'd know what it was about?"

I racked my brain. Other than Eric and Jeanie, I hadn't told anyone else about my Whitefish Bay theory. I thanked Miranda and picked up the phone.

"Cass Leary speaking."

There was a pause and a click on the other line. "You look good in green," he said. "That was one hell of a performance you gave in court the other day. Killian Thorne's whore? I'm impressed."

I froze. Green? I'd worn a green suit at the guardianship hearing four days ago. There had been press outside, but only a few people in the gallery during testimony. I tried to picture who I'd seen there. My brothers. A few local attorneys waiting for their own hearings to be called. Rayna DeWitt. There were others. Not many.

Then he began to hum and the air went right out of the room. "Don't say a word," he picked up the lyrics.

"Who is this?" I motioned for Jeanie to hand me a pen. I clicked on the speaker.

"Just a concerned citizen," he said. "Pretty lady. What a sweet family you're trying to make for yourself." He started to hum the lullaby again. Jeanie shot out of her chair and ran down the hall.

"I appreciate that," I said. "It's nice to have someone on my side."

There was a long pause. I thought he hung up. Jeanie rushed back into the room. She had a small voice recorder in her hand, the one Miranda used to dictate notes to herself. She hit the record button and set it next to the phone. Almost immediately, he started humming again. Just one verse. Then the phone went dead.

I checked the caller ID. This time, it came from an unlisted number.

"Damn," Jeanie said.

"He was in court with us," I said. "At Jessa's hearing. He knew what color suit I had on and heard me testify about Killian Thorne."

Jeanie clicked off the recorder. "I think it's time to call Detective Wray again."

Chapter 37

I GOT HOME the same time Matty and Jessa pulled in. Jessa's cheeks were flushed as she climbed out of Matty's car. She had a smile on her face. A real one. It brightened when she saw me and she ran to me. I squatted down and held my arms out to her as she came. She would have hugged me. I had no doubt. But just before she ran into my waiting embrace, the broken parts of her got in the way. She hesitated. Her smile stayed in place, but her steps faltered.

It's okay, I wanted to say. But Dr. Spencer warned us about saying things that made Jessa feel like there was something wrong with her.

"Did you have fun?" I asked.

"She was a natural," Matty called out. "She was pretty much skating rings around me after just an hour."

My brother exaggerated. He'd been good enough to make the Delphi High hockey team a decade ago. But Jessa's blush deepened. She had real joy in her eyes and I stood up and planted a big, sloppy kiss right on my brother's cheek.

"Come on," I said. "You know what happens after ice skating? Hot cocoa. With marshmallows!"

Jessa scrambled up the porch steps and started peeling off her boots and coat. I hugged Matty again.

"You're brilliant," I said. "She loves you."

"I'm not kidding. She was really good. She seemed almost ... normal."

"She is normal," I said. "Come on, let's get you inside. You look like you could use a cup of cocoa too."

A car pulled up and parked on the opposite side of the street. Matty stiffened, recognizing the government plates on it. Eric Wray stepped out and gave him a polite nod. My brother and Eric were cool to each other. Eric was used to seeing Matty at his worst, involved in bar fights down at Mickey's.

"I've gotta go," Matty said. "I promised Tina I'd take a look at her furnace."

"Oh?" Tina was Matty's estranged wife. She'd filed for divorce three times in the last five years then always dismissed. It wasn't that my brother hadn't given her cause. Still, it tugged at my heart because I knew how much he loved her and hated that his drinking had screwed so much up between them.

"Don't get excited," he said. "It's just about the furnace."

"Well, three months ago she'd have probably shot you just for setting foot on the lawn. I'll take it as progress."

"Matt," Eric said as he walked up.

"This a social call or official business?" Matty asked. Eric started to answer, then cleared his throat. He realized there was no good way to answer that. Eric didn't know, but I hadn't said a word to Matty or Joe about the calls from the Lullaby Guy or the Whitefish Bay murders I'd asked him to look into. For one thing, as part of my sister's case, it was privileged. For another, I didn't need either of them trying to play armchair detective on me.

"Never mind," Matty said. I knew he didn't like my

friendship with Eric. Matty's distrust of cops came hardwired in his DNA. "I'm already late getting over to Tina's. Give Jessa an extra kiss for me."

"You staying here tonight?" I asked. I couldn't keep the smile off my face.

Matty grinned. Just the furnace, my ass. I took a breath. Hell, I didn't want to see him get his hopes up or heart broken again. But I knew his marriage was his business for now.

"Just behave," I warned him. "Come on," I said to Eric. As Matty slid back into his truck, Eric followed me in the house.

"I've got some milk warming on the stove," I said. "Hot cocoa's coming up."

Jessa had curled up on the couch and was flipping through her recordings on the DVR. She settled on Princess Beula's castle. It was the unicorn princess she was so fond of. Eric caught it and he dropped his eyes.

"Follow me into the kitchen," I said.

I poured Jessa's cocoa and brought it to her. "Extra marshmallows," I said. "It's not too hot but take a small sip, okay?"

Jessa nodded and sat up on her knees. I'd given her a little spoon and she started swirling the marshmallows. She gave me a look and I couldn't help but smile. "Let me guess," I said. "You want whipped cream *and* marshmallows?" I held the can behind my back. Jessa smiled and I sprayed the top of her mug with a big, heaping swirl of the stuff.

"Girl after my own heart," Eric called from the kitchen.

With Jessa content with her cartoons and cocoa, I joined Eric back in the kitchen. We sat at the table.

"Out with it," I said. "You've got that serious cop look on your face. You came to tell me I'm crazy again to try connecting dots that don't exist in Whitefish Bay."

Eric took a spoon and started stirring his own cocoa. He wasn't lying. He sprayed a perfect cone of whipped cream on the top of his mug.

"Actually, no, that's not what I came to say. First, your Lullaby Guy. I've asked the sheriff's office to review security footage from the day of the guardianship hearing."

"Geez. And you think I'm grasping at straws? How many people do you think went in and out of that courthouse that day?"

Eric shrugged. "It's something. There's a camera down the hall from Judge Epperle's. We can look at who went into the courtroom and cross check it."

"How many favors did you have to call in for that?" I asked.

Eric didn't answer. He took a sip of his cocoa. When he set it down he had a thin, white whipped-cream mustache. I turned to Jessa. She was watching him and it made her smile. She bunched her shoulders, holding in a laugh. Eric stuck his tongue out and licked the cream. Jessa put her hand over her mouth.

"She thinks you're silly,' I said.

"She's right."

"Okay, so the surveillance footage isn't why you came here. What is it, Eric?"

He set his mug down. "Cass, this can't go any further than this room. I mean it. Not Jeanie. Not Vangie. Nobody. I'm stepping over so many lines to even bring you into this. But …"

"You're my client, remember?" I pointed to the refrigerator. I kept Eric's five-dollar retainer taped to it.

"There was something taken from the crime scene of the Kent murders. Jessa, it was a family photo out of a frame on their baby grand piano."

My lungs started to burn. White spots floated in front of my eyes.

"Breathe," he reminded me. "Now, it doesn't necessarily mean anything. But …"

"But nothing! Jesus. Eric, we need more. If this is the same guy … if there's even a chance …"

"I know," he said. "And I'm not giving it up. Give me a little more time. I'm looking to see if there are any other similar unsolved cases. This is likely a coincidence. But it's worth pursuing. I just don't want to make too many waves about it just yet. There have been leaks to the press on this case all the way through. We can't afford to have any more. Other than you, I'm not even sure who to trust."

His phone buzzed. He pulled it out of his back pocket. He clicked it off rather than answering. "Anyway," he said. "That's where we are right now. I wanted to tell you in person. It's getting late. I should go."

I acted on instinct. I reached for him, putting a hand on his forearm. Eric's eyes blazed. My heart fluttered and I drew my hand away. "Thank you," I said. "You might be the only person other than family who's keeping an open mind about my sister. That means … a lot."

Eric shot me a devastating wink as he rose from the table. I started to walk him out. He stopped by Jessa's chair. She had her cocoa mug in two hands as she looked up at him. "See you around, pretty girl. You take care of your Aunt Cass, okay? She tends to get into trouble."

Jessa's eyes shifted to me. We'd been careful not to use the word aunt or uncle when it came to Jessa. I was afraid of confusing her. But she seemed to accept the term as Eric said it. Maybe that was one more small breakthrough on a day chock-full of them.

Snow crunched outside and headlights shined across the lake.

"You expecting someone?" Eric asked.

I leaned down so I could see out the window. A white van pulled up. "I am not," I said.

Eric's face changed as his gaze followed mine. "I'll get that," he said.

I made a slight move, standing in front of Jessa as Eric went to the door. He opened it. A middle-aged, balding man stood on the step holding a clipboard. He wore a navy-blue jumpsuit and some kind of white embroidered patch on his breast pocket.

"Can we help you?" Eric said, puffing his chest out.

"Titan Security?" the man said. His tone was pleasant, but deep.

Eric turned back to me. "Cass, did you schedule this? It's a little late, don't you think?"

I let out a sigh. "This is probably Joe. He's been on me for weeks."

"Gotta say I'm on his side here," Eric said, smiling. Then he turned back to the guy. "You mind showing me your work orders? I'd like to see what Joe's thinking. You good if I offer a little industry opinion?" Eric turned back to me.

"By all means," I said. Eric stepped to the side.

Jessa reached up and gripped my hand. Hers was hot and sweaty. She was still wearing long johns under her jeans and sweater. I'd forgotten to tell her to take those off.

"Well, hi, there, princess," the installer said. Eric had stepped outside. The guy was standing on level ground. Eric was on the top step of my porch.

Jessa's grip on my hand tightened. She started to tremble. Shit. This was exactly the kind of thing Dr. Spencer warned me about. Not too many strangers all at once.

Eric caught on. "Come on," he said to the guy. "Let's walk to your van and talk there."

Jessa screamed. The sound of it shattered my heart, hollowing me out. She wrapped her arms around my leg.

"Jessa? Baby?"

"Don't let him!" she shouted. Jessa's voice rose. "He'll do it again. Don't let him do it again!"

Eric moved. "Take her upstairs," he shouted. "Now!"

I tried to scoop Jessa up in my arms but it was as if she'd gone feral. She kicked and scratched, screaming the same words over and over again. "No! Don't let him do it again!"

"What's happening?" I said.

Eric knew. He saw something. He made a move, putting himself firmly in front of the man. "Run!" he yelled. Then he launched himself at the guy, spreading his arms wide, throwing his body in front of Jessa and me.

I stood frozen, staring at Eric. He jerked backward, then turned. He took a staggering step forward. His expression had changed. His eyes widened. He cocked his head to the side then dropped to his knees. I watched with curious stillness as a spot of red blossomed on his white shirt.

Behind him, the man stood holding a gun with a silencer attached. He'd shot Eric straight through the chest at point-blank range. Eric knelt with a rigid back for one horrifying moment, before he slumped to the ground and his blood poured across my wood floor.

Jessa stopped screaming. "Well, hey, there, unicorn princess," the Lullaby Guy said as he stepped over Eric's body and came toward us.

Chapter 38

JESSA WAS BEHIND ME. The man advanced, raising the gun. He pointed it straight at my head. I felt frozen. Stuck in glue. Then Jessa made a small, whimpering sound. I put my hands up, palms out as I took a slow step backward. I chanced one look down, locking eyes with Jessa.

She took a ready stance, her legs slightly apart. She was small, but strong and defiant. A single tear fell down her cheek as she pointed one steady finger straight at the Lullaby Guy.

There was nowhere to tell her to run. She had a couch behind her. The stairwell behind that. Even if she made it there, he'd have a clear shot to pick her off if he wanted. The only thing I could do was keep my body between her and the gun. Just like Eric had tried to do.

"The man you just shot is a police detective," I said. "If he dies, they'll never stop coming after you."

The man smiled. He had a straight row of yellow teeth. I noticed tiny details, my heart thundering so hard it made me lightheaded. I took a deep, slow breath. I couldn't afford to lose it. His blue jumpsuit had white paint stains down one leg. He wore beat-up tan work boots, the left shoelace was coming untied. He'd carefully combed back what remained of his hair. I could almost count each brown strand as it glistened with sweat. His eyes were blue, almost gray. A small scar cut through his right eyebrow. The little white patch on his jumpsuit said Christopher.

"Christopher," I said. "Is that your name? Christopher? There's no place to go. This is Finn Lake. Delphi. Everybody knows everybody. Your van out there? Guaranteed, at least four of my neighbors have already seen it."

Christopher took a step toward me. Jessa clung to my legs. I put a hand down on her head, willing her to stay calm.

I couldn't take my eyes off his gun. Cold and black, a nine millimeter. He'd put three bullets from that gun into Sarah Dale. He'd likely used it to cave Ben Dale's skull in. All while Jessa watched.

"Here, chick, chick," Christopher said. He dropped his gaze to Jessa. She dug her little nails into my thigh. I moved my body ever so slightly, angling it so there was no way he could get a shot off without it going through me first.

"Such a pretty little bird," he said. "You were naughty though. It's not polite to hide."

"Aunt C-Cass?" Jessa's tiny voice cut through me, nearly driving me to my knees. She trusted me. Right now, I was her world. She'd just said the two words I'd prayed so hard to hear. Only now, she may have to use them to beg for her life.

"If you go now," I said, "you'll have a chance. A head start. The longer you stay here, the easier it will be for them to catch you."

Christopher tilted his head. His eyes shone. It was almost full dark outside. The snow came down sideways. My eyes went to Eric's lifeless body on the floor. His blood soaked between the floorboards. His skin seemed so white.

"They won't catch me," he said. "They never catch me. Not even you."

"They will!" Jessa yelled. I moved fast, scooping her up in my arms.

"Get on the floor!" Christopher yelled. "Face down. Hands out so I can see you. You move, you get a bullet."

I moved slow, carefully setting Jessa on the ground. I gave her a small nod. She lay down on her stomach. I positioned my body so I half covered hers. She was still exposed enough if he wanted to kill her. But I wanted her to feel me close. I needed her to know I would die for her. I would. Only he hadn't killed us yet.

Christopher started to move around the room. His eyes darted back and forth. He kept the gun trained on us as he stepped over me and headed for the kitchen. I looked toward the door. Eric's body was right in front of me. He lay face down. I watched for any sign of life. Just the slightest movement of his back to let me know if he was breathing. But he was still as stone. Still as death. Pain tore through my heart. God, he'd lost so much blood.

Christopher started to whistle the melody to "Hush Little Baby," as if there were any remaining doubt who he was. He opened drawers in the kitchen. From the corner of my eye, I saw him pull open my junk drawer next to the sink. He came back to us, carrying a roll of black duct tape I kept there.

"Let's play a game. Cover her mouth," he said, pointing the gun at Jessa's head. "Move too fast and I win, she loses."

He tossed the duct tape so it landed right next to my hand. Jessa pleaded at me with her eyes. I kept my face neutral. I tried so hard to convey a message to her with my eyes. Trust me. Do what I do.

"Now!"

I jumped as he shouted. I tore off a length of tape. Jessa turned to me. She understood. As carefully as I could, I covered her mouth with the tape. I mouthed an "I'm sorry." She gave me a little nod.

"Hands next," he said.

I closed my eyes and let out a sigh. But Jessa moved. She sat up and held her wrists out for me. She kept one eye on Christopher.

"Good and tight," he said. I wrapped the tape around Jessa's wrists, binding them together. The loud, ripping noise it made echoed through my soul. I knew if we survived this, that sound would haunt me until the day I died.

He walked closer. The gun was no more than two inches from Jessa's back.

"She's scared enough!" I shouted. "You win, okay? You've got the gun."

Christopher squatted down. He cocked his head to the side, regarding me with animal-like curiosity. I felt my pulse thumping in my jaw.

"Put your hands behind your back. Fold them together."

I saw something go through Jessa's eyes. She sat with her legs drawn up. She made a little movement with her feet. I was afraid she was thinking of trying to kick out. Christopher slowly rose. I took a chance and locked eyes with her, making a short, jerking shake of my head. No!

"Hurry up!" Christopher yelled.

Fear clawed at my heart. He meant to bind my hands next. Once he did, I didn't know how to fight back if I got the chance. I couldn't pull Jessa behind me or hold her. This was my one last chance to make some kind of move before giving up that kind of control.

Christopher's calm smile sent a chill into my bones. I had no control at all. It was an illusion. He kept that gun pointed right at Jessa.

Slowly, I put my hands behind my back, clasping them together as he'd asked. Christopher knelt down. He was right behind me, his breath against my ear. He smelled of body odor and motor oil. He moved, bringing the gun down. I acted on instinct, rearing back. The back of my skull connected with the bridge of Christopher's nose. I heard a crunching sound.

"Bitch!" he shouted.

Jessa scrambled backward, pressing her back against the couch. Her breathing came ragged behind the duct tape.

"Run!" I shouted.

Christopher shoved me forward. My cheek hit the floor hard. It put me inches from Eric. With my hands still free, I grabbed his shoulder, trying to roll him. He was dead weight. No movement.

I kicked back as Christopher got to me. The wind went out of me in a whoosh as he drove his knee into the center of my back, pinning me to the ground. I tried to scream but no sound came out.

It didn't matter. Jessa was on her feet. As Christopher struggled to get control of me, she ran out the double doors heading straight for the frozen lake. I wanted to yell to her. It was the wrong way to go. She made no sound. I wanted her to scream and cry and head for the nearest neighbor. But logic had no place in Jessa Dale's mind that night. Nor mine either. She was driven by terror and the cold memory of what this man had done to her parents. She went for open spaces and what felt like freedom. If I had magic, I would have willed her wings to fly.

But I had no magic that night. I had only my own fear and adrenaline. Even that leached out of me; my limbs grew heavy as Christopher pulled my arms back. I kicked upward, but had no leverage.

I heard another ripping sound then smelled plastic. He used the duct tape and bound my hands behind me. With incredible strength, he hauled me to my feet by my hair. He pushed me forward until my cheek pressed against the window.

Jessa was a small, dark dot, running across the lake. God, I prayed. Please let someone see her.

"Time to go," he said.

My heart lifted as he grabbed me cruelly by the arm, wrenching it nearly out of its socket. I tripped on the runner I kept near the door. I landed hard, cracking my knee.

"No!" I shouted, my breath coming back to me with a fury. Everything hurt. My lungs burned. My knee exploded with fiery pain. Christopher pulled me to my feet and shoved me outside. He raised the gun and pointed it straight at Jessa's running form on the lake.

She was putting distance between herself and the house, but not enough. He had a clear, unobstructed shot. His aim might not be true, but I wasn't willing to take that chance.

"You scream, I shoot," he said.

I looked frantically to my left and right. My neighbors' houses were close, but we had privacy fences between us. Christopher had parked his van at an angle, shielding my porch from the street.

He ripped off a piece of duct tape with his teeth and slapped it to the side of the house. I struggled against him, but he had me pushed against the door. He produced a filthy cloth from his pocket and shoved it in my mouth as I opened it to scream. I choked on it. The rag tasted of gasoline. As Christopher pulled me toward the van, he slapped the tape across my face, sealing the fetid rag in my mouth and stifling my screams for help.

Strange things ran through my mind. Old self-defense classes I took in college. True crime documentaries. The second location. Never let them take you to a second location. That's how you die.

I kicked for all I was worth, grunting and gagging against

the rag. But Christopher was so much bigger, so much stronger. He lifted me off the ground with ease, holding me against him with one arm, the barrel of the gun under my chin. With his free hand, he opened the van door.

He pushed me until I stumbled through the open door of the van. I tried to shove past him, reaching for the steering wheel. If I could fling myself on the horn. Christopher over-took me, throwing his arm around my neck.

He raised the gun. I thought of Ben Dale. I tried to dodge the blow, but he brought it down against my temple. Lighting flashed inside my brain. The last thing I heard was the heavy van door closing behind me before black sleep dragged me down.

Chapter 39

THE GROUND WAS MOVING. Wet grass. I'd fallen asleep with something heavy on top of me. I tried to turn. Couldn't. I saw a man, dancing, laughing. He was on the side of my bed, just out of reach. He said my name, over and over. Every time I tried to reach for him, I couldn't find my hands.

Someone was pounding a nail into the wall. It was so loud. Couldn't they see I was trying to sleep? They used enough force to shake the floor.

Light stabbed through me. Pain flooded my senses. I shivered from the deathly cold. It wasn't a hammer blow I heard. It was heavy footsteps coming down rickety, wooden stairs. My cheek was stuck to cold, wet cement. I realized with painful clarity that I'd vomited.

"Wakey, wakey!"

It was Christopher. He'd changed out of the Titan Security jumpsuit. He wore a plain red t-shirt with holes in the armpit and blue jeans, painter style with deep pockets and loops for tools.

I opened my mouth to ask where we were. The rag and

duct tape were gone. I realized if he hadn't removed them while I was unconscious, I might have choked to death. Small favors. It meant he wanted me alive. For what?

I struggled to sit up. My hands were still bound tightly behind me with tape. He'd done the same to my ankles. A cramp tore through my side as I got myself up, twisting awkwardly until I pressed my back against the cement walls.

This was a basement. Light stabbed through high, glass-block windows. It was so cold. My teeth chattered so badly, I couldn't form words.

Jessa.

I scanned the room, squinting, trying to force my eyes to adapt to the dim light. It was a rectangular basement. No walls. Probably a ranch-style house. How far had we come? I remembered nothing about the drive. I was nowhere.

Christopher started to whistle. The room was sparse. The furnace and hot water heater stood in one corner. Spider webs decorated the exposed rafters above me. There was a simple, wooden workbench along one wall. That's where Christopher went. He carried a cardboard box then set it on the floor in front of the bench.

One by one, he emptied the box's contents. With his back to me, I couldn't make out what he had in his hands. I grew bolder, scooting forward so I was in a shaft of light.

Morning. It had been pitch black when Christopher shoved me into his van. Eight o'clock at night? Nine? Now, I think it was full morning. Had I been out cold for twelve hours? My stomach growled. My throat burned. My limbs were stiff and hard to move. Yes. I might have been out that long.

God. Jessa. What had he done with her? I didn't know what to wish for. If she'd kept on running and gotten away, she couldn't have survived a night outdoors. Early February in southern Michigan, and the temperature got well below zero with a fierce wind chill on top of it. Plus, we were supposed to get up to six inches of new snow on the ground. Before I came home from the office, they were already canceling schools for the next day.

Christopher stepped away from the bench. He gave me an oddly pleasant smile as he dusted off his hands and walked back up the steps. The hammering sounds of his footsteps made my head ache worse than any hangover.

I tried to move my jaw. Pain stabbed through me. He'd struck me on the side of the head. The bones of my face felt heavy. My left eye wouldn't open all the way. I scooted forward, closer to the bench. Should I try to pull myself to my feet? With my ankles bound, I could still do it. But I didn't trust I could keep my balance. Dizziness set in just from that small movement. I probably had a concussion.

I tried to focus on the workbench and the box Christopher had brought down. Icy terror hollowed out my chest as my brain caught up with what my eyes were seeing.

They were photographs. I counted six of them. He'd tacked them to the wooden board behind the bench. Family photos.

I managed to bring myself up to a kneeling position. My badly bruised knee felt like raw hamburger meat. At least I didn't think it was broken. I got close enough to see the faces in the photos, though I already knew what I'd find.

He'd put Ben and Sarah Dale's photo smack in the center. It was the same one I'd stared at a thousand times, committing it to memory. Sarah had her head slightly cocked, as if she were trying not to laugh too hard. Ben's eyes sparkled as he held his wife against him. Jessa sat between them, her mouth wide open. She couldn't hold back her laughter like her mother did. For weeks, I'd wanted to see her happy like that again.

The photo to the right of the Dales belonged to Steven

and Amanda Kent. It was a wedding photo. Steven sat on a bench, his wife stood a few feet in front of him, looking down at her bouquet.

There were four other photographs. Three couples. And another with a family of four. Ten people. Fourteen including the Dales and Kents. My God. Had this monster murdered fourteen people so far?

For the first time since I heard Jessa's breakthrough scream, I knew I was going to die.

I'd been cold. Now sweat poured down my face. I heard Christopher's footsteps above me. He was humming to himself. That same damn lullaby, but he sang just the first two lines of it over and over as if he didn't know the rest.

I could scream. I had no idea where we were or if there was anyone close enough to hear me. Had it really been almost twelve hours since he dragged me from my house? Were we driving that whole time? God. We could be absolutely anywhere.

I had to think fast. If I could just get enough leverage to push myself to my feet. With my ankles bound, I couldn't walk. But maybe I could hop a little. To where? To what?

I looked for anything I could use as a weapon. A sharp edge. A rusty nail. Anything. There were little metal brackets on the wall of the workbench. At some point, they must have held pliers and hammers. Now it was bare. I went to the ground, pressing my uninjured cheek against the floor. Cobwebs danced as my breath hit them. I squinted, trying to see underneath the workbench.

Christopher's footsteps came closer. He was at the top of the stairs. He started to whistle. I didn't recognize the tune but it was a welcome respite from "Hush Little Baby." Why did he keep singing that? I had to bite my swollen tongue past the urge to yell for Jessa. I didn't know whether to wish for that or not. I just prayed she was safe.

But Christopher was too calm. Too methodical. There was no hurry in his steps. He started to come back down the stairs. I rolled to the side, pushing myself away from the workbench. As Christopher opened the door at the top of the steps, more light shone down.

I saw a new shadow beneath the workbench. There was a piece of something there. Metal maybe. I prayed I'd have enough luck and I could figure out how to get it. And maybe for even more luck and it would be a damn razor blade.

"Careful," Christopher said, smiling. "That floor's dirty. Nasty little critters down here. I set a mouse trap. I found some roach bait behind the water heater."

He let out a little laugh that chilled me. The fucker was jovial. He had another picture tucked beneath his arm. He held a push pin between his teeth and positioned the photo next to the others. He pressed the tack through it then stood back and admired his work.

"Oh, pardon me," he said. "You like it?"

He stepped to the side. I strained to see what he'd done even as part of me wanted to look away. I was playing right into his game.

Christopher didn't give me a choice. He lunged at me, hauling me to my feet. I screamed from the pain that shot through my stiff limbs. He pulled me to the workbench and turned my head so I had no choice but to look where he wanted. I could have shut my eyes, but I had to see.

A gurgled cry ripped from my throat. He'd tacked up one of my family photos. It was an old one. I kept it in a cedar chest at the top of the stairs at the lake house. In it, I was thirteen years old. It was the year before my mother died. She'd taken us to the department store and we posed in front of a fake sky background. Joe had been an asshole that whole day. Sullen. His smile was forced. Three-year-old Vangie sat in my lap, grinning. She held a stuffed rabbit. Matty sat in the foreground. He was four years old and had taken my mother's sewing scissors the week before and cut jagged bangs. My mother couldn't reschedule the photo session or she'd lose her deposit. It was enough of a reason to set my father off on an alcohol-fueled rant that ended in a busted coffee table and my mother's tears. I hated the picture. It's why I kept it hidden away.

"Pretty little princes and princesses," he said. "Happy as can be."

Naked jealousy dripped from his voice. I might never be able to reach under that workbench, but I'd just found my first weapon.

"Happy? Is that what you think of these people? Of me?"

What secrets lurked behind his eyes? He was a madman. But as he stared at those photos with contempt, I knew he was seeing something from his own past. God, I'd seen this kind of thing a million times from the witness box as I readied my next question on cross. It didn't happen all of the time. Some little question. A memory. A glimpse into what drove them.

"They're not happy, Christopher," I said. "That boy, my brother? My father once hit him so hard he cracked a ring. Joe had to get ten stitches just below his eye. They've retouched it, but if you look real close, you can see it in that photo."

He looked.

"My sister Vangie? Surely you've already heard what happened to her when I got old enough to leave town. She was raped, Christopher. By a school teacher. I mean, it made national news."

"Shut up," he said, but his calm had evaporated. Now he was sweating.

"Ben and Sarah Dale? They couldn't have children of

their own. Sarah was in a car accident when she was seven. Broke her pelvis. Her mother was driving, blitzed out of her mind on Christmas Eve." I was making it up. But I'd sprinkled in enough of the truth, I hoped he bought it all.

"There's no such thing as a perfect, happy family, Christopher," I said. "The people in these pictures? Liars. Cheaters. Abusers. Abused. All of them. Whatever they did to you ... whatever they told you ... it wasn't your fault. You're not to blame."

He reared back as if I'd struck him. "What did you say? What did you fucking say?" He charged me, grabbing my face in his hand. Pain seared me where he'd struck me before. Spots swam in front of my eyes and it got hard to breathe. I had to stay awake. I couldn't let the blackness pull me back down.

I fell gasping to the floor as he let go. I landed even closer to the workbench. I saw the piece of metal clearly now. It was no more than an inch away from me. If I could get to my back. If I could sit up and inch my way against the bench, I just might be able to grab it and hide it in my hands.

"I said it's not your fault," I said. "Whatever your parents told you. They should have protected you. I know what that feels like. You have to believe me. I've tried to run from all the shit my parents did to me too. All the way to Chicago. Big law firm. Big job. You were in the courtroom that day. You heard what they made me say. I've done bad things, Christopher. Things I can't take back. I know the kind of pain you feel. You're not alone."

He was snarling like a dog. Pacing.

"Sluts," he said. "Liars. Sluts. Fuckin' big shot! Who's the big shot now? Got some blood on your fancy floors now, don't you? Choke on it!"

He curled his fist and drew it back. I flinched. He froze

just an inch from my face. I slowly opened my eyes and Christopher started to laugh. Then he did the one thing I didn't expect. He pulled me up, forced me to sit. He pushed me against the bench, right where I'd been trying to get.

Christopher's gaze locked with mine. But it was like he was somewhere else. He saw someone else when he looked at me. His mother? Some girl who'd rejected him? There was no way to know.

I strained my shoulders, pulling backward. I slapped my bound hands against the ground, trying desperately to find that piece of metal. It was flat, with sharp edges. From what I'd seen, it might be part of a paint scraper.

My pinky touched something that moved. I slid my hands toward me, dragging the piece of metal.

"They can't touch you anymore," I said to Christopher, hoping I could keep him here but not here. So far, it was working. "I know what it's like. I promise you. I can help you make it so they can never hurt you again. It's what I do." It was all bullshit, but it sounded like the truth. I think.

The metal got caught on something. I couldn't drag it forward. Christopher's eyes flickered. He was red-faced, breathing hard. He curled his fist again and I thought surely this time he'd strike me.

He didn't though. He drew a hard hand over his face, sucked in a great breath of air, then turned his back and charged toward the stairs.

I got bold. I reached back and dragged the metal all the way out from under the bench. Using my nail, I managed to lift a corner of it off the ground. It was enough. The metal fit into my two palms. I clasped my hands together, hiding it if he turned me around. The edge was sharp enough to cut the meat of one of my palms. If I could just work it enough to scrape against the tape. I wouldn't have to slice all the way through. Just a little. Just enough to weaken it so I could pull my hands apart.

If there was time.

"Christopher!" I called out. He pointed his shaking finger at me, then charged back up the stairs.

I was alone. I had a crude-as-hell weapon. And I had precious little time.

Chapter 40

I DROPPED the metal shard twice. My shoulders screamed with pain from being bent behind me for so long. I pushed past it. I found if I could wedge myself against the wall for leverage, I could draw the sharp edge of the metal against a piece of the tape binding my wrists. If my hands were in front of me ... if I wasn't doing it blind, I would have made quicker work of it.

Sweat poured from me as I grunted through my efforts. I heard Christopher humming, singing, and whistling upstairs, but he didn't come back down for a long stretch of time.

I got careless. As I wedged the metal edge against the tape for another pass, my grip slipped. The metal sliced my palm.

"Shit!" I whispered. Scooting away from the wall, I saw a few drops of blood on the ground. If Christopher came back down, if he saw ...

I heard water running and pots banging. My stomach growled as the aroma of cooking meat wafted down. I grew lightheaded from so many hours without food or water. But the longer Christopher stayed occupied, the better my chances of cutting through that damn tape.

My thoughts wandered. At some point in the process, I dozed off. I saw Jessa running across the lake. First, I dreamt she reached the other side. Then she didn't. Then I saw Christopher gaining on her.

Clanging metal jolted me awake and again I forgot where I was. Christopher was still upstairs, banging around in the kitchen. God. Jessa. All I could do was pray for her safety.

I tested my bindings. They held tight. My efforts had been worthless so far. My hand throbbed from where I cut it and I'd dropped the piece of metal. Twisting around, I found it again and worked up a new sweat getting it back between my hands. I nearly dropped it again as Christopher came back down.

"Time to go," he said. He had an oddly bright smile on his face as he came to me.

Panic set in and I crab-crawled backward away from him. Christopher reached down; grabbing me under the armpits, he yanked me to my feet. He picked me up easily, throwing me over his shoulder, fireman-style. I screamed and tried to kick, but my strength left me.

He bounded up the stairs with me. Upside down, my stomach churned. If I had anything in it, I would have thrown up down his back. The room was a dizzying blur as he charged through the kitchen, up from the basement. Christopher deposited me into a chair at the kitchen table.

"She sits and smiles," Christopher said. "She makes the dinner and everyone is happy. Nobody yells. Father doesn't make her cry."

What the actual fuck?

He'd set four places at the kitchen table. Perfectly neat with cheap China bowls atop matching dinner plates. Two forks, a spoon, a table knife. My heart raced. If I could get free. If I could grab one of the knives. They weren't sharp, but if I could gather the strength to stab him hard enough …

With renewed urgency, I tried to work the piece of metal against my bindings.

Humming, Christopher went to the kitchen. He had a large silver stewpot on the stove. Using hot pads, he brought it to the table. My stomach growled loudly, betraying me as he used a ladle to scoop out the broth into all four bowls.

It was some kind of stew. Bits of meat floated at the top. It smelled wrong, but my stomach didn't care.

"It's been such a long day. They're all tired. How was school? What did you learn?"

"What?" I asked. I took in my surroundings. Other than the kitchen table, I saw no other furniture in the house. I could see part of the living room. It had beige shag carpet and a wooden front door with three little diamond cut-out windows. Was this Christopher's house? There was one hallway to the right of the living room.

"Shh!" He put a finger to his lips. "Grown-ups are talking. Mother doesn't speak unless Father asks her a question. He works so hard all day. He doesn't need to hear her nag. She always nags. Dinner needs to be on the table when he walks in, or else."

"Of course," I said.

The steam from the stew spiraled up, filling my nostrils. I was so damn hungry, I was about to put my face in it. Christopher wasn't watching me. His eyes glazed over, playing whatever distorted childhood memory he was in right now. I used it. Working the bindings. It got easier now, sitting upright in that chair. If I had five solid minutes …

Christopher stuck a finger in the stewpot. He drew it away quickly, waving it in the air. He'd burned himself. Then he slammed his fist against the table hard enough to make the plates jump.

"She's supposed to take it off the heat so it's just warm enough when Father sits down!"

Should I apologize? Was I Mother in this creepy fantasy? Then Christopher charged away from the table and down the hall.

My pinkies cramped and ached from trying to work the metal at such an odd angle. I pulled my wrists in opposite directions. The tape held. God, I didn't care. I didn't care if I sliced myself down to the bone if I could just get loose. I worked harder. Christopher rummaged through something down the hall.

I wedged the metal between my palms and pushed for all I was worth. I felt something pop. The tape snapped. Pain speared down my spine. But the tape broke. I grabbed the knife. Scanning the kitchen, I looked for Christopher's gun. Could I be lucky enough that he'd left it behind?

My legs were still bound with duct tape. I reached down and started to cut through it with the kitchen knife. I almost had it. I couldn't overpower Christopher. But if I had the element of surprise.

"Always whining." Christopher's voice reached me from down the hall. "Sister's so ungrateful. She gets everything."

This was my chance.

Then Christopher came back. Except he wasn't alone.

He carried Jessa over his shoulder just like he'd carried me. And she wasn't moving.

Chapter 41

"Jessa!" I screamed, dropping the knife to the floor. I put my hands behind me so he wouldn't see what I'd done.

Christopher put Jessa in the chair beside me at the table. Oh God. Thank God! She was okay. Her eyes widened and filled with tears when she saw me. He'd taken the tape off her mouth but her hands were still bound in front of her with duct tape.

"It's okay," I whispered. "You're okay." I blinked hard, trying to stop my own tears.

She stared straight ahead, her face blank. Only a tiny, frantic pulse in her neck betrayed the terror I knew Jessa must feel.

I had to keep it together for the both of us. I'd acted way too soon. If Christopher figured out I'd freed my hands, he could use Jessa to threaten me. I couldn't let Jessa see my hands were free either. Any tiny reaction from her and I'd lose my advantage.

"Always something." Christopher stirred the pot. "It's not hot enough. There's not enough salt. He asks for one simple thing."

Christopher dropped the ladle and slammed his palms against the table. He hovered over me, just inches away from my face. I kept my hands clasped behind me, praying he wouldn't see the broken tape on the floor.

"You get to live in this house. What do you do all day?"

He was his father, perhaps. Was I the housewife in this twisted memory of his?

"I'm sorry," I said. "Let me just heat it up a little longer. It'll just take a second."

"Too late!" he yelled. "Not the point." He picked up the ladle and threw it across the room. Jessa jumped but kept silent. For the moment, it almost seemed like he'd forgotten she was there.

A phone rang from deeper in the house. My heart raced. That was my ringtone. I kept stock still. Christopher glared hard at me.

"No calls during dinner!" He smacked the table again and headed toward the sound of the ringing.

God. My phone. Surely by now someone had figured out we were missing. It was a beacon of hope. The police could track me that way. I shot a quick look at Jessa.

"You're being very brave," I whispered. "Just do what he says for now, okay? I'm going to figure out how to get us away from him. Can you stay calm for me like you are for just a little while longer?"

I realized she'd been taking care of herself already for God knew how long. He'd gone after her while I lay unconscious in that van. He must have thrown her in back right along with me. Had she thought I was dead? This poor, sweet little girl had already seen so much. Still, she sat with her back straight. She wasn't panicking.

Jessa slowly lifted her eyes and focused on me. All at once, the last couple of weeks of progress washed away. She looked hollowed out like the day I first saw her in the hospital in Toledo.

"Jessa, did he hurt you? Did Christopher hurt you?"

I tried to get a better look at her. She didn't appear to have any bruises or cuts, at least where I could see. God, if he'd done anything to her …

Jessa squeezed her eyes shut then shook her head.

"Okay," I said. "Just don't say anything, okay?" I hated that I was telling her that. More than anything, I wanted to hear the sweet sound of her voice. But there was no telling what might set Christopher off.

Christopher had my phone in his hand. It had stopped ringing and he stared at the screen. He paced near the front door. "No calls during dinner!" he screamed, then threw the phone hard at the wall. He'd used enough force to make a dent in the drywall. The screen shattered. Jessa jumped, then stared straight ahead.

I stared at the table knife in front of Christopher's place setting. If I made a move for it, Christopher would know I'd freed my hands. It was no match for the gun he held so close to Jessa. There was no way I could act fast enough to save us both. But if I could at least save Jessa. She was worth dying for.

"People are going to come for me," I said to Christopher, trying to pierce through his delusion. "You know that, right? I told you back at my house. You killed a cop. People will have seen your van. You can't get away with it this time. But if you let us go, I can tell them that. They'll go easier on you."

He snarled like a dog. "Shut up. You don't talk unless I ask you a question."

"I'm a lawyer, Christopher. But you already know that. You came to court to watch me that day. I can help you. Let Jessa go and I'll make them listen."

"Lawyers lie," he said. I couldn't tell if he was here or in that loop from his past.

"I don't," I said. "You were in the courtroom. You heard what they said about me. It's all true. I have very powerful friends, Christopher. People who care what happens to me. I can get you out of this. But you have to do something for me."

"We're a family," he said. "Everybody stays."

Shit. I was losing him again. Christopher pointed the gun at me. With his other hand, he smacked the side of his head as if he were trying to drive voices out of it. I couldn't decide if we were better off with him in the past or the here and now. Which would make him less likely to pull that trigger?

"Dinner's going to get cold," he said. "You talk too much."

He pointed the gun at Jessa. My heart leaped. Silent tears fell from Jessa's eyes.

"Christopher," I said. "Look at me."

He did, but he kept the gun trained on her. "Who left you?" I said. "Was it your mother? Do you want me to help you find her? Your father?"

"So perfect," he said, his lips curled in a snarl. "They sit there in their pretty house eating their pretty dinner. And I burn!"

He lifted his shirt. I sat back hard in my chair. He had dozens of tiny, circular burn marks all over his chest, his stomach, all the way up to his neck. They were the exact shape of cigarette butts. God, he'd been tortured.

"Every night. Perfect dinner. Smiles. They don't know I can see them. I screamed once from my window. They kept right on eating."

Who? Was he talking about neighbors? I took a chance.

"They didn't know," I said. "If they'd known they would have helped you."

"They knew!" he screamed. Jessa jumped in her seat.

"Little house on the cul-de-sac. Pretty pictures. They don't like to know what it's really like."

"I told you," I said. "Nobody's perfect. Everyone has things that hurt them. They have pain. It's not what you see in the pictures. You're not alone, Christopher. I see you. I won't let them hurt you anymore."

He smiled, but his eyes were cold and dead.

He bolted up from the table and went to the kitchen sink, taking the gun with him. He hummed that damn lullaby again. I turned to Jessa.

With the water running and his humming, I felt fairly certain he couldn't hear me. "I'm going to get you out of here," I said. "When I say, I want you to run. Just like you did before. Only this time, he won't be able to follow."

Jessa's eyes flicked to Christopher then back to me. Her bottom lip quivered and she slowly shook her head.

"He knows how to stop you," she whispered. "He always knows. He keeps coming back."

My heart broke for her for the thousandth time. If it took the last breath in my body, I would find a way to make sure she was safe.

Christopher shut off the water and came back to the table. "Time to eat," he said, smiling. "Then it's time to go."

Adrenaline poured through my veins. He was right. It was time to go.

Chapter 42

CHRISTOPHER CAME to the head of the table. He pulled the gun out of his back pocket, pointing it at Jessa as he took his seat.

"Enjoy your dinner," he said.

"I ... uh ..." My hands were free but he still didn't know that. If I could get him to come close to me, leave the gun behind.

"I can't," I said. "I can't use my hands."

He slammed his fist against the table again. "Ungrateful! You have everything you could ever want. You don't work. I come home and this house is filthy. Children crying. You know I need peace."

I looked hard at Jessa. Her face had changed. Her jaw dropped. She was looking down at my hands. She finally noticed the loop of tape on the ground.

"It's okay," I said, matching the sing-song quality of Christopher's voice. "We won't say another word unless you ask us to. We know how hard you work."

Jessa clamped her mouth shut. God bless that sweet, sweet, beautiful, smart child. Six years old. She'd seen the worst horrors the world could bring. But she was still fighting the only way she knew how.

"That's better," Christopher said. "Now eat this meal!"

Did he want us to just stick our heads in the bowls like dogs? Jessa leaned forward, clearly thinking the same thing.

Christopher let out a sigh and threw his napkin to the table. He rose. Pushing himself away from his seat, he nearly toppled the table. The soup sloshed in my bowl, dripping over the side.

"You'll clean that up!" he yelled. My ears rang from it.

I gripped the edges of my chair as Christopher came around. He picked up the gun and pointed it at me.

"I said, you'll clean that up!" He grabbed my arm, jerking me forward. He pulled so hard I couldn't keep my hands clasped behind me. In one terrifying instant, Christopher saw the tape on the ground. His eyes widened.

"You made the mess!" Jessa yelled, drawing Christopher's attention. She picked up her bowl with her bound hands and threw it across the table. It was just a moment. A split second. Dear God, he raised the gun to point it at her.

I grabbed my bowl and threw it in Christopher's face. He reared back, temporarily blinded as the hot soup scalded his face.

"Run!" I yelled to Jessa. Instead, she dove beneath the table.

Christopher pulled at me. But his movements were clunky and erratic. He swung the gun wildly. He got one shot off. It ricocheted against the wall. Jessa screamed. I dodged Christopher's next blow.

It was so heavy. So unwieldy, but it was the only weapon I had. I grabbed the stew pot and threw it at Christopher. Some of the soup spilled over my arms, scalding me too. But I knocked Christopher backward. The gun fell out of his hands and thumped loudly on the ground.

I pressed my advantage and lunged at Christopher. If I could disable him long enough for Jessa to get away again.

"Go!" I screamed. "Out the door! Now!"

I kicked, scratched, bit, flailed for all I was worth as Christopher and I toppled over. He was badly burned, his face already a mass of red welts. But he opened one angry eye. He got his hands on my shoulders and shoved me backward. I slid across the slippery floor, landing up against the wall.

I kicked out, hoping to trip him as Christopher advanced on me. I found the small knife that I'd thrown to the ground. I held it in front of me, ready to impale Christopher on it.

Then a single, deafening shot rang out.

Time froze.

I scrambled to my feet. Jessa sat against the wall, shaking as she held the gun in front of her. Her shot went wide, just grazing the side of Christopher's already burned face. He gave her an eerie grin.

"Sister is so ungrateful!"

As he made a move for her, I vaulted forward, burying the kitchen knife deep in his belly.

This time, when I yelled for Jessa to run, she did. She dropped the gun and scrambled for the front door.

Chapter 43

SOMEONE I CARED about told me this was the man he'd want on the case if a person he loved was murdered. Now I understood why. Detective Brett Carey stood like a stone mountain at the end of my hospital bed.

"You'll all get your statements," he said. "And you'll all come through me. If I find out even one of you talks to that kid without me knowing about it, I'll fucking end you."

A detective from Whitefish Bay had just arrived. Two agents from the Ann Arbor field office of the F.B.I. waited just down the hall. Carey turned back to me. His eyes were red-rimmed and full of concern as he shut the door behind him.

"I'm sorry," he said.

I couldn't help it. This got a smile out of me. "No, you're not. You were doing your job. And my sister wasn't doing anything to help herself. As long as you do the right thing now and get her down here, I'm willing to call us square."

"Working on it," he said. I reached out, trying to shake his hand. My IV pulled at my arm. I was okay. Just second-degree burns on my arm, the self-inflicted cut on my hand, and a little dehydration. I wasn't even being admitted.

"His name is Christopher Fielding," he said. "Up until a year ago, he lived near Albuquerque. His first two murders took place there."

The police had the family photos he'd displayed. Fourteen murders. There were three other cases in Florida he may also have been responsible for.

"What the hell was he doing in Ann Arbor?" I asked.

"It may take months before we can piece it all together. What we have so far? He worked for Titan Security originally in Little Rock. That's how he got access to most of these homes. In every case, the homeowners had installed a Titan system within the last two years. Anyway, he got laid off but relocated here six months ago."

"Is he talking?" I asked.

Carey shook his head. "No. You hit an artery. He lost a hell of a lot of blood and the burns on his face ... some of them are third degree. Doctors are certain he'll pull through though."

"I need to be with Jessa now."

I swung my legs over the bed. They weren't planning to admit me overnight. Not Jessa either.

"She's asking for you," Carey said.

My heart thundered. "She's still talking?"

Brett Carey's smile cracked wide. "She won't shut up. It's like music. Dr. Spencer's with her. She was able to give a brief, official statement identifying Fielding as the man who killed her parents."

I dropped my head. So much damage. So much loss. "She's an amazing kid," Carey said.

"Yes, she is."

I got to my feet. Everything on me was stiff and creaked

as I tried to walk. Carey dove for the wheelchair in the corner of the room. I put up a hand to stop him.

"I'm okay. I want to walk. You mind leading me to Jessa's room?"

He looked over his shoulders. "The nurses are gonna kill me."

"I'll take my chances. After that, I'd really like it if you went back to the jail and oversaw Vangie's release personally. The longer she waits to see Jessa, the worse it is for both of them."

"I'll get her here," he said. "That's a promise."

We made it two steps out the door before my brothers came charging down the hallway. Joe's face was sheet white. Matty looked ready to murder Carey when they locked eyes. I got between them.

"It's okay," I said. "Believe it or not, he's on our side. Now, come with me. Let's go see our niece."

Joe made a choked sound. He broke. Lunging for me, he threw his arms around me. "Jesus," he said. "I thought … when we got there … when Wray …"

My brain was still a little fogged over from running on about twelve hours of pure adrenaline. It took a beat for me to realize what had happened. The lake house. It had been Joe who got there first. He discovered Eric's body and Jessa and me missing.

I met Carey's eyes over my brother's shoulder. "Has someone got in touch with Eric's family? His mother lives in North Carolina now, I think." I tripped over Eric's name. I'd pushed thoughts of him away until now. My fight against Christopher had given me no room to let grief in.

"Yeah," Matty answered. "His partner called her, I think. She was going to catch a flight or something and they were hoping she'd make it before he got out of surgery."

Time froze again. The bright fluorescent lights of the hospital hallway made my eyes burn. I couldn't breathe.

"Surgery?" I said. "He was ... is he ..."

Carey's face fell. "Oh Jesus. You didn't ask. I didn't ... shit. He's alive, Cass. Eric Wray's a tough son of a bitch. The shot punctured his lung and he lost over half his blood volume, but your brother's a hero. If he'd shown up at your place maybe even ten minutes later, there'd have been no chance to save him."

"Eric's alive?" I asked again. It couldn't be true. He was lifeless. There was so much blood.

"Yes," Joe said, finally letting me go. "He's alive. He's not out of the woods yet, but he's got a chance. He's here, actually. A couple of floors away. They life flighted him right here to U. of M."

I couldn't feel my feet as Carey and my brothers walked me down the hall, around the corner, and into Jessa's room.

Chapter 44

COLLETTE SPENCER SAT beside her bed. Jessa was busy coloring a picture. She looked so small, a little gaunt, but she had a huge smile for me as I walked in the room. She tossed the coloring book page at Collette, scrambled off the bed, and ran into my waiting arms.

"Hey, honey," I said. "I missed you."

Jessa had tears in her eyes as she pulled away. I showered her with kisses. "You were so brave. You did just what I said. It's going to be okay now. I'll make sure of it."

"I was worried," Jessa said. Brett Carey was right. The sound of her voice was pure heaven. "I didn't want him to hurt you too."

"I know. He won't. The bad man will never hurt anyone ever again. I have some news for you though. See this big guy standing over there?" I smoothed back a lock of hair from Jessa's face. She looked up at Detective Carey, her eyes big.

"He's going to go get Vangie and he's going to bring her here so you can see her. Would you like that?"

Jessa stepped out of my arms. She walked up to Brett. He

squatted down so he was at eye level with her. "Your aunt is right," he said.

"Go right now," Jessa said. "I wanna see Vangie. I miss her."

Brett gave her a nod. Jessa reached out. Carey's badge hung from a chain around his neck. Jessa took it, running her small fingers over it. "Do you catch bad guys?" she asked.

A tremor went through Carey's jaw. "I try to," he said. "Sometimes I'm not as fast as I want to be."

"Sometimes they're faster," she said.

"Yes," Carey answered. He was a big man. Strong. Formidable. But Jessa's words nearly shattered him.

"Sometimes you need help," she said.

"Yes. I always need help. You helped me so much, Jessa. More than you know."

"Do I get one of these now too?" she said, turning the badge over.

Carey smiled. "You know, I think I can find you one. How about I bring it back with me when I get your mo—. Uh ... when I bring back Vangie. How does that sound?"

"Sounds good," she said. "But will you hurry?"

Brett Carey choked up. He blinked hard, trying to hold back a tear. "Yeah," he said, locking eyes with me. "I promised your aunt the very same thing."

A nurse came to the door. "It's getting kind of crowded in here," she said.

"Jessa." Collette Spencer rose. "Can you hang out with your Uncle Matty and Uncle Joey for a few minutes? I'll be right back."

Nodding, Jessa climbed back up into her bed while Matty and Joe went to her. Joe gave her back her coloring book and remarked on how good a job she'd done. I put a light hand on Brett Carey's chest as we all walked into the hall, closing Jessa's door behind us.

"She's okay?" I asked Dr. Spencer. "What she's seen ... what she did ..."

"Kids are resilient," the doctor answered. "I won't lie. It could be years before she's mature enough to fully process everything that's happened. But yes. I think she can be okay. She's powerful. With your help, she slew a dragon today. And she's surrounded by people she knows love her. That's one special kid in there."

It was my turn to blink back tears. Collette Spencer knew what I needed. She came to me, her arms open wide.

"It would do you some good to talk to someone for you," she said. "I can give you a name."

I wiped under my eyes. "Maybe."

The same nurse waited beside us. "I'm sorry to interrupt," she said. "But I got a call at the desk from the surgical floor. Your friend is waking up. He's asking for you."

"Thank God," I said.

"Go," Collette said. "I'll keep an eye on things down here. Detective?" Carey had moved to the end of the hall. He was on his cell phone. Collette turned back to me and whispered, "I'll make sure he keeps his promise about Vangie. With any luck, she'll be here before you get back down."

"Thank you," I said while the nurse guided me to the elevators.

Chapter 45

MY HEART FELL to the floor as another nurse peeled back the curtain in front of Eric's bed. His skin was ashen. He had more tubes and machines hooked to him than I could count. But his eyes brightened with recognition as he saw me approach. Groaning, he tried to pull the oxygen tube away from his nose.

"Stop that," his nurse said. He had the look of a body-builder and he towered over Eric's bed. Eric Wray knew when he was outmatched. He dropped his hand from his face and reached for me.

"No excitement," the nurse said. "And no more than five minutes. Your friend needs rest."

"Got it," I said, clasping Eric's hand. I couldn't stop the tears from streaming down my face. The nurse pulled the privacy curtain back. I dropped my head and pressed it against Eric's shoulder.

"You okay?" he asked, his voice an unfamiliar croak. "God. I'm so sorry. I should have acted quicker. I should have seen. Just ... tell me you're okay."

"Me? Jesus. I thought you up and died on me. I'm so

sorry. I tried to fight. I didn't want to leave with him. And Eric, you just took a bullet for me. And for Jessa. You saved our lives."

Eric started to cough. The agony of it tore through him and his eyelids fluttered. But he settled himself. I straightened his pillow.

"I'm on a lot of drugs," he said. "So you'll probably need to explain all of this again. But that was the Dales' killer?"

"It was. He's killed many more. The couple in Whitefish Bay. They think maybe even up to a dozen or more unsolved murders nationwide. He worked for Titan at one point. He was able to use that knowledge to override their home security systems. It's how he targeted. He was so messed up, Eric. Badly abused as a kid, I think. He got it in his head that everyone around him had this perfect life and nobody was there to step in for him. So, in his twisted mind, I think he was avenging some little boy inside of him. It's so sad. Such a waste. But it's over. He can't ever hurt anyone again. I ... uh ... I kind of stabbed him. I had some help though. Jessa."

"Shit," Eric said. "Is she okay?"

"She will be. At least, I think so. Carey's working on getting Vangie here. They're dropping the charges against her, of course."

Eric got a faraway look. For a moment, I thought he was about to drift off to sleep. It might have been for the best. He turned to me though. "I'm sorry, Cass. I should have protected you. I should have believed you sooner or pushed harder on your theory. You were right. I'll be damned you were right about all of it."

I smiled. "Haven't you figured out by now I usually am?"

He shook his head and smiled. God, it was good to see. Heat flooded through me when Eric's eyes caught mine.

"I thought you were dead, you asshole," I said, my voice strained. "Don't ever do that again or I'll kill you."

My emotions washed over me like a tsunami. I saw Eric as he was. Nearly dead. Bleeding. I meant what I said. If Eric hadn't been there, Fielding might have shot me instead. Eric had stuck his neck out more than once for me on this case.

Before I could think it fully through, I leaned forward and pressed my lips to Eric's. I think part of me just needed something concrete, something to feel. But ... another part of me wanted something more. I had almost died too.

It was just a moment. But as I pulled away, everything changed. His face broke into that lopsided, infuriating smirk.

"I think maybe they've given me more drugs than I realized," he said. "But did you just kiss me, Leary?"

"No, Wray, you're stoned," I quipped. "Get some rest."

As if on cue, the nurse poked his head around the curtain. "Five minutes are up," he said. "Time to see if we can get Detective Wray to pee." He held a plastic urinal in his hands, waving it back and forth.

"Yeah," I said. "That's all you. I'll check back in a couple of hours."

Eric's eyes glazed over. He really was stoned. With any luck, he'd forget the last five minutes. I gave him a peck on the forehead and left him to his nurse.

When I got back upstairs, my heart swelled as I came down the hall. I heard my sister's laughter coming from Jessa's room.

Matty and Joe stood out in the hall, looking in. Joe held his arm out. I tucked myself beneath it. Joe kissed me on the head as we watched together.

Jessa sat on Vangie's lap. She showed her the picture she'd colored. Vangie placed soft kisses on her daughter's head. Her eyes were swollen from crying as she hugged Jessa close.

"I'll stay with you now?" Jessa asked. Vangie looked up and caught my eyes. Hers held a question.

"Yes," Vangie answered as she kept her gaze locked with mine, her meaning crystal clear. It was up to me to make sure what she said stayed true.

"I love you," Vangie mouthed to me. I mouthed it back. Then she whispered, "Thank you."

I stepped into the room. "That's a super brave kiddo you've got there," I said.

"Aunt Cass is like a superhero, Vangie," Jessa said.

"So I've heard," Vangie said. "Of course, she's always been one to me."

"No way," I said. "Jessa's the powerful one. We're just lucky we get to know her."

I reached forward and caught Vangie's hand. She held mine in a vice grip. Later, I'd give her a fierce hug and make her promise me that she was okay. She and Jessa would sleep in my room in the big bed with the view of the lake. I'd take the guest room, for now. We could conquer the rest of it starting tomorrow.

"I like the lake," Jessa said. "Uncle Matty's teaching me how to ice skate. He said we can build a snowman and it'll stay there until the ice starts to melt. Then we watch it sink into the water. Can we do that?"

"We can do anything you want, sweet pea," Vangie said. "I'm not going anywhere ever again. Pinky swear." She hooked her pinky with Jessa's. God, they looked so much alike.

"Come on," Joe whispered; he'd stepped into the room. "Let's give them a few minutes. Jeanie just showed up."

I kissed Jessa and hugged my sister. Then I followed my brother out into the hallway.

Jeanie Mills looked a hundred years old. She had bags beneath her eyes and her hair stuck out in odd peaks. She threw herself at me, grabbing me in a bone-crushing hug that nearly knocked us both to the floor.

"I'm okay," I said. "We're all okay. Even Wray. It's over."

Jeanie didn't believe me. I walked down with her to the family waiting area. She made me tell her the story three times. Christopher Fielding was the killer. Jessa told the police everything she remembered. We stopped him. He would never kill again. Vangie was free. Forever.

"She wants to take Jessa home," I said. "Jeanie, we have to figure out a way to make sure that happens. It's different now, right? Now that Vangie's been cleared, Ben and Sarah Dale's will prevails, right? That stupid P.P.O. they tried to get won't change that?"

Jeanie took my hands. "It's okay. God, Cass. I was coming to your house to tell you. This morning. When I got there, all those police cars ... I nearly died."

"I'm sorry," I said. "I didn't mean to put you through that. Wait, tell me what?"

"Marty and Geri Dale withdrew their petition. They weren't willing to produce their financial records. I've gotta look harder into it, but I'm pretty sure your hunch was right. I think they tried to buy Lois Reese from the F.O.C. to change her recommendation. It's over, Cass. Vangie's path is clear. No judge in the world would dare try keeping her from Jessa now. There will be a home visit and all of that, and she's going to have to prove she's got the means to care for her. And a place ..."

"She has a place," I said, smiling. "My place. We'll figure out the logistics later, but Vangie and Jessa are finally coming home."

I swear, the circles under Jeanie's eyes lightened then and there. Her smile warmed me as she pulled me into another bear hug.

Epilogue

Finn Lake
Two weeks later ...

IT WAS SATURDAY MORNING. This Michigan winter had been harsher than most. Though spring would officially come in just a few weeks, the snow and ice would linger all the way into April. The day we brought Jessa home from the hospital, my brothers had moved heaven and earth to erase all trace of Christopher Fielding's presence in our lives and my house was clean.

This morning, new snow had fallen, covering up the rink Matty made. He wasted no time heading back out there with the snow blower. Joe went to help him.

Jessa brought out her skates. She sat on Vangie's lap as my sister taught her how to lace them. I'd done the same for her nearly twenty years ago. It seemed the past and the present blended together that morning.

Just this morning, Judge Epperle signed the order granting Vangie full guardianship of Jessa. It was a new beginning for both of them. They were beginning to heal the broken parts of each other. For now, Vangie wanted that healing to take place here in Delphi. There were a million reasons for her to leave. Martin and Geri Dale were right about one thing. The ghosts of Vangie's past lived here, but she wasn't afraid of them anymore. The strength of our family helped to keep them at bay.

I would help her manage the trust Ben and Sarah set up for Jessa. Vangie had just put in an offer on a beautiful house on the lake, just ten houses down from me. I'd gotten the call earlier in the afternoon that the sellers accepted. I planned to tell her when we came in for hot cocoa later. We'd celebrate.

Jessa would start kindergarten again at the new elementary school in Delphi. Matty had plans to walk her there on her very first day.

Jessa still had a long way to go in her recovery. She would still have nightmares. But little by little, she would become part of our family and we would help her feel safe. She would be loved. She was a miracle.

I brought my own skates out and gave them to Vangie to wear. She put them on and she and her daughter toddled their way across the yard to the lake's edge. Matty had just finished clearing the circle.

My brother Joe stood behind me. "Look at her go," he whispered. "I can't get over how much she looks like Vangie."

"She's strong like her too," I said.

"You're the strong one, Cass," he said. "You've been strong enough for all of us. Remind me never to doubt you."

I looked up at him. "You doubted me?" I was teasing. So was he.

"I mean it though. Once again, if it wasn't for you, Vangie would be ... and Jessa ..."

"Shh," I said. "No need to think about any of that now.

Or ever. We do what we have to do. What we've always done. And what we'll do again."

"I suppose," he said. "I just wish ... I wish Mom were here to see this. Vangie reminds me of her too."

"Mmm. She's here, Joe. I can feel it."

He let out a sigh. I leaned against him, bringing my hand to his cheek as we watched our sister and her daughter begin to find their way. Holding Vangie's hand, Jessa glided across the frozen water. Her cheeks were rosy red. Her smile coming easier. And her sweet laughter echoed over the lake, stirring my heart like music.

Up Next for Cass Leary

CLICK TO BUY

Cass's darkest regret just knocked on her front door. She thought she was done defending shady mobsters. But when Killian Thorne calls in a favor, Cass realizes her debt has yet to be paid. And if she wants to keep her family safe, she must find a way to let a known hitman walk free...

Don't miss Devil's Bargain, the heart-stopping third book in the Cass Leary Legal Thriller Series.

Turn the page for details on how to grab a free, exclusive copy of *Crown of Thorne*, the bonus prologue to the Cass Leary Legal Thriller Series.

Newsletter Sign Up

Sign up to get notified about Robin James's latest book releases, discounts, and author news. You'll also get *Crown of Thorne* an exclusive FREE bonus prologue to the Cass Leary Legal Thriller Series just for joining. Find out what really happened to Cass before she came back to Delphi.

Click to Sign Up

http://www.robinjamesbooks.com/newsletter/

About the Author

Robin James is an attorney and former law professor. She's worked on a wide range of civil, criminal and family law cases in her twenty-year legal career. She also spent over a decade as supervising attorney for a Michigan legal clinic assisting thousands of people who could not otherwise afford access to justice.

Robin now lives on a lake in southern Michigan with her husband, two children, and one lazy dog. Her favorite, pure Michigan writing spot is stretched out on the back of a pontoon watching the faster boats go by.

Sign up for Robin James's Legal Thriller Newsletter to get all the latest updates on her new releases and get a free bonus scene from Burden of Truth featuring Cass Leary's last day in Chicago. http://www.robinjamesbooks.com/newsletter/

Also by Robin James

Cass Leary Legal Thriller Series

Burden of Truth

Silent Witness

Devil's Bargain

Stolen Justice

Blood Evidence

Imminent Harm

First Degree

Mercy Kill

With more to come…

Mara Brent Legal Thriller Series

Time of Justice

Price of Justice

Hand of Justice

With more to come…